THE HONEY PLAIN

ELIZABETH WASSELL was born in Manhattan, and studied fiction writing with Grace Paley and Edna O'Brien. She has worked as a restaurant critic, a barmaid, an English lecturer and a public relations writer. Having travelled and lived extensively in Europe, particularly England and Ireland, she has now settled in West Cork. While she has published in various magazines, *The Honey Plain* is her first novel.

The Honey Plain

Elizabeth Wassell

WOLFHOUND PRESS

First published in 1997 by
Wolfhound Press Ltd
68 Mountjoy Square
Dublin 1, Ireland

Wolfhound Press receives financial assistance from the Arts Council/ An Chomhairle Ealaíon, Dublin.

British Library Cataloguing in Publication Data
A catalogue record for this book is available from the British Library.

ISBN 0-86327-595-8

Cover design: Brenda Dermody, Estresso
Cover illustration: Eva Byrne
Photograph on first page: John Minihan
Typesetting: Wolfhound Press
Printed and bound by the Guernsey Press Co. Ltd., Guernsey, Channel Islands

Do Sheán

'Proceed, proceed. We will begin these rites
As we do trust they'll end in true delights'
William Shakespeare
As You Like It

'With that Diarmaid rose up and he gave three kisses to Grainne in the presence of Fionn and the Fianna. A pang of jealousy and anxiety seized Fionn on seeing that, and he said that Diarmaid would give his head for those kisses.'

Toraíocht Dhiarmada agus Ghrainne
(The Pursuit of Diarmaid and Grainne)

Chapter One

H *er eyes were hazel, deepening from moss-green to brown to nearly black. They were beautiful in a face less than beautiful, although she was disarmingly pretty when she smiled — but those eyes! Large, wide, slightly upswerving at their outer corners, they gazed solemnly at him from her unremarkable face. Her brown hair was so thick, it flared a bit from her brow and temples, and rippled down to the middle of her back. Once, when she tilted her head forward, a curl spilled over her cheek and clung there, and his fingers literally ached with the desire to push it back behind her ear and to touch her throat. He was alarmed by himself. After all, she was just a girl, in an audience.*

Dermot had come to Galway to present a paper at a conference whose theme was 'The Feminine Voice in

Early Irish Poetry', just his kettle of academic fish, it would appear, although lately he had soured on most things feminine. Furthermore, the conference organiser, a nervous young woman with woolly hair, called Maeve, had asked him to speak on 'The *Femme Fatale* in Irish Mythology'. *Femme fatale*, indeed! The only reason he consented to participate in these tiresome academic gatherings was that they enabled him to escape, if only briefly, the *femme fatale* in his own bed.

He no longer enjoyed life on the road, the obsequious organisers of lectures and conferences, eager to impress him while all he wanted was a stiff drink and some sleep; the pompous university types, the gushing students, the tedious dinners, the impersonal hotels. But lately he said yes even when bossy impresarios like this Maeve woman invited him to speak. Anything was better than the unease at home, and anyway, there was money in it, and he liked Galway, its seaport bustle.

He arrived two evenings before his talk. Maeve had booked him into a bed and breakfast along the Claddagh, the famous old fishermen's village bordering Galway Bay. But he saw no fishermen, only a parade of suburban houses, each displaying, neat as an open palm, a small lawn adorned with tiny grottoes, capering stone nymphs, stone mermaids balanced on miniature fountains, grinning plastic frogs. Such kitsch splendour, while a silver vapour fumed in the sky, and the pewter sea was thronged with gulls. Why, he wondered, did those houses need their pools, and stone swans that never moved, with that vista before them of

10

brine-washed sky, seaweed, and real swans in the bay? Then, the day after his arrival, as he was walking along Bourke Road, he began to understand: these people didn't look beyond their gardens; the sea and swans did not concern them, they were too absorbed with trying to outdo each other. Each succeeding house was more elaborately decorated than the last, with the one labelled B & B, his temporary home, the most opulent of all: a mossy sundial, a bird bath, a swing, a rocky pool, a stone mermaid combing stone hair.

His hostess, Mrs O'Malley, was a diminutive old woman whose skin shone like a white-and-rose china cup, and whose hands worked excitedly while she talked. Her breakfast room was decorated with an alarming 3-D plaster Jesus, mounted behind a glass panel, faceted on maroon velvet, his white hands dolefully extending an anatomically correct Sacred Heart from which plastic blood flowed. Overlooked by this extraordinary icon, Dermot had that morning eaten a breakfast lavish enough for a large family: eggs, black and white pudding, sausages, grilled mushrooms, warm crumbling brown bread, pot after pot of tea. That was why he was walking now, even though a light rain had begun to fall from the sunlit sky; it was hours after the meal but he still felt bloated, and was afraid that without exercise he'd slumber through the talk tonight, which, delivered by a local academic famous for her verbosity, was bound to be unbelievably arid, and a soporific even if he were not full of Mrs O'Malley's wholesome food.

He was strolling along the promenade when a girl

with copious nut-brown hair, sporting a green coat, approached him. 'Hello,' she said, 'Are you a guest at Mrs O'Malley's?'

Her accent was American. 'Yes. Are you? I didn't see you at breakfast.'

'I glimpsed you. I had already eaten. Mrs O'Malley's breakfasts are pretty daunting, aren't they?'

'Indeed. I believe I ate a dozen eggs this morning.'

They laughed. She seemed to hesitate, and he said, 'Would you like to walk a bit?'

She swung in beside him. It was still raining lightly, glinting filaments striking their cheeks and hands. The wind was fairly strong. A gaggle of small children wheeled past them on bicycles, three boys and one little girl with a pennant of hair streaming out behind her. He had wanted to walk by himself, but even now, so weary and bitter, he had to admit that he still enjoyed the company of a woman. She seemed a nice creature; he had registered her pretty eyes, the candour of her gaze, and he liked how her hair fluttered across her face so that she had to keep drawing it back with her hand. 'Are you here on holiday?' he asked.

'No. I'm only at the B & B temporarily, until the flat that I'm taking becomes free. I'm a painter,' she said, amending hastily, 'An apprentice painter.'

'You have come to Ireland to paint?'

'I don't like the light in America, because it's so harsh, and hard.' She indicated the silver sky. 'I'd like to try to paint this light.' She paused, then continued, shyly, he thought, 'The glow on these clouds, it's like light under water.'

12

Chapter One

He took a small purplish stone from his pocket and examined it. 'Some say the Irish light can't be painted, because it's so changeable.'

'I'd like to try, though. Probably I'm not good enough. But I'd like to try.'

They stopped before a cluster of boulders festooned with bladderwrack.

There was a tang of iodine, the sap of sea plants. She asked, 'And you, are you here on holiday?'

He was overtaken by the impulse, universal throughout Ireland, to torment a guileless American. In summer, when the island was infested with tourists, opportunities for this particular kind of mischief abounded: the Cork farmer savouring his pint in a local pub while informing a group of Americans that the real Blarney stone isn't in Blarney at all, but up in a remote Donegal village to which he gives them directions; the two men smoking their pipes who innocently tell a vulgar American in a big car that the road to Bunratty Castle is 'right; then left; then drive straight on as though the devil himself was after you,' when they are actually directing him over a fairly high precipice. But now it was spring, with dismayingly few opportunities to practise misleading Americans, so that this girl beside Dermot was a choice victim. He hesitated, then said seriously, 'I am here to study *slobhagóns*.'

'Oh.' He could see that she was struggling between honesty and the desire not to appear ignorant. Honesty prevailed. 'What are *slobhagóns*?'

He massaged the stone with his thumb before pocketing it again. 'You might see one, if you look carefully. There, amongst the rocks.' They both looked out at the wrack-garlanded boulders, gleaming with spume. He smiled. 'Well, perhaps not today. They are very shy and, besides, this isn't really *slobhagón* weather.'

They resumed their slow walk. The little cyclists returned, pedalling untidily by and screaming with laughter. She asked, 'What do they look like, *slobhagóns*?'

He was silent a moment. 'They are related to sheela-na-gigs, but they don't really resemble them.'

Again she struggled. 'What are sheela-na-gigs?'

'Cousins to *slobhagóns*. Would you like to walk through town?'

She consented, and they strolled past the new hotel, where his conference was taking place; then up past the great bulk of the old millhouse, with, beneath, the Corrib river coursing furiously towards the bay. Gazing down at the swollen waters, the girl said, 'Those waves could be the curving grey backs of *slobhagóns*. They do wear grey camouflage, don't they, when they frolic in the river?'

He gave her a startled look; she was grinning. Not stupid, he thought admiringly, not stupid at all. 'Come on,' he said, laughing, 'Let's walk a bit more.'

He was tempted to tell her the true reason for his visit to Galway, but he liked the fact that she didn't recognise him, that they were just a man and woman walking along the curving roads. It was a cliché: well-known people bemoaning their eminence as though it were an affliction, lamenting that they were cultivated

14

not for themselves but for their fame. But, cliché or no, it was true in his life, on a modest level, of course. He was no pop star to be assaulted by hysterical adolescents in restaurants and airports, but he was famous enough, in certain circles, to have had to develop a kind of radar. Dreamers and schemers, groupies and acolytes, he'd learnt how to recognise them, and deal with them, so much so that the ability to absorb and return the homage of women (while avoiding deeper feelings or awkward entanglements), the ability to dismiss undesirables, to flatter possible patrons (and patronesses!), to handle annoying journalists, all this was by now second nature to him.

And the fact that he had a more essential nature, a real self, and that this real self was seldom honoured, or even addressed, had more or less ceased to trouble him. Only it was pleasant, now, to realise that this girl was responding to just Dermot, a man. Like an explorer who dips under a thicket and discovers a secret copse, she had broken unwittingly through the brambles of his notoriety and come upon the place in him that was undefended, unwary, unseasoned by the attention of girls and women. And because she was not a groupie, he could respond to her more honestly, also; he did not regard her as a sort of temporary muse orchestrated by destiny to soothe him this time around, as opposed to the blonde before and the redhead who would come after. She was no muse, no fantasy in flesh; why, he didn't even feel attracted to her, particularly. He wasn't thinking, *How come she is at the same bed and breakfast as myself? This couldn't be an accident. Perhaps we will make love, she and I.* She was just a rather nice American with big eyes in a nondescript face, who was trying to be a painter, and whom he would forget as soon as he returned home to Dublin.

Only after she had wandered off to go to a bookshop did he realise he didn't know her name. Well, he thought, he would ask her tomorrow at breakfast, or he'd inquire from Mrs O'Malley — these bed and breakfast people knew everybody's business as well as their own.

Chapter Two

That evening, the lecture was followed by a dinner at long tables in the hotel dining-room. The food was execrable ('What *is* this?' exclaimed the man on Dermot's left, a lupine Institute professor called Doyle, peering through his glasses at his plate of wan meat covered with muddy sauce), but the wine was good and plentiful.

'Perhaps it's elk, or reindeer,' suggested Dermot, replenishing both their glasses.

'No, no, my good man. I have had the pleasure of reindeer, in Stockholm. Excellent meat, as are the women.' He gave his wolfish grin. 'But *you* are off corn maidens, I would imagine.'

Dermot smiled noncommittally. He liked Doyle's keen mind and acerbic sense of humour, and he even liked the suggestion of corruption, like a sulphur smell, that clung to the man's cynical, dapper person. But he was wary, as well, of such a spirit, corroded by disappointments in love and work.

Fastidiously nibbling on a morsel of brown bread, Doyle continued. 'You needn't worry that you would be committing some breach of honour, if you talked honestly about your difficult marriage. After all, it isn't as though everybody doesn't *know*!' He considered his plate again; then pushed it away with a delicate shudder. 'Your Fiona is a redhead, no? Ah, so is Mrs Doyle. It *is* true, what they say about the redheads being fiery — and troublesome. The solution—' he inclined his head towards Dermot, as though to impart a profound confidence; his smile was a perfect crescent, scalloped into his lean face; '—the solution, my dear boy, is to *hang-glide.*'

'Hang-glide?' repeated Dermot blankly, picturing Doyle floating through the air above Dublin, his academic gown fluttering around him, a Gaelic Batman.

'Exactly. Take it easy, to employ a crude Americanism.' He made a sweeping motion with his hand. 'Easy does it, you know? A bit of amusement here, a bit there. A place for everything, and everything in its place.' He gave a sly cackle. 'But then, you are talented with the ladies; everyone knows that.' He pointed to Dermot's forehead, where there was a small constellation of cinnamon-coloured freckles. 'Women think your little spots are quite adorable, did you know? Anyhow, the solution is simple. You must simply be an adroit juggler.'

'It might be difficult to juggle while you are hang-gliding. And incidentally my wife is *not* fiery. She's frosty, and dejected, and disappointed. Probably because I've let her down so much.'

Ignoring this, Doyle carried on. 'I have considered approaching you with a little scheme. I was thinking that perhaps you and I could get a flat somewhere, a small place, for entertainment purposes.'

'For entertainment of ladies?'

'Precisely. A nice couch, a bit of booze, some carefully chosen records. Very discreet, and no possibility of spouses stumbling in while one is, shall we say, profaning the marriage bed.'

Dermot paused. 'An interesting notion. I'm afraid, however, that I have tried your juggling and hang-gliding formula, and, for me, at least, it hasn't been very successful. It is a bitter thing, a loveless marriage, in which you cannot ease your wife's pain, nor she yours, nor, either of you, anyone else's.' He gave a bleak laugh. 'A misery-go-round.'

Doyle served them more wine. 'But you take it all too seriously! Love is a purely physical relationship. A series of sensations along the epidermis, a succession of agreeable stimuli.' He laughed. 'You see, you are stimulating me to poetry.' He touched his napkin to his rosy mouth. 'It's all so easy! You stroke her, and her flesh sings, her dough rises, her goose is cooked, her circle is completed. She touches you, your little forest goes on fire, the wind surges in your sails, your brain cells ease into ecstasy mode, your toes curl as your heart distends. Simple. Why confuse this pleasant series of mutual stimulation with philosophical anguish, and ravings about love, which has yet to be satisfactorily defined?'

'Thank God for that,' murmured Dermot. 'Imagine love being defined by academics!'

'Ah, Dermot, you and love. You have quite a *thing* about it, don't you? Even carving it out as your especial area of expertise — academically speaking, of course.'

'Which doesn't mean I know the first thing about it.'

'Your modesty becomes you. I don't know anyone who *does* know the first thing about it. But of one thing I am certain.' The waiter placed their dessert before them, bowls of what looked like pink mortar. Doyle gazed at his with silent loathing, then resumed. 'What I am certain of is that love must be kept in its own compartment, or else it becomes intolerably messy, and throws everything off balance, *everything*.'

'I am surprised at you,' Dermot replied mildly. 'Surely even a man as proudly cynical as yourself must believe, at least on some level, that love is the one thing we should not restrict to a compartment. We should try to make love the centre of our lives; it should inform all that we do; don't you think?'

Doyle made a *tut-tut* sound. 'Really, my boy, you speak like those undergraduates who are enamoured of Eastern religions, or those doleful ladies in the agony columns, advice to the lovelorn. Isn't there any cognac in this dreadful place?' He swivelled his head like an indignant bird; then sighed resignedly and said, 'Anyway, speaking of the feminine voice, what do you think of our Maeve?'

'She's a bit strident.'

'A *bit*? She laughs like a factory hooter. There she is now, making goo-goo eyes at you.'

Sure enough, at a table parallel to their own, Maeve, eating her pink dessert with apparent relish, was dimpling across at Dermot.

'Not very pretty,' observed Doyle cruelly. 'Looks rather like a sheep with that dusty hair. And those protuberant eyes are quite unpleasant. Feminists! So tiresome, and they're taking over the world.' He touched Dermot's sleeve. 'Let me caution you, old boy, be careful what you say tomorrow. It is not politically correct these days for members of the male persuasion to discuss *femmes fatales*, if you know what I mean. You don't know yet what it's like to be mau-mau'd by the bull dykes. The lady terrorists in the audience will be more than eager to punish you for your effrontery.'

'What effrontery?'

'Even thinking about women as objects of desire is punishable by castration nowadays, if you are a man, that is. A lesbian would of course be applauded for salivating all over the lectern with lust over some girl's anatomy. But not an ordinary mortal man, oh no. His penis would be slashed, his balls plucked like grapes. Anyway, good luck tomorrow.'

'Thanks,' said Dermot glumly.

'Not at all. I'm looking forward to it. Should be lively sport. By the way, where is your kip? Not here in this appalling Americanish hotel?'

'No. Maeve was good enough to book me into a very pleasant guesthouse.'

'Not Mrs O'Malley's in the Claddagh? Why, I'm there as well.'

Dermot gave him an astonished look, and Doyle explained that he slept late, and took his breakfast at one or two in the afternoon, Mrs O'Malley being so motherly and accommodating.

'Still,' said Dermot, 'the house is so small, I'm surprised I haven't had even a glimpse of you.'

Doyle gave his sickle grin again. 'Oh, I skulk about; nobody ever sees me. But the house is indeed small. I believe the only other guest is a little American.'

'I know. With brown hair. She spoke to me today, on the promenade. A funny face, she has.'

Doyle plucked a brown cigarillo from his pocket. 'I am shocked at you. I thought you were a connoisseur. She's actually rather attractive. If one has a discerning eye. And the accent is not too pronounced, thank God.'

Doyle's insouciance and blithe misanthropy were beginning to annoy Dermot. 'You have spoken to her?' he asked.

'Dear me, yes. Quite an interesting girl. Her father is what's-his-name. MacCormack, the senator. That must be one of the reasons she came to Ireland. Trying to be an artist, you know, and doubtless wanted to escape the burden of the famous name. And I believe she has friends here in Galway.' He blew an elegant scarf of smoke into the air between them. 'A pleasant morsel, I'd say. And convenient, her being in the same house.'

Dermot gulped down the last of his wine. 'She struck me as a bit too thoughtful for your kind of sport, Doyle.'

'Really? Do you mean that *your* kind of sport, presenting yourself as vulnerable and wounded in love, would appeal to her more? Oh, yes, yours is a quite effective strategy; I've seen you in action. Girls of a certain temperament go all moist at the prospect of soothing poor, bruised, handsome you. But—' He thrust his finger into Dermot's chest, and screwed it lightly. 'I saw her first, old boy.'

Dermot gave an impatient sigh. 'I assure you, I have no intention of tangling myself up with a naive American who believes she's a painter. My God, I've enough woman problems, these days.' He further thought, though didn't say, *But the last thing that poor girl needs is a dose of your brutal charm.* Then he wondered why he was feeling faintly protective of her, a young woman he didn't even know, or care about.

Chapter Three

Next morning, when he went down to breakfast, the girl was there. He took the place next to her at Mrs O'Malley's large table, laden with milk jugs, china bowls full of jam, baskets of brown bread, and dishes of butter moulded into curls, food for an army.

'Good morning,' she said. 'I was looking out at the sea, just before, and I think I saw a *slobhagón*.'

'How unusual. They're normally quite bashful.' He gazed across Bourke Road at the rain-soaked fields, and, beyond them, the Atlantic, blue and silver under a mother-of-pearl sky. 'How close did the *slobhagón* come? Did you see its flippers?'

'Goodness. I didn't know *slobhagóns* had flippers.'

Mrs O'Malley bustled in with Dermot's breakfast. 'Oh, yes,' he replied when she had gone, 'and they are quite deft with them. Why, the lady *slobhagóns* use their flippers to play water camogie.'

'Ah. Is water camogie a popular sport among *slobhagóns*?'

'Only the ladies, of course.'

'I see. Have the *slobhagóns* a rich cultural life, generally?'

He poured milk into his tea, and gave her a serious look. 'Yes, indeed. You should hear their Flippermonic Orchestra.'

She laughed. This morning, her hair was in a rather fetching disarray, piled up on her head with tendrils escaping onto her shoulders. Her eyes, he saw, were green-brown, the colour of forests. He supposed Doyle was right; she was not unappealing, but he preferred tall, elegant women to American imps with untidy hair.

'You must excuse me,' he said abruptly, 'I have a talk to prepare for tonight.'

He made to leave, but she asked, 'At the conference? I will see you there, then. This guy who was at art college with me in America is one of the organisers, and I promised him I'd help serve drinks at the reception. I didn't know it was you who would be speaking, but now I can look forward to it.' She grinned; then glanced at the chair beside her. 'Did you know that a man who must be a colleague of yours, Professor Doyle, is here at this guesthouse also?'

'You have met Doyle, then? An entertaining fellow, isn't he?'

She gave him a sidelong look. '*He's* certainly convinced that he is an entertaining fellow.'

He tried not to smile. She asked, 'Will you be talking about *slobhagóns* tonight? You know, you haven't told me your name. Mine is Grania MacCormack.'

Dermot introduced himself, and said, 'No, not *slobhagóns* this time. They merit a conference all to themselves, you see.' Then he excused himself, and hurried up to his room to work on his paper. At about one, he heard Doyle stir and trudge down to breakfast, but he didn't call out to him. For some reason, the very thought of Doyle was slightly distasteful to him now.

* * *

Earnest students clutching paper and pens; grizzled professors; younger academics trying not to look nervous; local poets, artists, and thinkers wearing the Galwegian uniform of rumpled fisherman's jersey, threadbare scarf, and jeans; a journalist or two: all were gathering in the large, airy reception hall for drinks and glad-handing before Dermot's talk commenced. Maeve, in an angry red dress with floppy red bows, seized Dermot's arm the moment he came in.

'*Hello*, Professor O'Duffy. *So* glad you're on time. You look splendid. I'm so excited about your talk tonight! We *must* have a tête-à-tête afterwards, you and I! Have I told you, I've read *all* your books—'

He managed to unfasten himself, murmuring that he would like a drink. Then he pushed through the thickening crowd up to the table where bottles of wine and whiskey were arranged in regimental columns. The young American, Grania, was there, pouring drinks into plastic cups. When she saw him, she grinned, and brandishing a wine bottle, exclaimed, 'I will be your Ganymede tonight.'

He smiled back. 'Ganymede? The cup-bearer of the gods? Well, you are a delightful cup-bearer, but I'm not any kind of a god.'

'Still, if you require a cup-bearer to stay you with flagons, I'd like to apply for the job.'

'The job is yours. May I have some of that nectar?'

She laughed up at him, and, without thinking, he pointed a finger at her and said, 'You know, you are dangerous.'

Doyle, wearing an elegant black coat, materialised on his left. 'Well! If it isn't my family.' He touched Dermot's hand in a proprietary way. 'I have decided that we three are family, since we are living together, as it were.' He gave Grania his feral smile. 'May I have a whiskey, my dear? You are looking very well this evening.'

It was true, Dermot thought. Her hair was floating around her shoulders, and she was wearing a pretty, rather demure green dress. Why hadn't he thought to compliment her first? Doyle, narrowing his eyes significantly at Dermot, announced, 'I'm off to speak to that *Irish Times* girl in the corner. But I shall return!'

Dermot gazed morosely at his back. 'That man is dangerous.'

Grania laughed. 'I thought *I* was dangerous.'

Looking into her amused eyes, he laughed as well. 'You're dangerous to *me*, but he's dangerous to *you*.'

At that moment, Maeve appeared, and clutched his arm again. 'Dermot, my dear, you must come with me.

Your talk is about to begin.' She turned haughtily to Grania. 'Please give the professor no more wine. He must go now, to prepare for the evening.'

'Yes, of course,' replied Grania evenly. Dermot said, '*Gracias*, Ganymede,' and they smiled while Maeve gave them both a baffled scowl.

* * *

It's always the same, Dermot thought, placing his sheets of inky foolscap on the lectern, and looking out at the rustling, expectant crowd. Always this nervousness, sudden shyness, his voice feeling tight and dry as if unconnected to him, always the conviction that he will fail, the whisper, curdled with contempt, in his head (his mother's whisper, he sometimes thought), *So, do you really think you have something valuable to say, to all these people?*

His eyes, moving over the audience, discovered Grania, her hands folded in her lap, her thickly lashed eyes looking solemnly up at him. And that was when he felt it, arrested by her, feeling it not in his mind but in his body, although not in his stomach as one might expect, but in his throat, a sudden constriction there, and, when she moved her head and a brown curl tumbled forward across her cheek, he felt it in his fingers, a literal ache of desire to smooth the hair back behind her ear, to touch her nape, her throat, the hollow between her collarbones. But he was registering this curious response to her with only a portion of his mind; mainly he was preoccupied with the audience as a whole, sounding the climate in the room, how these academics

28

and artists and writers would respond to his talk. Anyway, he thought, slightly annoyed with himself, more annoyed with Grania, *She's just a girl, in an audience. There have been so many girls, and so many audiences.*

* * *

'Good evening. I should like to begin by asking you to forgive the vulgar French term with which my paper is entitled. *Femme fatale* evokes, for me at least, sultry celluloid goddesses, parodies of feminine sexual power, but sometimes a brightly coloured fly is called for to attract the fish. And now that we are all happily splashing about in Galway's academic waters, I should tell you that my real subject is the difference between the temptress heroines of Greek and English literature, and the headstrong women who wrought so much havoc in Early Ireland.' Dermot cleared his throat. 'Because of Helen, Troy was pillaged and burned, but Helen was a passive agent, mere plunder for a furious and foolish man. Why the Greeks and Trojans battled so long over such a mute love object is surely a matter for the psychiatrist, not the scholar. Whereas Deirdre, the great heroine of the Ulster cycle, is a tempestuous, obdurate creature, determined to cause damage. She is not chosen by Naoise, she goes out and stalks the poor dolt, who hasn't a chance; no matter how brave he might be in battle, he and his brothers are at the mercy of her demands. She hasn't an iota of respect for her protector, the King of Ulster, and blithely wreaks destruction all round her, until Emain Macha is laid low, like Troy. Did the early Irish want to be manipulated by beautiful women?' He paused again. What was wrong with him? He had intended to give a strictly scholarly paper contrasting the concept of the beguiling woman in classic Greek, English, and Early Irish literature, but here he was bellowing like a mad bull. He had better lower the volume.

Dermot focused on the sheets of foolscap before him, and read his carefully prepared paragraphs on Helen of Troy and Chaucer's Criseyde, only to falter once again when he came to Guinevere of the Arthurian cycle. Stubborn but mercurial, governed by caprice, Arthur's queen happily exploited men who, bound by honour, could not gainsay her. Guinevere! Who was this bitch who had weakened the king, and smashed the Round Table? Arthur and his knights offered homage to the ideal of honour, but the strength of Woman was that she had none. Leaving men shorn of their friends, leaving them with only honour, a flavour grown bitter as bile in their mouths. And even that is not enough for them! After cruelly sundering Naoise from his boon companions and making him betray his king, Deirdre must cause general slaughter, the laying waste of Ulster's capital!

By this time, the audience had begun buzzing like a swarm of angry bees. So it was no surprise that when Maeve (still simpering and oblivious) bustled up to the lectern to call for questions, the air was thick with flapping hands.

'Yes, Professor Talon,' said Maeve, indicating a large, grey-haired woman with enormous spectacles. Is she really called *Talon*? Dermot wondered.

'Professor O'Duffy, after reading your texts on love in Early Irish literature, it is quite illuminating finally to experience you in person.' She paused, a charged pause, and looked level at him through her immense glasses, which enlarged her eyes so that they resembled two fishbowls. 'Quite illuminating,' repeated Professor Talon. 'You obviously subscribe to the narcissism of the patriarchy, whereby women exist merely as projections of the masculine psyche, without rich and complicated lives of their own. Man is permitted to create and accomplish, but Woman is merely his inspiration, his ideal, or his undoing, but always his ancillary, always an embodiment of something in himself, never her own self, entire, as he is entire.'

Dermot said, 'But I don't subscribe to such a notion at all. In Early Irish society women were nearly equal to men. And they were poets, delighting in male beauty, making men into their muses. Men and women were equal as lovers, friends, bards—'

Professor Talon interrupted. 'Please, let us focus on tonight's presentation. In the Irish sagas, women are depicted as either weak and insipid, or else powerful troublemakers. And, as you stated, Woman as Big Trouble is a theme we can discern in most mythologies, from Pandora through Helen of Troy and, of course, Eve, the mother of all our miseries, as an Early Irish poem declares.'

Maeve, beside him, was wringing her hands, and he saw that beads of sweat had collected on her upper lip. Poor Maeve, he thought irrelevantly. She was a dedicated impresario, and had considered his presence here a *coup* for herself, but the truth was that when it came to the province of scholarship she had not a notion of what was really going on. She had wanted him to please the audience so that she could savour her own triumph, and all she knew now was that her group were not happy. The Talon woman had mentioned Pandora, but it seemed that it was Dermot who had opened a Pandora's box tonight, loosing demons who were seething and swirling in the air.

Despite Maeve's conciliatory murmurs, the relentless Talon continued to sweep the room with her ocular headlamps. 'Professor O'Duffy, why do you promote such an unenlightened idea of women? Do you not see how men's fear and loathing of women is the reason for the establishment of the patriarchy? Men declare that females are ineffectual and weak, but, unconsciously, the patriarchs are terrified of the great power of the feminine, and that is why they feel compelled to keep women down. Do you realise that you, yourself, by presenting women as dangerous temptresses, are fostering their oppression? Do you not see that when men accuse women of tempting and enticing them, they are renouncing responsibility for their own behaviour? If a man is driven mad with lust for a woman, is it the woman's dilemma, or the man's? Is the woman responsible for his lust? Do you honestly believe that women are Deirdres and Guineveres, *femmes fatales*? Are even present-day women mere archetypes, whose function it is to serve the desires and fantasies of men, men who cherish to themselves the exclusive right to

32

be fully human? Do you ever write about real women, who piss and shit like you? Do you think modern Ireland is *not* a patriarchy? Are you—' She pointed an admonitory finger at him, and the hushed hall resonated with her indignant cry, 'Are you not a *gynophobe*?'

'Gynophobe?' he repeated.

Another woman, thin, with unkempt hair, jumped to her feet. She was rather beautiful, but Dermot registered something disturbing, nearly wild, about her face; then realised that her eyes were slightly crooked. She also thrust a finger at him. 'Yes, O'Duffy, a gynophobe! Don't know what it means, eh? Fear of women, terror of their bodies, of their genitalia.' Her askew eyes glared at him. 'Oh, you love our bodies when they belong to you, when they are instruments of your pleasure. But when we take them back, when we define them, and use them, on *our* terms, when we use our breasts not to *tit*illate you but to feed our babies, when we let you see that we bleed every month and that this does not soil us, when we are not ashamed, then what you feel is fear, and loathing.'

'Don't tell me what I feel,' replied Dermot hotly, trying to control his temper. 'I am no — er — gynophobe. And the old Irish sagas are full of women pissing and fornicating and bleeding. Just look at Queen Medb!'

'Ha!' crowed Professor Talon. '*Wonderful* example, O'Duffy. The bit of earth where her menstrual blood flowed was called Medb's Foul Place. And her poorly timed menstruation contributed to the defeat of the men of Connaught!'

The other woman, whose eyes seemed to be pitching dangerously in her angry face, shouted, 'You still don't get it, do you, O'Duffy? It is all right for men to spill torrents of blood during a battle, but the natural, beautiful, and mysterious issue of blood from Woman is abhorrent to Man. He hates Her body, hates the Glorious Cunt, and why? You know why! She, Woman, creates Life, she created Him, and so He fears and resents Her, and is jealous. Yes, jealous, jealous, jealous.'

'Absolutely,' declared Talon. 'Down with penis envy! The only real envy is cunt envy.' In a calmer voice, she went on. 'That is why we have created the Sheela-na-Gig Society. To exalt and exult in the private powers of women.'

From the corner of his eye, Dermot saw Grania give a little start, and remembered that he had spoken to her about sheela-na-gigs. Now she was probably expecting someone to bring up *slobhagóns*.

Maeve, he saw, was pale as tallow, and her lips were trembling. She doubtless hadn't liked the references to her mythological antecedent, Queen Medb or Maeve, whose menstrual flow was said to have burrowed three great channels in the earth, and poor Maeve herself beside him in an ill-chosen red dress. Now she quavered, 'Please, ladies and gentlemen. This is a scholarly occasion, and surely talk of defecation and — and — genitalia is unseemly and — and — inappropriate for such a gathering. Please let us *keep to the subject*.'

A third woman, businesslike in sober brown suit and white blouse, shrilled, 'No one has been talking about defecation! Menstruation is not defecation. And why shouldn't we celebrate our bodies? For men, the eternal truths are battles and business deals and the power of money, while for women, the essential things have always been blood, the womb, the hearth, to say nothing of the war between the Catholic Church and the clitoris. Why shouldn't the truths of our bodies matter?'

Defecation? Menstruation? The Catholic Church and the clitoris? Dermot was sympathising with the hapless Maeve. He'd thought this audience was assembled here to consider 'The Feminine Voice in Early Irish Poetry', but now he was feeling as though he'd stumbled into the wrong conference, or into one of the recurring nightmares he used to have, years ago, in which he would be speaking before an attentive academic group only to realise suddenly that he was bollocks naked. Professor Talon was saying, 'For those amongst you who might be unfamiliar with the term, sheela-na-gigs are female figures decorating the portals of many medieval Irish churches. Usually, these ladies display their vulvas, opening the labia with both hands, and grinning or grimacing. As caution: the Tooth Mother naked at last? Or fertility symbol, the replenishing generosity of Mother Earth? To invite men back through the door of bliss? Nobody knows, but we of the Sheela-na-Gig Society prefer to believe that the sheelas' position celebrates the Feminine Mysteries, which the patriarchy have tried to usurp, pillaging our power to serve their fantasies. From classical mythology to the Roman Catholic Church, men have idealised women as objects of desire or prayer, but has the patriarchy ever regarded or honoured us as ourselves, as *we* see ourselves? For example, did the Blessed Virgin ever go to what Americans quaintly call the bathroom? I am a woman, and my love goddess is not the insipid Aphrodite of the patriarchy with her sickly yellow curls, my Persephone is not the helpless concubine of a cruel god, my Blessed Virgin is not an impossibly virtuous patriarchal fantasy! We must take back our power, our mysteries! I ask you to do a daring thing, to imagine a world where the feminine powers, the goddesses if you will, are defined by women themselves, instead of being defined for us, by men. Perhaps in that world the masculine powers would exist only as women's fantasies and projections, to give the boys a taste of their own bull. The goddesses would be vital, complicated, and powerful, while the male figures would be — well — whatever we wanted them to be. He-man, footservant, daddy, baby boy, useful *man*ikins, our male models, with their limited attractions on display for our delectation.'

Part of the hall erupted in applause. Professor Talon gave Dermot a smirk; the light was glinting off her spectacles so that he couldn't see her fishbowl eyes. She'd certainly spoken eloquently, more so than he had done, faltering over his sheets of foolscap. Obviously she had carefully prepared her tirade. Dermot sighed; Doyle was probably right, these women were guerrillas; that Sheela-na-Gig would have launched into her diatribe no matter what he had said; she and her cronies had been waiting, poised, to bury their Talons in his unsuspecting flesh the moment he stopped speaking. They don't even ask a proper question, he thought peevishly, they just use *my* time, *my* platform, to spout their propaganda. What do they care about scholarship? All knowledge had to be dragged back to the revenge of the gaping vulva; he felt giddy, as if he were about to be swirled down into a vortex, an enormous bidet or toilet bowl. And something tilting him even further off-balance was the niggling suspicion that the argument of these outspoken ladies was not entirely unsound. Thank God Maeve was so flustered that she had not offered him his right to reply, but was mumbling her thank yous, trying to smooth angry feathers and bustle everyone back into the reception room for more booze and delightful gabble.

Dermot decided he wouldn't mind a stiff whiskey; then he would slouch off to Mrs O'Malley, whose gutted Christ extending his wounded heart was beginning to seem appealing, a kindred spirit. But at the drinks table he stumbled into Doyle, that silky, insufferable bastard, who smiled, and cried, 'Marvellous talk, O'Duffy. I enjoyed every syllable. And weren't those high-spirited women just great? Clearly you have a new academic future as a whipping boy.'

'Ah, Doyle. How did I know you would enjoy the bloodbath?'

'My friend, I did caution you. But you are right; it is possible my response is slightly less than generous. Yes, I must confess that your suspicions are not groundless. I did indeed enjoy the spectacle of you opening your mouth and inserting both feet into it. A sheela-na-gig gone wrong, if you want to adopt the terminology of these new and fearful scholarly ladies. No wonder they wanted to tear you apart.'

'You should be commended for your honesty.' Dermot moved brusquely past him, to where Grania was again positioned behind the bottles.

'Hello,' she said pleasantly. 'Perhaps you'd like a restorative?'

'That would be kind. A large whiskey, Ganymede.' While she poured he asked gruffly, 'Were you also made angry tonight?'

She gave him an amused look. 'No. You spoke well, though I suppose a man who ventures into the field of love nowadays is the equivalent of a condemned prisoner placing his head on the block. Maybe you should focus on *slobhagóns*, next time out.' More softly, she went on, 'Don't you think Professor Doyle must have some *slobhagón* ancestors? There is that watery *gleam* on him, with the little beard.'

Dermot laughed, and felt immediately better. He finished his whiskey and manoeuvred out through the crowd, managing to avoid both Talon, who appeared to be talking intently to Doyle, and the damp and fluttering Maeve. All he wanted was sleep.

Chapter Four

B ut his night was torn by dreams.

He is alone on a wind-scoured plain, and the *femmes fatales* of legend, a brigade of them, Circe, Helen of Troy, Criseyde, Deirdre, all dressed in white, are walking towards him, arm in arm, their hair streaming out behind them, and all of them with Fiona's face! Those eyes narrow as daggers, that proud jaw, a monstrous regiment of Fionas, come to reclaim him, as Emer did Cuchulain!

He gave a mute cry, and realised he was thrashing in the bed, his legs tangled in the sheets, his pyjamas bunched uncomfortably. He stared at the ceiling, flushed with a faint glow from the streetlamps along Bourke Road. Someone was rustling in the corridor, Grania or Doyle, he supposed, going to the loo.

Guessing it was about two o'clock, he tried to close his eyes again.

His mother is moving in her heavy shoes through the farmhouse, which is also Mrs O'Malley's house; he recognises the plaster Christ, and the butter moulded into curls on the breakfast table. Silently he follows her into the kitchen, and regards her dark head inclined over the cooker beneath the painting of the Blessed Virgin. These are familiar things, freighted with a kind of pain, and he is confused: Is he twelve years old, or fifty-eight, his current age? Without speaking to his mother, Dermot walks out the back door and into the summer fields. They are drowsy with flowers, and the grass is so green the colour seems to leak into the air, blurring the light so that it burns green as bottle glass. He feels the familiar green sickness in his body; he is twelve years old, and the air smells of loam and flowers, but he knows that it is wicked to touch himself. He lies on his stomach in the grass, half-closing his eyes against the sun, and feels Her hair fall over his face, Her breath on his cheek. He gives a groan of desire, but then a rough hand is wrenching him up — it is his mother — but when he looks, he sees not his mother but *them* again, the army of Fionas, bearing down on him....

Dermot cried out. His pyjamas were clammy with sweat, and his heart was pounding so heavily, he had a sensation of bruising in his chest. The dream-images were beginning to dim, but Fiona's winter-blue eyes, her hair, more muted now she was past fifty, but still red, her milky skin drawn taut over the strong bones of her face, these details of her presence seemed to hover briefly in the dark room. Fiona! Shorn of the intervening years, unalloyed somehow because of the two dreams he'd just had, Dermot's grief and bafflement struck him full in the heart. *Why* had things gone so wrong? And when? When had his lovely girl darkened into the morose and chilly creature with whom he was living now?

Oh, he'd known she was sorrowful when he married her, a bright woman in her mid-twenties, more handsome, arguably, than beautiful, with that defiant face of hers, and the burning hair. But it wasn't her imperious good looks that had haunted both Dermot and many of her other fellow university students. It was her mysterious silences in the midst of their raucous, uneasy, adolescent banter, the way her head would suddenly dip, like a flower drooping on its stalk, while she frowned, or sighed enigmatically, long lashes veiling those light eyes so that no one could read their expression. And these charged silences of hers, along with her air of melancholy, were all the more intriguing for being so at variance with the bold quality of her beauty, the high cheekbones and exotically tapering eyes, the proud carriage. And she was so tall, a modern Maud Gonne.

Yes, Dermot had been intrigued, enthralled by her. She had seemed so different from all the others. He recalled how they had thronged the big hall, gawky boys with raw knuckles and damp overcoats, shy girls with bedraggled hair and unravelling scarves, all of them smelling of wet wool and cigarettes, all hormone-crazed, ignorant, grubby, loutish, their shrill nervous cries eddying around Fiona who appeared impervious to them, standing tall and composed in that grimy hall which resembled nothing so much as an immense lavatory, while her red hair seemed to flare and crackle around her white face.

Almost immediately she had developed a reputation for mystery. Her suitors had glimpsed their own fantasies in the pool of her silences, comparing her to film goddesses like Bergman or Garbo, or else to the dreamy Celtic maidens of their schoolbooks. What could be more exciting than a woman who was beautiful, intelligent, *and* an utter enigma?

There was no doubt that he had liked it, wanted it, her dolour, her remoteness; he had wanted to soothe her, or so he'd always thought. Only lately she had begun to seem his dark opposite.

He could locate its origins in all kinds of things — his failure to understand her double depression after the loss of their child — her brokenheartedness at the miscarriage, allied to a physical, hormonal depression. Instead, he had behaved as if she were still her old efficient self, expecting her to cook and launder, imagining, even, that such ordinary labours might comfort her, when really all she'd needed was to be looked after. But it had been his baby as well, he had also been grieving; why could they not have comforted each other? Why, instead, had vaster and vaster silences, a tundra of silence, continued to expand between them, chilling their hearts? He supposed most men of his generation would have had trouble understanding

Fiona's particular kind of bereavement at that time, but with a mother like his, he hadn't had a chance. In the back of his mind he'd been convinced that all women were ailing, complaining, demanding. No wonder he had been lured to girls, and not women, with the benighted attitudes he'd had: women collapsed into bilious blobs, their faces invariably began to pouch with disapproval, but girls were always sweet, pliant, and full of possibility.

Ah, but if only Fiona had told him, taught him. He'd thought that was the crux of love: you travelled over wastes, suffered grief and famine and fear — in other words, you confronted your own blundering self, of which you were ashamed; in dread and trembling you let this other person *in*, to where you were terrified, and she did the same, fearing the same things, derision, rejection, loneliness. And instead of those familiar blows, what were you dealt? Grace! Sudden grace, through love, the gentle rain from heaven anointing your two bruised spirits.

He had longed to know Fiona's secrets, was convinced that their closeness could reside in their otherness; there she was, with all her own stories, all her history and hunger and dreams, a mystery, another country. But she told him so little! He knew now that her mother had been an alcoholic, and her father a ruthlessly ambitious man who had visited all his hunger for success on Fiona, before withdrawing from her emotionally at the same time as he'd recoiled from his drunken wife, as though mother and daughter were one and the same, and beyond redemption. But it had taken her so long to reveal these things. Poor girl, let down by her feckless drunk of a mother, convinced by brutal experience that men were false and cold; then whom does she marry? A cad, who blithely betrays her! But would he have done so, would he have flown into other women's arms, if she'd been warmer, more open, if she hadn't managed somehow to absorb her father's hardness into herself? Even when they were newly married, their love had been barren of a certain necessary sweetness. Exciting, it had been, and splendidly exhilarating, but he'd felt the absence of sweetness, had ached for it, even then.

And he and her other admirers had been wrong about her passion. With her flashing eyes, her red hair, Fiona had seemed as though she might be all fire, if only she would allow some ardent man to release her from the spell of those wistful-seeming silences. But he had now to admit that she was cold, so cold; he could not warm himself there. It was not fire, but ice, which had scorched him, when he'd looked for the first time into those blue and blazing eyes.

Yet now, in this dream-cargoed darkness, he had also to admit that despite his self-justifications there was a good deal of truth in the things Fiona said about him. His own mother, now dead, had been a stern woman, with work-roughened hands and a bitter, resolute face. Ah, but she'd had reason to be bitter. After the death of Dermot's father, she had expected her ten-year-old son to begin managing their fairly prosperous farm. But he, a dreamy boy (and a virtual moron in the realm of practical things) had been inclined to abandon the farm work suddenly, as though summoned by a voice, and wander off for hours through the woods with their green shadows and clouds of green-gold light, returning home at dusk with pollen all over his clothes and the faraway look in his eyes which his mother had loathed. And chagrined by her increasing coldness, he'd become even more clumsy. How bereft he'd felt as a child, as though he had lost his father and mother both, and how determined he had become, as he got older, never to feel so bereft again.

By the time he was twelve years old his love of the woods and fields was supplanted by a love of girls, their sweet voices and mysterious bodies. And when he was finally quit of the farm, and attending university in Dublin, there began what Fiona would later disparage as his pattern of profligacy.

During his rollicking university days, Dermot had known what he was up to, even without the dubious benefit of psychoanalysis. By making love to all those girls he was ensconcing a mother in every port, keeping every portal open. By encouraging this woman here and that one there, he was making sure that never again would he feel the emptiness, the barrenness, of that loveless parish of his youth. Girls for him were money in the bank, collecting love interest! And there was a further complication: in his early youth a schoolmistress had taken a maternal interest in him. Solicitous, tolerant, demonstrative, she'd been everything his mother was not, his first 'other woman', and on the days when he had gone stealthily to visit her, murmuring an excuse to his mother, knowing that he was betraying her, his heart had thrilled at its own wickedness, and with fear that he might lose her if she ever came to know that he was calling on Miss Flaherty, drinking her milk, eating her scones, and suffering her to place an affectionate hand on his curly head.

So one woman had never been enough; the double — or triple — life had been his solace. If one girl let you down, your other love, your sweet secret, could be the lamp in your sky.

But what had he really been looking for, throughout his career as a bit of a rogue, both before and during his marriage? Dermot did sense that probably he had always been much more in love with love itself, with the sweetness each new tryst had seemed to promise, than with the pretty girls themselves. And while as a child he had loved and longed for his mother, he had also hated her, hated her still in the place in himself which was like a dank cave or a lightless wood, so deep, this secret vault, he could never really understand what was housed there, had only smelled the fear of it, sometimes, in bad dreams.

Was it true, therefore, that some dimly comprehended desire for revenge on his mother compelled him to behave badly to Fiona? (And he did behave badly to her, had cuckolded her shamelessly, again and again.) All he knew was that by the time he married her, he had already grown tired of fleeting encounters; no fresh new face, or eager new body, could bring him enduring love; the predictable affairs with their murmured seductions, their drunken embraces in strange rooms, had begun to leave him lonely, and hungry. The double life had become a fractured life, as though when all was said and done his dalliances were just a means for keeping some fault open, keeping the wound in his psyche alive. And so he had come to his bride ready, aching, even, for a different life, for blessings, and grace. What, then, had gone wrong?

He had let Fiona down, there was no question. That girl with her tapering blue eyes and thick red hair, that elegant lady whose composure could collapse like a house toppling, who sometimes resembled an animal caught in a snare, frightened by the approach of even a rescuing hand. She had needed him, needed surety, consistency — and he had not been up to it. So much for his position as an authority on love, a voyager in the country of the heart! His female disciples might consider him a beacon to light their way, but he had failed to carry such illumination into his own life. His attempts to succour his own wife had misfired so badly, his flights to other women lately had been more in search of ordinary human sweetness than anything sexual; indeed, the sexual element was often minimal, or nonexistent. Oh, it was a long time since he had glimpsed the love god Aengus with his bright head garlanded in birds. And if this bitterness continued to afflict his heart, he would have to deconstruct poor Aengus into some ornithological archaism, in the manner of those cynical scholars for whom literature was a gimmick, a meagre source of mammon to be parroted with diminishing conviction each year to the ever-eager young.

He sometimes thought it would be better if only Fiona would get angry. But she was never angry, only cold, or else lachrymose, forever gazing out their bedroom window with a book forgotten on her lap, a cigarette drooping from her hand, as day deepened into evening. Had he been a fool to think that mere words could ease her sadness, that if she only spoke of her past (not a considered account, neatly fashioned into anecdote or myth, but the raw truth of her feelings), then it would be like sunlight transforming a mountain lake? Anyway, since it seemed she couldn't speak, he sometimes longed instead for a burst of ordinary anger, a shout, a cry, anything to shatter the silence. But she was never angry.

Dermot switched on the reading lamp, but soon realised that the customary pile of books on the floor by his bed would offer no relief; he might as well go out for a walk.

He threw on his clothes and Burberry, and moved quietly through the still corridor and out into the road. It was three o'clock, and the moon was full over the sleeping houses, whose gnomes and mermaids looked less kitsch and more magical at this hour. He swung to his left, towards town, and saw a figure a number of feet ahead of him, at the lip of the Bay, gazing down into the water. Why, it was Grania, and he had a mad thought; perhaps she had come out to look for *slobhagóns*! Her hands were thrust into the pockets of her green overcoat, which was buttoned up to her throat, its collar flaring. As he approached, he saw that she was staring fixedly at the swans, snowy blurs in the black water, heads folded under wings as they huddled against the quay wall.

Hearing his echoing tread, she looked up angrily. Then, 'Oh, it's you,' she sighed, and gave a low laugh.

He immediately understood. 'Doyle?' he asked, and also laughed. Again he thought, How plain she is, with her smudgeen of a nose and big doll's eyes. She grimaced. 'Yes. Professor Doyle. The Casanova of Irish Letters.'

'Oh, my dear, how awkward.' He touched her shoulder solicitously. 'I thought I heard someone moving in the corridor, about an hour ago.'

'It was going on all night. He'd come rasping and rustling at the door, and I'd open it and say something politely discouraging; then he'd go off looking wounded, only to come back in half an hour, still snuffling. So, finally, I bolted.'

Dermot suppressed a grin. 'You know, some women think Doyle is immensely attractive.'

'I'm sure they do. He's oily, pedantic, self-regarding, and supercilious. Those are very attractive qualities. Anyway, what are you doing up and about at three in the morning?'

'Couldn't sleep. Nightmares, and I do mean mares, not stallions. Doyle may be a magnificent machine for scholarship and sex, but I don't seem to make the grade. I take it all too seriously, it seems. The thin-skinned have no place anymore in the arena of political correctness. I dreamt that I was being gelded, probably at the same time Super Scholar was drunkenly dreaming of ravishing you. If this goes on, I'll have to throw love to the birds.' They looked down at the sleeping swans.

'I enjoyed your talk,' she said after a while. 'But it's true, you know, what those ladies were saying. They might have seemed ferocious to you, but you must admit they weren't completely wrong. A woman these days isn't pleased to be an incarnation of something in a man, his yearning, or his idea of beauty, or something; she is herself, after all, just as he is himself.' She paused. 'We want the same things that you do.'

'Oh? And what is that, pray?'

She seemed embarrassed. 'Just — to fulfil our promise, I suppose, to flourish in whichever province we choose, and to have equal love. The Deirdre you described was chosen by someone for a role, but she rebelled, and fashioned her own, which, of course, the man *she* chose may not have appreciated. It's bondage which creates calamities.'

He was silent a moment, stung. Tomorrow would be the conference's last day; Doyle would speak in the evening; then he and Dermot, along with everyone else except for the Galwegians and this curious girl who was sojourning here, would return home. Home! He muttered, 'There are so many kinds. Of bondage, I mean.'

Grania regarded him, and again, suddenly, he was made uncomfortable by her. As earlier, at the conference, he was too vividly aware of the slightest aspects of her presence: her rough lashes, the pleat at her mouth's corner, her bright hair under the lamplight, even the texture of her overcoat. It occurred to him that she might be wearing only a nightgown, or might even be naked, underneath that coat. Curiously enough, this was not a lecherous thought, but a flicker of protective concern. There was something about her that made him want to put his arms around her, but not in the old way of casual desire. Certainly she was fetching, and he was all too conscious of the pulsations of attraction between two people at such a witching hour. But, beyond all that, and the romantic backdrop of gaunt warehouses, cloudy swans in moonlit water, and the invisible Atlantic spreading out towards Aran and the Clare shore, it was some kind of aroma or aura he felt, a tug of interest beyond the ordinary. He wanted to know more about her, to take her hand and walk with her along the sea wall, slow and romantic like a schoolboy. But again he felt a rush of concern: perhaps she was too lightly clad, and he should get her back to Mrs O'Malley's before she caught a cold. Heavens, what a welter of emotions for an ageing, supposedly sophisticated academic to feel. Maybe he should get *himself* back to bed, before he went daft entirely.

To his surprise, Grania was regarding him with lively good humour, and to his even greater surprise, she suddenly took his hand, saying, 'Why don't we return to Mrs O'Malley and her stone swans? I think we'll be able to sleep, now.'

So, firm as Fiona had ever been, but with a shyness and gentleness he had not encountered for years, she brought him back to the guesthouse. Walking over the lawn, they took care not to stumble over the mermaid, combing her stone hair in the moonlight. Then they were in the corridor, but, as he was busy formulating a warm goodnight, he discovered that she had drawn him past his room towards her own. At the door, she touched a finger to her lips. Was this goodbye, then? His heart gave a sickening thump — of disappointment, of relief? But then he realised she wasn't dismissing him, she only wanted him to be silent for a moment, and when he heard what she intended him to, he had to muffle a snort of laughter. Through the wall came the shuddering snores of Doyle in alcoholic repose.

'I think I'm safe,' she whispered, and guided him in through her door.

It was nearly dawn, and the sky had changed; a watery light was muffled in the curtains now, making them look membranous as a moth's wing, but the room was still in shadow. Silently he took her in his arms and kissed her lips; he was still wearing his Burberry and she was still bundled in her overcoat; his hands moved up and down over the rough back of it. She drew away slightly to let him undo her buttons. He was fumbling, as so often. Despite his reputation as a lover, he was always terribly shy the first time, daunted by the mysterious body, suddenly revealed, and by his own sudden nakedness. And since the sad failure of his marriage he'd become too afraid and self-protective to abandon himself in the arms of any woman.

But she was patient as a good child suffering the ministrations of a clumsy adult, and when he had finally removed the overcoat, letting it drop to the floor, he saw that, as he'd suspected, she was wearing only a nightdress. It was a long, childish, flannelette thing, but somehow it, and her in it, were more appealing to him than those gossamer negligées favoured by vamps in old films.

He drew the nightdress over her head, then she huddled shyly against him. He wanted to caress her, to touch her breasts, but, respecting her timidity, he kept his hands only on the warm skin of her back, which moved with her breathing under his palms. He settled his cheek on her hair.

'Let me take your clothes off,' she said presently, and, while she unbuttoned him, frowning with concentration, he regarded her body, pale, slim, with small breasts and plump, delicious thighs.

'You are pretty,' he murmured.

'I'm not. But you are very handsome. You make me think of medieval paintings, with those slender knights who move along dream-meadows, under the turrets of a castle.' She touched his face, his hair. 'I like your blue eyes, and your lovely iron-grey curls, and those freckles.'

They got into her unmade bed, and kissed again. His hand glided over her breast, the curve of her hip, but after a few moments he realised that he was not able for this. Into her hair, he said softly, 'I am so sorry, my dear, but I am afraid that I will let you down tonight. It isn't that you don't delight me—'

She kissed his brow. 'Don't apologise. I feel the same. I don't know, it's just ... a little too much? You will be leaving soon, and maybe I will never see you again.' She paused. 'Have you a wife, Dermot?'

He answered flatly, 'I do, and she is quite miserable, and so am I. We bungled our marriage, a long time ago, and there is no way back. But we keep on; I don't know why.'

'I was married, too. A brief, disastrous marriage.'

'Is that why you came to Ireland?'

'Yes, to escape all that, and my father. And also to paint, as I said. But despite my boldness tonight, I don't think I am really made for casual encounters. One night, and then you're gone....'

'We could arrange to see each other again. I often come to the west.' But even while he said this, his heart was heavy; did he really want to engage in random exchanges anymore? The fly-by-nights which had once eased the ache in his marriage had now become themselves a burden. Did he truly want to pursue girls until he was doddering, a balding eagle squawking after ever-younger chickens while the crowd laughed at his unseemly antics? And he really would like to see this endearing young woman again, for talk or love or both: he felt totally at ease in her company, as though he'd known her forever. But what had he to offer her, besides a series of furtive embraces in a series of indifferent rooms?

'How old are you, Grania?' he asked softly.

'Older than I look. Nearly thirty-two. How old are you?'

'Ach, I'm an old man. Fifty-eight.'

'Fifty-eight isn't old!'

He laughed, and continued to stroke her hair. He was relieved that she was not so very young, that she'd been married, lived a bit. An awkward nineteen-year-old would have been too absurd, even for a man as desperately lonely as himself. But thirty-one seemed rather late to embark on a career as a painter. What was she up to? Why had she waited so long? Was she, perhaps, talentless, and had she flown to Ireland in a desperate try to evade the knowledge that her dreams of artistic success would never bear fruit? Somehow, he thought not. There was something, a vivacity in her, an intelligence. How good her paintings were he could not know, but he suspected she had *something*.

She said, 'Yes, I'm sure we could arrange to meet, here and there, now and then. But I don't know if I should see you again, after this. It would be stilted and strange. Somehow I didn't think you were married. Do you mind if I tell you that you seemed untried to me somehow, childlike or something, as though you had never been married....'

He squeezed her hand. 'Hush, dear. It's all right. Why don't we just sleep, in each other's arms? This night was wonderful, in its curious way.'

But, to his surprise, their candid talk had stimulated them. Instead of resolving and concluding things, and soothing them towards sleep, their discussion of his marriage, and her misgivings, seemed to have opened them up, quickened them into passion. Suddenly she was kissing him, her hair falling over his face. And, just as suddenly, desire flared in him, a fierce, dry heat. Hoisting himself up, he looked down at her, at her body: small rosy breasts; narrow waist; full hips; and at her face, flushed, with strands of gleaming hair across it, the lips parted, the hazel eyes gazing at him. Clothes had rendered her figure indistinct; he could not have foreseen the delicacy and opulence of her form, like a Renaissance nude, or perhaps her sudden beauty had to do with a glow, a light, that he felt in her, but she was not a dream. Through the disordered strands of hair it was her own face that looked at him. He took her in his arms and touched and kissed her; she murmured something, and her own hands moved over him. When he entered her it was easy.

'Grania,' he whispered, taking a sudden sweet pleasure in speaking her name, 'It's been so long.'

* * *

At ten o'clock Dermot's eyes opened, and he was overwhelmed by a feeling of happiness which coursed through his body; he felt it in his chest and throat and wrists and hands, like a lost music. The immediate sources of this joy, this delicious sensation, seemed to be the muted sunlight pouring in through the window, the distant soughing of the sea, and the smells of coffee and bacon from Mrs O'Malley's kitchen, as if he were back in love with the world. He smiled, and, still bleary with sleep, threw out his arm and touched a warm, naked shoulder. Only then did he realise he was not in his own room, and that the true reason for his happiness lay beside him.

Grania stirred, and peered at him through her rumpled hair. 'Good morning,' she said tentatively, almost apprehensively, as though afraid he might be regretting everything now, and look at her with dismay. But he was delighted, and ready for more lovemaking. He kissed her, and she nestled against him. 'So hard you are,' she breathed.

'And you,' he answered, 'are all damp and slippery, like a *slobhagón*.'

She sighed with pleasure. 'Have you made love with many female *slobhagóns*?'

'Only a few. And only in my reckless youth. It was an extremely foolish thing to do, you see. The *slobhagón* gentlemen are very jealous.'

'What do they do when they're jealous?' she asked drowsily, nibbling at his nose and winding her arms around his shoulders.

'They threaten to turn the poor fellow over to the sheela-na-gigs,' he answered, coming into her, with great pleasure, again.

After an exchange of sweet sounds, and a mutual consummation so lovely that it seemed predestined, a coming together decided before the beginning of the world, they lay amused and entwined, breath mingling with breath.

'And what would the sheela-na-gigs do to the hapless man?' Grania asked.

He smoothed the damp hair back from her forehead. 'Well, *slobhagóns* make love gently, a kind of flipper music. But sheela-na-gigs are voracious, insatiable, grinding the life out of the poor man night and day, as if he were caught between two millstones. His balls are crushed forever, and his poor male appendage whittled down to a stump. "Not big enough! Not big enough!" cry the sheelas, capering round his forlorn member.

Only if he has great magic can a man survive the fury of the sheela-na-gigs.'

'Sounds terrible,' she murmured sleepily, 'I think I'd prefer something more soothing.' She reached out for him again. And, miraculously, he was there.

Chapter Five

They decided to meet at breakfast, as if by accident. They reckoned that the sweet but old-fashioned Mrs O'Malley would be sorely flustered, if not offended, were they to descend hand-in-hand to the dining-room, and as for Doyle, 'At least we needn't worry about him,' said Grania. 'He seems to always linger in bed until the afternoon.'

So Dermot had his bath and then took his place at the big table. Mrs O'Malley had thoughtfully left *The Irish Times* on his chair, and he was reading a whimsical article on the magical properties of white heather, and drinking his first cup of tea, when there was a rustling across from him. But when he lowered the paper, already smiling, it was not Grania his eyes met, but a tousled, pouchy-looking Doyle.

'Why, Doyle, you're up early,' he cried, trying to conceal his dismay with jauntiness.

'Don't *shout*, O'Duffy,' grumbled Doyle. 'I drank too much and ate too little last night, and even a fool should be able to regard me now and discern that I am in less than good health. Good God, I ought to be cosseted, not *screamed* at. Where is that tiresome woman with my tea?'

'You're very grumpy. Why don't you go back to bed?'

'Because I must write my lecture for tonight. Heaven forbid I should go in unprepared and fall straight into the lioness's mouth, as a certain scholar-cum-lover managed to do yesterday. Ah, Mrs O'Malley. Just a boiled egg today, please, and *gallons* of tea. Thank you.' He passed a hand over his face. 'I couldn't even have a shower this morning. That American baggage was occupying the bathroom, as those doxies always do. They must be trying to wash off the guilt for being American, certainly not because they are smothered in the oils of love.' He took a piece of brown bread from the plate at the centre of the table, and began buttering it vehemently. 'Those spoilt creatures wouldn't recognise *amour* if it struck them across their overfed faces!'

Dermot said mildly, 'This particular American girl doesn't look overfed. And I thought you liked her.'

Doyle glowered at him. 'She has a funny face. *You* said she had a funny face.'

'But *you* said it was a pretty face.'

At that moment, Grania appeared, smiling, her hair, still wet from her shower, clinging in scalloped curls to

60

her forehead. 'Why, Professor Doyle,' she said, 'you're up early.'

'No thanks to you,' he growled, almost inaudibly.

Mrs O'Malley appeared with Dermot's enormous fry, and Doyle's lonely egg. Grania said, 'I'd like poached eggs, please, and black and white pudding, and bacon, and sausage. And grilled tomatoes and mushrooms, please. And coffee.'

Doyle glared at her. 'You eat rather greedily, don't you, my dear?'

'I'd say I eat with a healthy relish. Goodness, you are taking sickroom food. Are you ill, Professor Doyle?'

He vigorously salted his egg. 'No, I am merely weary. And I—' He looked up just in time to see Grania give Dermot a deep smile, and a long look from her dancing eyes. He stiffened in his chair. Dermot could see what he was thinking: Not only had he been scorned, but he'd been scorned for a lesser scholar than himself, which meant, by definition, a lesser lover, since intelligence was without doubt the rudder of the emotions. Certainly O'Duffy might be good-looking with his bright cheeks and curls, but any love inspired by appearance was a meagre thing compared with the love which flared from the sword of the mind!

'Well,' said Doyle, 'It seems some of us have become rather *cosy* overnight.' He smiled at Grania. 'But you mustn't take our dear boy too seriously, Miss MacCormack. He is a scamp, you know. Why, the groves of academe are fairly littered with the hearts he has broken. I hope you haven't let him tamper with yours.'

Grania's cheeks whitened then burned red, but she answered steadily, 'I am moved by your concern for me, but I'm quite capable of looking after my own heart, thank you.'

'You shock me, Doyle,' said Dermot softly. 'I wouldn't have thought that you would recognise a heart, broken or sound, if you fell over it. You have always considered heartlessness a virtue, no? And yet you are giving a young lady advice about how to protect hers. Anyway, you ought to have some more tea, dear man. You're looking quite green.'

Doyle, mechanically spooning up egg, opened his mouth to fire a return salvo, but at that moment Mrs O'Malley appeared, bearing Grania's coffee and a message for Dermot: 'A telephone call, Professor O'Duffy. You may take it in the pantry.'

Another religious picture adorned the wall above the phone, a Madonna in the throes of the kind of pious ecstasy one could easily confuse with nausea — eyes turned up, mouth open — with a wizened-looking baby Christ in her lap, flailing its misshapen fists.

'Hello?' said Dermot.

'Dermot?' replied Fiona wearily. 'I am in Limerick, as it happens. I came down with Daddy yesterday, to visit my brother, which means I can drive up to Galway and collect you this evening; you needn't take that awful bus. Daddy might come as well.'

He stared at the Virgin with her boiled-egg eyes. He had intended to leave tomorrow morning, so that he could have one more night with Grania, and now he felt suddenly, violently bereft. His throat thickened with disappointment, and he was close to tears — ridiculous! He barely knew this girl, and would be leaving her tomorrow, anyway. Why should the deprivation of one night affect him like a blow in the stomach? Had he had some romantic notion that this night would unfurl forever, that he and Grania could navigate their little bark of love past all the shoals of his circumstances, and conquer time? In the past, love affairs had bestowed on his life some of the sweetness absent at home so that, replenished and sweetened, he could return to Dublin and Fiona, and sustain the charade he believed that *she* believed she needed. But why did that formula of the double life seem suddenly impossible now? Surely he should simply be glad to have discovered Grania. Whenever he missed her, or the days with Fiona became too unhappy, he could simply concoct some excuse to visit Galway and see the girl, provided she agreed to such an arrangement, and then she would restore him, and enable him to go back, heartened, to his difficult life in Dublin. Wasn't that the reason for taking a lover, to make a bad marriage tolerable? Well, he'd discovered the ideal lover. Why, then, was he miserable now, and not rejoicing? Suddenly he pictured Doyle's lean, savage face: *The solution, my dear Dermot, is to hang-glide.* But he didn't seem to have the talent for hang-gliding anymore, or else, absurd though it might seem, he was already partly in love with the brown-haired woman in the next room. Already, last night, she had helped to make his body and heart whole again; how could he return to a half life, after such a healing?

'Dermot,' repeated Fiona, with a sigh. 'Are you listening? I'll come by tonight, to the conference, and then we can return home straightaway.'

'I had wanted to take another night here,' Dermot said dully, 'and return tomorrow.'

A pause. 'Fine. If Daddy comes along he might like some more time in Galway. He'll go to the Great Southern, of course, but, as for us, have you a double or a single room? If it's only a single, ask them to change it. Two beds, please. I've been sleeping badly lately. Perhaps a midnight walk by the Claddagh would be a tonic. How did your talk go?'

'It was splendid. I was attacked by Furies, plural. Indeed, a crowd of them.'

'What? The musical group? Do they go to academic lectures?'

The impossibility of extricating himself from all the ironies made Dermot decide to conclude. 'Never mind. Till tonight, Fee. And it'll be grand to see your father.'

Dermot meant the last statement sarcastically. Fiona's 'daddy', Finn O'Reilly, a square-headed, blunt-spoken, coarse-mannered farmer, had idealised his daughter before growing cold to her when she failed to make a splendid marriage at university, and when his relations with his own spouse were withering. And then, after Fiona finally married Dermot, a mere college lecturer, a social nobody, he had all but abandoned her. But Fiona had continued to adore him, to curry his favour, and since the recent death of his wife he'd begun to warm slightly to her, if not to her pathetic husband. Old Finn, whose wealth was recently

Chapter Five

acquired, had cherished dreams of a rising barrister or
a diplomat for Fiona, someone whose prowess would
advance Finn himself, not an insignificant intellectual
with empty pockets. Even after Dermot became relatively famous in Dublin's academic and literary circles,
'Daddy' remained stubbornly unimpressed.

When Dermot returned to the table, Doyle was gone,
his napkin thrown over his egg cup like a cowl. Grania
said, 'I think our Professor Doyle lost his appetite.'

Dermot stared down at his cooling plate. 'Mine
seems to have diminished as well.'

'What is it, Dermot?' she asked, touching his hand
on the table. 'That phone call?'

He sighed. 'Will you come for a walk with me, out to
Salthill? We can maybe talk there.'

* * *

Grania told him that as a child she had visited English
sea resorts, and had been intrigued by their dilapidated
Victorian hotels, invariably called The Queen, The
Grand, or The Royal, dignified as matrons in threadbare shawls, and positioned on high slopes from which
they could command a disapproving view of the
promenades. There, a vulgar glamour would prevail:
tinselly dance hall music, neon gambling parlours,
carousels, ladies of the evening, hawkers of candy floss.

But Salthill was her first *Irish* sea resort, and she was
seeing it in late spring, with the promenade nearly
deserted, the hotels and amusements arcades still
closed, and over the entire area the romantic desolation
of an abandoned carnival. Hand-in-hand, they strolled

past the shuttered discos, fish-and-chip shops, and newsagents, onto the long concrete promenade.

Presently they wandered into a pub called O'Connor's Real Irish Shebeen, a dark place with stuffed birds rearing gloomily out of the corners beside oil portraits of de Valera and Parnell, and, occupying one entire wall, an immense cauldron suitable for cooking a wild boar or stag. The room was empty of customers but for a frail old lady wearing a genteel blue suit and drinking what looked like a double whiskey, and her consort, a gaunt man absorbed in *The Connaught Tribune* and clutching a blackthorn.

After two pints of Guinness, they walked again by the sea, under a milky sky flushed here and there with a clear gold light, and every so often he paused to take her in his arms; the sea-smell clung to her hair, and her lips were warm. He placed his hand on her head and kissed her temple, her ear, the pulse in her throat. He still hadn't spoken to her about the telephone call, but she was patient, settling her cheek on his chest, gazing quietly out at the ocean, the mythical realm of *slobhagóns*.

He was just about to tell her of Fiona's imminent arrival, when she said, 'You are quite a famous man in Ireland, aren't you, Dermot?'

He took her hand, and they continued walking. 'Well, being a famous scholar is not exactly the same as being famous. Although it is true that the Irish cherish their writers, even those who only produce academic texts, like myself. And I suppose I was canny, or lucky, in my choice of subject matter. People are always

interested in reading about love. But I believe *your*
name is quite well known.'

'My father is famous, in America, although not as a
man who's wise in the matter of love! He's a shrewd
politician, and would regard those who love ardently
as soft-hearted fools. Which is not to say he doesn't
have plenty of admirers. His fame attracts sycophants,
and gushing girls, and so on. He seems to feel the girls
belong to him, like spoils or trophies. Spoils rhymes
with goils, for him, I'm afraid, which makes it hard to
be his daughter. I do love him, but he can't help con-
descending.'

Dermot divined that, despite her cool response at
the breakfast table, Doyle's remark — about the groves
of academe being strewn with the hearts he'd broken
— had upset her: was she about to find herself caught
up in a different version of her father's slippery game?
She was going on hotly, 'And I also despise how male
painters seem still to believe that women should simply be models, that they should be content to exist not
as real people, but as inspirations for masculine crea-
tivity. And what happens when the painter sickens of
his model, when she fails to inspire him? Then he
moves on to the next one. But what if women were just
like him, wanting the same things, work, and the fruits
of their work, and a real love?' She was suddenly silent,
as though afraid she had lost her composure, which
indeed she had. Her cheeks were burning, and he could
swear there were tears in her eyes. She mumbled,
'Anyway, I want to paint *light*, and, when I draw portraits, I am not so vain as to think — Oh, I don't know.'

She stared down at her feet. So, she was trying to tell him that she was afraid he might use her for a time to kindle his cerebral energies then drop her for a more novel companion. Damn that Doyle! He considered what to say to her now; then decided on the truth.

Stopping, he cupped her face in his hands, and murmured, 'You know, Grania, I think I am a little bit in love with you. And I didn't bargain for that at all.'

She looked level at him. 'What are we going to do?'

With a chill, he realised he had forgotten about Fiona. He dropped his hands, and tried to tell her, haltingly, of the broken state his marriage was in, and yet how he and his wife seemed to depend on each other, so that tonight Fiona would arrive, resignedly, frostily, to take up the burden of himself, once again.

'Oh, God,' Grania said bitterly, 'She's coming *here*? I knew I shouldn't have got involved in something like this. If this marriage of yours makes you so deeply unhappy, why do you remain in it? Surely it can't be good for her, either?'

Dermot gave an irritable sigh. 'It's so easy for you Americans to abandon a marriage. It's like what you do when you have grown tired of an old car. You just blithely trade it in for a newer model.'

'I wasn't talking about trading something in for a new model. I was talking about your unhappiness!'

They glared at each other. She said, 'You probably enjoy it. You can indulge in as many naughty affairs as you please because, of course, you need them for comfort, since she makes you so miserable, and you can feel marvellously daring for how boldly you deceive her, thrilled by your own exploits, and, even if she is not deceived, that's all right too, because your affairs are a perfect punishment for her. Lucky you. You get everything. Except simple happiness.'

He said quietly, 'I didn't think you could be so spiteful.'

'Of course not! How could you have known? You don't know me, and I don't know you. And now—' Grania's voice broke, and immediately his anger dissolved. He fumbled in his pocket for a handkerchief, and pressed it into her hand. She dried her eyes; then looked down, biting her lip. With a sigh he drew her against him and whispered, 'I don't know why women never carry hankies.'

Her answer was a forlorn sniffle. He squeezed her, and said with emotion, 'Grania, I don't want to lose you.'

'Me neither.'

'That's all right, then, that's all right. We'll think of something.' He gazed over her head at the sky, the wheeling gulls. 'In the meantime, why don't we go back to bed, for what the Old Irish called the conversation of bodies?'

She drew back and looked at him. 'That's a lovely expression. And maybe we can agree on a new dialogue, before Doyle performs?'

And my wife arrives, Dermot remembered grimly.

* * *

While they were walking back to Mrs O'Malley's a gentle rain began to fall, spattering the mossy quay. But by the time they came to the house, the rain had stopped, and the rinsed sky gleamed pearl and gold. Silently as possible, they hurried up to Grania's bedroom, but their timing was good: both Doyle and Mrs O'Malley seemed to be out. Grania gave him a towel, and, while he was drying his hair, she opened the window, and cried, 'Look, Dermot!'

He came up beside her, and gazed out at two rainbows straddling the sky, one vast crescent, with its smaller companion just beneath it. They extended from the Bay out to the Atlantic, curving over the promenade.

Grania said softly, 'I have never seen a rainbow before. And now, two of them! We must be doubly blessed?'

He brought her to the bed, and took off her damp clothes. First, they made love delicately, with a kind of sweet urgency, but then her cries and caresses began to draw forth from him a passion deeper and warmer than any he'd known in years, and before he knew it they were both panting, filmed in sweat, tumbling around on the dishevelled bed like a couple of lolloping seals, and Grania, clutching him, sobbed, 'I can't *stop*, I can't *stop*,' and he could feel that it was so; she was coming over and over with sharp, high gasps. They did indeed seem to be blessed, doubly, triply, quadruply, or any multiple of bliss one might desire.

But after a short sleep, from which he was roused by her hair, bristling against his face as she moved her head on the pillow, his elation collapsed. Tonight, these hours would be a memory; even now while he touched her hair, her cheek, she was receding from him into the past. Of course, he would manage to see her again, but, for now, the thought that tonight he and Fiona would be practically next door, together in his room, while Grania slept alone in this bed, was nearly too painful and embarrassing to contemplate. Grania had told him she intended to leave the guesthouse shortly; a Galwegian artist friend of hers was preparing to embark on an extended holiday abroad, and in his absence she would settle into his flat and studio. But for at least a few more days she would be living here in this room, with her clothes, books, and drawing materials bundled into the cupboards, so that he couldn't very well suggest she tactfully disappear tonight, to make this passage easier for both of them, and, if he moved to another bed and breakfast this afternoon, before Fiona arrived, she would doubtless smell a rat. So there was nothing for it. This episode would have to be undergone, but, staring up at the ceiling, with Grania nestled against him, Dermot felt like the greatest blundering idiot in the world.

Chapter Six

Strange, he thought, this echo of last night, the same crowd, yet for him nothing was the same: he observed the now-familiar Maeve with her rough hair and glassy smile, and the excited students, grizzled war-horses of professors, journalists, gawkers, and hangers-on, all the fun of the off-season academic fair. And of course he glimpsed Professor Talon, her bosom festooned with a thick necklace, probably composed of testicles, he thought. His eyes sought Grania, who was not serving the drinks tonight, but had decided to come to the conference because her friend on the organising committee had invited her, and because she was curious to see how Doyle's performance would be judged by the lady zealots: would they clamour for his blood as they had for Dermot's yesterday, or would that wily goat contrive somehow to gratify them?

Earlier, Grania had said to Dermot, 'I suppose it might be easier for both of us if I kept away from your conference tonight, and I suppose I could sleep over at a friend's apartment. But I don't want to skulk through Galway this evening for fear of glimpsing you and Fiona. I know that you're married, and, when she appears tonight, we'll all just have to behave like grown-ups.' But after this firm declaration she had blanched and swallowed painfully, and Dermot, while admiring her pluck, had wondered whether any of them — he, Grania, Fiona, or the oleaginous Doyle — would be remotely capable of conducting themselves like grown-ups if anything were to go wrong. Rather late in his life, he was learning that, no matter how intelligent one was, emotions could always surge up from underground and upset everything, cracking the mask, toppling the apple cart, banjaxing the band-wagon.

With a catch in his chest, he saw Grania now, talking to a young woman whose motorcycle jacket was emblazoned with the clarion call 'Sheela-na-Gig Society', written in strong red letters above a particularly fierce-looking sheela. He sighed; the crowd really did look nearly the same as yesterday, although, last night, before he had thrown himself into their collective maw, the anti-gynophobes had greeted him with cordial smiles, while now a nearly palpable chill was wafting towards him from their corner. Talon mouthed a hello across the room, but her fish eyes were glaring, and even the cloying Maeve was pronouncedly cooler, giving him a remote smile, as though he were a nice but not very bright student. But as far as Dermot was concerned the greatest alteration since the evening before was in his own, previously untenanted heart. He could barely look at Grania, and his eyes kept wandering to the door, through which Fiona might appear at any moment, accompanied, perhaps, by Big Finn.

When he felt a hand on his shoulder he nearly jumped in the air, but it was only Doyle, smiling like the crescent moon.

'Nervous, my dear O'Duffy? I should think nervousness might be *my* privilege tonight, since I am speaking.' He carefully removed a mote of lint from the sleeve of his fine English suit. 'But actually I am at this moment quite confident in myself as a lecturer, thanks to you, dear boy. One feels secure in hazarding that, after last night's performance, the general current this evening will flow upwards, if you know what I mean. To be blunt, there are very few mistakes I could make tonight which would equal your dazzling gaffes of yesterday.' He sipped from his glass of mineral water. 'And, speaking of gaffes, your lovely helpmeet arrived at the guesthouse just after you left. I took it upon myself to escort her to your room, where she is now freshening up. She should be along shortly. Really, O'Duffy, you are rather a fool. I have been telling you for years that you must handle these things more tidily. Wives and mistresses all thrashing about in the same B & B! Positively distasteful. You must develop greater *style*, my friend; I am afraid that you are rather long in the tooth to insist on behaving like a lovesick adolescent. Surely you are not still inclined to disdain my wise advice about keeping love in its proper compartment? Love and its attendant complications ought never to encroach on one's marriage, old boy, *never*. But you seem to be the poorest hang-glider since Dan Cupid was a boy. You deserve disaster! You're certainly courting it, letting a slip of an American warm your almost-marriage-bed.'

'What did you tell my wife?' asked Dermot evenly.

'What did I tell her? Why, just that I was delighted she had come in time to hear my talk. And that you have seemed to be enjoying yourself a very great deal in Galway. Excuse me, Dermot old fellow. I'm quite parched and must have more water. I never drink wine or spirits before I lecture, a recipe for success I recommend to you. *Ciao.*'

Dermot looked round, and saw that the woman with crooked eyes was approaching him. Her handsome but asymmetrical face made him think of a cracked teapot. Certain that her intention was either to revile him or ask him to make love to her (or both) he hurried into the Gents, and took a deep breath.

Was he vain to presume that so many of these academic women were in hot pursuit of him? Perhaps, but long experience had borne out the truth of this presumption. And his area of scholarship had fostered it all. Despite the fact that he was blatantly a self-satisfied fool who couldn't even get it right in his own marriage, he still doggedly continued to write about the great lovers of Irish legend and to discourse on this theme, so that many of the girls in his classes and audiences must have believed he had divined the truths of their hearts, *and* that they had fathomed the truths of his. And indeed he had sometimes felt as if he were an initiate; it had often seemed to him that a certain girl in a certain audience, her face shining up at him, was meant to be there, that it was no accident, her presence in the lecture hall, but a mystic synchrony. He supposed now that this was an example of how he had all too often glamorised the trivial, tumbling in and out of infatuations, rapt in romantic myths, and giving too little credence to genuine love, which, though housed in the ordinary, was after all more strange and rare than he could know.

His poor wife, she'd had to put up with a lot. He remembered a particular talk in Dublin. Dermot, a woman poet, and a male short-story writer had been invited to read from their current books. Warmed by the students' bright faces, uptilted as though to drink in his words, he had spoken well that evening, and afterwards his admirers (mostly women) had thronged the lectern with their questions and books for him to sign. Amongst this crowd, shyly proffering her copy of his *Love and Early Irish Mythology*, was a girl whose billowing yellow hair had arrested him during his talk. Now he said to her, 'Give me time to think of something special to write in the book for you. Come back in a moment.' She blushed, conscious no doubt that throughout the reading he had favoured her with special glances, and while the other guests clustered round he thought of her, that sweet face and profuse fair hair. And when he looked up from the last volume (thrust under his nose by a garrulous woman dressed, it seemed, in tea towels) to see that the lovely girl had not gone, but was still bashfully waiting for him as he'd suggested, his pleasure emboldened him to rashness. 'We might meet tomorrow, in the pub across the road,' he said, whispering because his wife happened also to be in the audience, inconveniently interfering with the marriage of true minds.

He and Fiona went to dinner, then, at a French restaurant. And over the entrées (*salade avec fromage de chèvre* for her, *poireaux remoulade* for himself) she remarked frostily, 'I noticed you were enchanted by a certain young woman in the audience. I overheard you congratulate that vulgar man, the one who sponsored your talk, on his pretty student, and then you and he had a cosy laugh. And while I was waiting for you at the door she came out with her pals, giggling and telling them that you had asked her to meet you tomorrow.'

He moved uncomfortably in his chair, angry with himself, and with the girl for her indiscretion. 'Indeed we did arrange to meet. To discuss Early Irish poetry. She is an enthusiastic student. And that *vulgar* man is buying you your sheep's cheese—'

'Goat's cheese.'

'—and this nice Côtes du Rhône.'

'Stop lying, Dermot. It isn't scholarship you want to engage in, with that girl. I saw you giving her burning looks—'

Inserting a ribbon of leek into his mouth, he asked nervously, 'Did anyone else see? It's a lecturing device, to try to focus on someone in the audience. And she was certainly noticeable.'

Fiona's eyes looked suddenly stricken; her poise seemed to dissolve, and the clamour of the restaurant to recede. He was about to extend a penitent hand to her, but she said in a quiet, wintry voice, 'I was at the back of the room, you didn't even look at me!'

'Then why did you have to place yourself where I couldn't see you?'

The waiter removed their plates. She asked, 'Why must you always slight me in public?'

He thought of the girl, her sweet smile. 'She was very pretty,' he said with brutal thoughtlessness, 'And why was she there, up so close to the lectern?'

Fiona crumbled a piece of bread in her hands. 'Do you think she was especially positioned in that particular place for you? You think providence arranged it?'

Her moment of vulnerability had vanished as though he'd imagined it. Now she was fastidiously eating her *rognons de veau* while gazing rigidly over his head, and the thought of extending his hand to her was inconceivable — surely she'd only withdraw her own, and give him her long-suffering smile. He nibbled at his duck, in its cloying orange sauce. Inexorably, she continued.

'You have to beguile them all, don't you, suggest to other women, in my presence, that you are available to them?' She drew a breath, then plunged on with determination. 'Dermot, if you have truly devoted your life to love, then why do you trifle with *my* love, why do you abuse it, and how can you indulge in the folly of believing that a pretty face was placed before you by the gods precisely for your delectation? Women do not exist so that they can appear in audiences to inspire you!'

It occurred to him just then that of course she was right, and, anyway, what the hell was he doing, he who had married this woman in order to renounce a life of trivial conquests, what the hell was he doing propositioning a giggling girl at a reading, and with Fiona in the same room? How lost was he becoming, how lost to himself? But what could he say, now? Simply, stupidly, that the blonde girl's smile had been a balm to his spirit after Fiona's reproachful silences and sighs? That the girl had seemed sweet, and his heart was famished for sweetness? That he was desperately in need of physical love, as his wife might also be, though she seemed not to know how to call out to him? But then the truth struck him, that the significant moment in this dinner had come when Fiona had looked at him with confusion and pain, and he, moved by that place in her which was simply full of need, had wanted to take her hand. But the tender moment had died, killed, perhaps, by both of them, by his bitterness and her coldness. And now, here in this Galway hotel toilet, he closed his eyes and thanked God he hadn't met Grania as a member of one of his audiences, thanked God she had come to reside in his heart so naturally, as herself. In the old days, he might even have relished the woman with crazy eyes; she'd have been good sport, perhaps, and sport had been what academic conferences were really for. But now all he knew was that his life had changed, literally overnight. Suddenly he no longer wanted easy affairs, or the loveless security of his life with Fiona, and, just as suddenly, he was scared.

He shuffled over to the urinal, and was peeing pensively, when the door opened and the woman with tilted eyes sauntered in.

'Sorry,' she said breezily, 'the Ladies was full. You don't *mind*, Professor O'Duffy, surely? Gents is such a misnomer these days, an old-fashioned concept, don't you think? We must campaign for unisex toilets in busy thoroughfares!' She laughed coquettishly while he bundled his shocked instrument back into his trousers. Then, 'Professor,' she cried, 'we haven't been properly introduced. My name is Cordelia Callaghan. And since I am using the Gents toilet, perhaps in future it ought to be called Cordelia's Foul Place. What do you think?'

She vanished into one of the cubicles. Oh, God, he thought, What next? and lurched out the door.

Chapter Seven

Emerging from the Gents, he scoured the big room with a quick glance, but Fiona had still not arrived. He gulped down a scalding whiskey; then followed the chattering crowd into the lecture hall. Immediately, he noticed Grania, towards the back. She gave him a hesitant smile; the place beside her was empty. He waffled; then thought, Why not? If Fiona were to come in, she would simply see him talking idly to a young colleague. And although he suspected that proximity to Grania now would be a kind of torture, it might soothe him as well. Anyway, he felt helpless, felt himself drawn to the chair on her left as if tugged there by an invisible cord, and settling down beside her with a nervous smile, he was once again forcibly struck by the most trivial details of her presence, the texture of her sleeve, the slope of her cheekbone, the burnished lights in her brown hair. He could tell that she was agitated, too; he was fairly sure that her lashes were starred with tears. Like a fool, like a schoolboy, he wanted to murmur an endearment: *sweetheart*, *darling*, but restrained himself, a true professional.

Doyle had appeared at the lectern, on which he was placing his clean, typewritten lecture, whose heralded (and cautiously vague) title was 'Women and Early Irish Poetry'.

'Ladies and gentlemen,' he cried, smiling benefi-cently at the audience, 'This conference, at which we have all so enthusiastically assembled, compels us to focus on the feminine presence in Early Ireland, so central and so important.' From the corner of his eye, Dermot saw that the Talon woman with her enormous glasses and brutal necklace was smiling eagerly. With approval? With cannibalistic glee? He supposed they would all know pretty soon.

Doyle proceeded, in elegant and learned fashion, to extol the feminine presence in Early Irish society, dipping into the Brehon Laws, under which women had nearly the same rights as men; then gliding over into the realm of poetry, where women composed, sang, and spoke in their own voices, ardent and clear as the voices of men. Or did they? Were they merely personae, male scribes, perhaps even clerics, assuming the voices of women? Beaming, Doyle presented his listeners with various readings of the old poems, asking was this lament, or that love poem, created by a woman, or by a man adopting the persona of a woman? By all appearances, Doyle (scrupulous scholar that he was) meant to encourage the audience to choose for themselves, but, as far as Dermot could see, he was slyly tilting the argument in a direction obviously meant to flatter the distaff side. Talon's face was at this point garlanded in smiles, and the woman with awry eyes was nodding excitedly, like a manager whose team was triumphing. Obviously, these Sheela-na-Gigs weren't excited because they smelled blood, as they had done last night. No, they were excited because they were *happy*, because they liked Doyle, they actually *liked* him; he was praising them so highly, his face was reddening with the effort, as though all this gushing about women bards and women warriors and women who in Early Ireland were able to throw over their husbands as easily as husbands could throw over their wives, as though all this effort were wringing the last droplet of energy from him, and working him up to the point of apoplexy. He had to pause now and again to smooth an immaculate handkerchief over his brow, and his eyes were glistening.

He was marvellous, though, Dermot had to admit, a real master fisherman, casting his deceptively brilliant flies before the gaping mouths and pulsating gills of the lady fish. Even Grania murmured, 'He does have a flair for not letting personal issues encroach on his professional life, doesn't he?'

'Hmph,' replied Dermot, unable to manage a more articulate response. Compared to this *finesse*, his own lecture, he began to realise, was an even greater fiasco than he had thought.

Doyle launched into a reading of the medieval Irish poem *'Aithbe damsa bes mora'*, 'The Hag of Beare', archly explaining that his pronunciation of the old Irish was only a putative reconstruction. He followed this up with a rousing rendition of the poem in contemporary English, and his low, clear recital, the measured stanzas alternately sweet and harsh, the old tidal rhythms, the woman's lamenting, wry, strong voice, all these washed over the still audience as if the sea were in the room, and Dermot could tell they felt privileged, as if they had been drawn into Doyle's scholarly quest, allowed to discover the poem with him, understand it for the first time, his intimates, his confidantes, in on the real thing. When Doyle finished, he took a swallow of water from the glass on the lectern; then asked his largely female audience, 'Was this poem written by a male clerical scribe, like myself?' Talon tittered. He went on, 'If so, then I am certainly flattered.'

The hall rang with applause. After it had died down a bit, Grania said, 'Don't look so morose; our Doyle is a cunning old wolf, but he was splendid, you must admit. I liked what he said about how the feminine qualities as imagined by men were a different thing from how women perceive and write about *themselves*. Very nice, I thought.'

'I don't remember him saying anything about the feminine qualities,' Dermot grumbled.

She grinned. 'I'm paraphrasing.'

He gave her a narrow look. 'You're teasing me. Did you really think it was a splendid lecture?'

'It was a *professional* lecture. You know he designed

it to butter up the ladies. I bet those Sheela-na-Gigs will be eating out of his hand, now.'

More than his hand, thought Dermot glumly, but kept this observation to himself.

Sure enough, after the question and answer period (consisting of accolades from that chatterbox Talon, and judicious praise from two male colleagues of Doyle's) the audience shuffled out to the reception hall, where Dermot immediately saw a graciously smiling Doyle encircled by eager women. He recognised the woman in the brown business suit from last night, and the woman with asymmetrical eyes, and Talon, of course, who had placed an intimate hand on Doyle's arm and was allowing her stout breast to brush against his elbow, and even Maeve, looking rabbitty but pleased: at least one of her academic lions had roared properly.

'Ah, my fellow scholar and gentleman,' Doyle chuckled, lightly disengaging himself from Talon's sturdy hand and sauntering over. 'And the young lady.' He gave Grania a brief, chilly smile then beamed at Dermot. 'O'Duffy, my boy, I believe I shall linger in Galway a few days more. It seems I shall be booked up for quite a while...' (he caressed his sparse beard) '...giving some basic instruction in *hang-gliding*.' Smoothing his hands down his lapels, Doyle continued. 'As I have been trying to explain to you, it is one of the more delightful modes of locomotion. And there are so many models at one's disposal, from the frail fluttery craft, to the heavier dirigible. And so many techniques to master, from the full flight forward into the wind, to the sideways dip, not to forget, if you are truly daring, the counter turn and reverse!'

Doyle's motor was only warming up to the infinite pleasures of his subject matter. As for Grania, although she obviously had no idea what the man was talking about, she must have felt the innuendo charging his snide words, for she had begun to blush. Dermot placed a protective arm around her shoulders, and said levelly, 'All right, Doyle, I take your point. I should think you ought to be careful, however. All that motion can make a man sick, especially if his heart isn't in it.'

'Ah, dear fellow, it is not my heart I am concerned about,' answered Doyle, with a crowing laugh. He smirked at the Sheela-na-Gigs, who were gazing admiringly at him; then strode over to the drinks table. Dermot was thinking he could use a drink himself, when a chillingly familiar voice, the loud, hectoring, cattle-jobber voice of Big Finn O'Reilly, assaulted his ears.

'So there you are, you blackguard, shamelessly making passes at other women in public! Have you no manners, or concern for your wife, or yourself, or my position in the world, you two-timing guttersnipe?'

Realising his arm was still draped around Grania's shoulders, he let it drop as he whirled round to see Big Finn (actually a shortish man, though burly; the 'Big' came from his wide fields), at the door, fists clenched, eyes glittering with anger — he did not resemble his daughter at all except for those ice-blue eyes, and a certain strength about the jaw. There she was beside him, her face white and utterly expressionless.

The hall was silent but for the sudden rattle of ice in a glass as someone gulped a drink. Dermot, horrified, felt as if he were floating up out of his body, as if he might look down and see the rigid husk of himself staring dumbstruck at the door through which Finn and Fiona were now striding. Finn was obviously fuelled to near exhilaration by his rage, and his aware-ness of an audience which he plainly assumed was already on his side, accustomed as they must be to Dermot's shameless antics. As indeed they were, only not for Fiona's reasons, but because of his tactless lecture, as well as the academic world's boundless appetite for scandal.

Finn continued gloatingly. 'Sure, I smelled a rat when I brought my daughter to your bed and break-fast, and Professor Doyle let us know what a *grand* time you've been having here in Galway. And in what way, I asked myself, would a *schoolteacher* be managing to have a *grand* time at a conference of schoolteachers?' He shook his blunt finger at Dermot. 'I'm not stupid, boyo, despite being a mere peasant as opposed to a fine college man such as yourself.'

With splendid abandon, Big Finn warmed to his task, a public dressing down of the weakling husband who had shamed his daughter once too often. At first he thundered, eyes grim and sharpened. Then suddenly he was pious, a priest clothed in virtue, hands clasped over his barrel chest, gaze sombre. Finally, abruptly, his manner changed again, grew sly and coarse. 'Good God, man,' he cried into the tense silence, 'sure I don't object to a frolic meself now and again, since boys will be boys. But you don't have to blunder about like a fool, letting the world and his neighbour know about it!'

Fiona had been silent all this time, her face chill as marble, but now, at last, she spoke, in a low, vibrant, strangely calm voice.

'It's true, Dermot, what my father is saying. I have tried and tried to improve you, to correct you, to save you from yourself, but it is simply thankless. You're like an errant child who will just not learn how to behave. And now you've insulted me one time too many. I suppose you haven't any shame left, or decency.' She looked at Grania, who was trembling.

'And you,' she continued in that same curiously fluent voice, as though she were reciting from a play, 'you, whoever you are. You should not have done this thing.' She indicated the spellbound crowd. 'These people are my husband's colleagues, whom he and I often meet, together, but, thanks to you, from now on all such meetings will be — will be *soiled* by humiliation. You have come into this place from another country, intruded into this world which does not belong to you, and you have humiliated me here, where I must live. You have damaged my world by engaging in a public affair with my husband.' She switched her gaze back to Dermot, who had been marvelling at her composure. 'No, you haven't any shame left. Making love to impossible people, insignificant groupies who clamber all over you, massaging your ego, manipulating you. You can never resist them, never say no to them. You feed on their flattery, you hunger for it. You will never stop, Dermot. You have never been true or loyal to me, and you never will be.' She drew a shuddering breath. 'And these girls care nothing about me. I am only the *wife*, an annoying impediment on the way to your bed.'

Dermot said quietly, 'You may be right, about the past. But this woman is not as insignificant as you say. She is—' He paused, dry-mouthed. Fiona and her father's display was so humiliating, he was unable to register fully that it was taking place, and was aware of the staring crowd with only a fraction of his consciousness. All that was completely real to him at this moment was himself and his spouse, staring at each other through a miasma of anger and pain. It was as if there were no one else in the room. He swallowed. 'She is not insignificant. She is kind, and intelligent, and I happen to love her.'

He could scarcely believe what he had just said, but as his own words echoed in his ears he realised they were true, and what he felt was a relief so tremendous, it was as though some sullen weight on his heart had finally lifted, so that he could breathe again.

Fiona stiffened. Then, still in that calm voice, she answered, 'All right, Dermot, very well. You love this girl. And I presume she loves you, as well.' He noticed her hands, white knuckled, clutching the stuff of her skirt. 'But if that is so, why do you persist in skulking about, and being so furtive? Do you think it's daring, and deliciously wicked, to deceive people, to conduct a secret life? Is that it? But it isn't fair to me. Can you not see that? And it isn't fair to this girl, either, whose time with you would have to be dealt out in small parcels. And it isn't fair to yourself, really, is it? You can't build a life on the quicksands of deviousness. You mustn't implicate me, and this woman whom you say you love, in such falsity. If you love her, then make a life with her, and leave me free, to make a new life for myself.' Her voice quavered, but she swallowed hard. 'I want you to leave, Dermot. I want you to go away, and I will keep our Dublin home, and try to soldier on. But I do not want you to use the house, and our lives, as a station from which to conduct a love affair with another woman. No more of that! Do you hear me? I want you to go.'

She had threatened so many times before to throw him out or else to leave, but on each of those occasions she had been either cold or full of reproachful tears. And now? He looked at her resolute jaw, the taut skin under her eyes, her straight shoulders, and was struck, as he had not been for so long, by what was fine in her. Why, this woman's heart might be breaking, but she was behaving bravely, and he was certain that this bravery of hers was exacting more from her, from her heart and her exhausted spirit, than he could possibly measure. He had a sense of how difficult he must have been to live with over the years, and how in the beginning Fiona must really have believed that her icy rebukes would improve him. And, however mistaken she might have been in her conviction that criticism and woebegone silences would buttress their marriage, still she did try, in her own way; she did sacrifice; she had loved him, in her fashion. Certainly, if she had failed him, he had also failed her. But now she was saying that she was willing to let him go, for the good of all concerned in this, his latest misadventure. And now, at what looked to be the last chapter in their marriage, her valorous words were recalling him to the first chapter, to the bright, beautiful girl he had once loved, so many years ago. He gazed at her, his old companion, and knew that what she said was true, and that he would not be able any longer to indulge in the thrills of a double life, not after today; he would not be a hang-glider anymore.

'All right, Fiona,' he said simply. He deliberately did not look at Big Finn, whose bulky, heavy-breathing presence he could feel beside her. 'I'll do as you ask.'

'Good. I have taken a room at Daddy's hotel in Eyre Square. And tomorrow I will go home. Good night, Dermot.'

Finn took her arm, and as they turned to walk out the door Dermot saw that her composure had begun to crumple, and that she was crying. Then they were gone. He looked about him, shaken and bemused, as though he had been dreaming. There they were, all of them: Talon, her mouth gaping open; Doyle, stroking his beard and smiling; Maeve, wringing her hands in that infuriating way she had; the journalists, looking avid as carrion birds. Then his eyes met Grania's.

She touched his hand, and immediately, as though her gesture were a signal, everyone began moving and talking, pretending nothing had disrupted them. Talon and the Cordelia creature, their heads together in deep conversation, converged on the drinks table, Maeve fluttered over to a journalist and began gabbling to him while he, ignoring her, caught Dermot's eye and gave him a rueful smile. The students, some with distressed expressions, others looking thrilled, broke into groups and commenced chattering. Nobody except for that kindly journalist looked at Dermot, as if his shame had rendered him invisible, or given him the kind of affliction from which passers-by avert their eyes. Grania said, 'Let's go.'

'Yes, in a minute. First, where is that shitbag?'

'Who? Doyle? There, talking to that lady.'

Doyle and the woman in the brown business suit were drinking wine and laughing *sotto voce*. Dermot strode over and gave Doyle's sleeve a wrench, aware that the man would be annoyed at having his fine English cloth tugged at by a sartorially inferior colleague. 'Look here, Doyle, come out of the room for a minute. I want to talk with you.'

'Very well, old fellow,' replied Doyle easily. 'Let us repair to the road. I imagine we could all of us use a breath of air after that unfortunate spectacle.' He smiled at the woman, who glanced at Dermot and blushed, embarrassed, no doubt, by his public flaying.

Doyle asked the woman to look after his glass; then they walked out of the hotel, accompanied by Grania, who could not have been enjoying the glances and whispers encircling her in the hall, although she had confronted them squarely enough, head high.

The three of them swung through the revolving door into the road. It had been raining again; the pavements were gleaming, and a light mist shawled the street-lamps. Doyle produced one of his pretentious cigarillos and said, 'My condolences, old man. A terrible bore, that sort of scene. But of course there is a certain kind of woman who savours public tirades.' He blew a scroll of smoke into the fog.

Dermot realised that this man had a lively contempt for him, regarded him as coarse, naive, unsophisticated — everything, in short, that Doyle the famous flying juggler was not. How ridiculous Dermot must seem to him, a perpetual lovesick calf, bungling everything! And, realising this, Dermot's anger increased mightily; he wanted nothing more in the world than to smash his fist into that wolfish face with its scythe of a smile.

'Listen, Doyle,' he said quietly, 'you corrupt, cunning, craven little bastard. What did you say to my wife when you met her at the guesthouse?'

Doyle laughed, blasting Dermot with his stale breath, a combination of cigarette smoke, alcohol, ancient coffee, and, Dermot was now sure, moral decay. 'Dear boy, I *told* you. I explained to her that you have been *amusing* yourself in Galway. Why, I was comforting her, O'Duffy, in case she feared you might be lonely. I told her she needn't worry about you, because you have been having a *delightful* time.'

Dermot clutched Doyle's lapels. 'You absolute shit! Does it never enter your conniving head that it is people's *lives* you are playing with?'

Doyle's cigarillo fell to the gutter, but he smiled, and replied soothingly, 'Now, now, old man, I understand that you are upset. But it's no good trying to make other people responsible for your blunders, you know, no good at all. I certainly did not inform Mrs O'Duffy that you have been fornicating with a little American, or anything of that sort. Now let us be civilised, dear fellow. Do stop damaging my suit, if you please.'

'Why? I want to damage your suit. But what I would really like to damage is your smug face.'

Dermot had the satisfaction of seeing his colleague blanch. He knew Doyle had consented to come out into the road because he was convinced that he, Dermot, was a wimp, a weakling, a uxorious self-pitying adolescent, which might indeed have been true up until this moment, but things, undeniably, were changing. He released the man's lapels. 'Take your glasses off, Doyle, you slobgolliper.'

'My dear man, please calm down.' Adjusting his coat, Doyle smiled uneasily. 'And what under heaven is a slobgolliper?'

'*Slobhagóns* gone wrong. Cousins to *slobhagóns*. Evil, black-sheep cousins. Take your glasses off or I'll take them off for you.'

'What nonsense are you uttering? What the hell is a *slobhagón*? Are you daft? And I will not take my glasses off. Look here, my good man, I am a highly esteemed Gaelic scholar, not a street urchin. I refuse to brawl—'

Dermot fired a straight left, the only punch he knew. It landed on Doyle's forehead; his spectacles flew off and spun into the road. Fists clenched, panting, he knew that he should follow up his advantage, but Doyle's confusion, his frightened, faltering movements as he tried to recover his glasses, were pitiful. Oh, how the mighty are fallen, Dermot thought.

But Doyle located his glasses, placed them in his coat pocket, and flung himself on Dermot. He was a filthy fighter, and surprisingly strong and wiry. He tried to butt his head into Dermot's stomach, tug at his hair, knee him in the balls, and he'd managed to fasten both his hands on Dermot's earlobes, and was pulling down on them like bell ropes, when suddenly he let out a yelp and sprang away.

'You bitch!' he screamed, whirling round to glare at Grania, who presumably had given him a toe in the behind. She looked levelly at him; then landed a punch flush on his jaw. He collapsed on the wet pavement.

'Ouch,' said Grania, examining her knuckles.

They gazed down at the supine Doyle, splayed in the gutter like a starfish. Dermot asked Grania, 'How'd you learn that?'

She smiled sheepishly. 'My father. He used to take me to Madison Square Garden. Some of the boxers were his friends. And he taught me a few moves, when I was small. He said I should only use them if somebody got fresh with me. But I never met a big enough louse, until now. Do you think he'll be all right?'

Two gangly young men slouched past, most likely heading towards one of the pubs up the road. They glanced down at Doyle; then threw Grania and Dermot a friendly grin. Dermot observed, 'Either young people these days are so callous that they enjoy seeing men unconscious on the pavement, or else Doyle is more disliked than I suspected.'

At that moment Doyle opened his eyes, groaned, and struggled to his knees, fumbling in his pocket for his glasses. Dermot helped him to his feet.

'Don't touch me, you homicidal maniac!' Doyle shrieked. His hair was in disarray, his cheek smudged with dirt, but he seemed unbruised. He produced a handkerchief and began scrubbing at his no longer impeccable coat. 'And you,' he suddenly pointed a finger at Grania, 'you American philistine! Just because you have a powerful American father, you think you can come over to Ireland and clout people. All you American-Irish political families are the same, drunk with power. You think you can have whatever you want, like sweets in a shop, everything is yours for the taking. Everything that has happened here tonight is your doing, you spoilt hussy. And since you are doubtless rich as Croesus, I shall post you the cleaning bill for my suit!'

He made to go back into the hotel, but Dermot seized his lapels again. 'Look here, my friend, I'll make sure you're sprawled out in the road a second time, unless you apologise to this lady. Understand? Since you met her you have insulted her in one way or another, and in my opinion she has been admirably forbearing.' He gave Doyle a shake. 'But no more. Say you are sorry.'

'Let go of me! I am not a sack of potatoes!'

'Not until you apologise!'

Doyle looked slowly from Dermot to Grania. 'Fine.' He gave her a forced version of his leering smile. 'My dear, if I have insulted your delicate sensibilities, I am most heartily sorry. Now let me go, old man. This evening has been entirely too sordid.'

Dermot released him, and he hurried back in through the revolving door, eager, no doubt, to entertain the Sheelas with the story of his valiant KO of that impossible O'Duffy. And he nearly had gutted him! Where had Doyle learnt those rough-house tactics? Then Dermot remembered: before hoisting himself up by the bootstraps into the higher echelons of the academy, Doyle, like Big Finn, had come from one of the border counties, where he'd probably survived a diocesan college, as savage and primitive a society as any described by the anthropologists. So knees in the groin and pucks in the neck were mother's milk to him. Under the smooth veneer, and the platinum glossed accents of Oxbridge, he was still an aboriginal bogman, responding instinctively to the war cries of his native place: *Gut your man, stick in the boot, maim him for life!*

* * *

They returned quietly to the guesthouse. Dermot was feeling nothing. They went to Grania's room, where she gently undressed him and settled him into bed like a child.

While she eased off into sleep the rain began again. A strong wind lashed it against the windows, where it spattered in quick, agitated bursts. He had a picture of Fiona crying, the big tears coursing down her face. He moved his head back and forth on the pillow but the image remained. Why did he have to cause so much hurt and harm?

What had he done? What had he done? A black panic was in him. How many nights beside Fiona in their barren bed had he dreamt of freedom? And now he had it, with her benediction, but, oh God, at what cost? The cars hissed through the rain along Bourke Road, Grania murmured something in her sleep.

Grania! Who was she? Perhaps Doyle had been right, calling her a spoilt hussy. These American-Irish political family dynasties really were so privileged, and so corrupt. This girl beside him had travelled all throughout her life in a limousine, luxuriating in the fool's gold of glamour American-style. Why, her family were regarded as royalty, practically, over there! So she might play at being a struggling artist (could she possibly be any good?) but that invisible carapace of wealth and privilege had always surrounded her, protecting her from pain, rendering her, probably, impervious to the needs of others. Did she care that Fiona was in anguish now? Did she know that she had caused Fiona's anguish?

'Grania!' he cried, overcome with anger.

Instantly she was alert. 'What is it? Oh, what is it?' She extended her arms but he recoiled.

'Grania, what have you done?'

She gave a little gasp. 'What is it, Dermot?'

'Does it matter to you that you would appear to have broken up a marriage?' She became very still. He went on, 'Probably you don't give a damn. After all, you have everything *you* want. Why should you care that you have inflicted so much pain on Fiona, and on me, who must suffer for her pain?'

She was silent for a minute; then another. He thought she might have gone back to sleep, when she said huskily, 'You are telling me that I am responsible for what happened tonight? No, you are actually telling me that I am responsible for the collapse of your marriage?'

'If it weren't for you—'

'Yes? You would have gone wearily on, living without love? Or something else would have happened, to bring about this *dénouement*? And you would not have been responsible for that occurrence either? I have never heard such self-deceiving rubbish in my life! Do you Irish ever leave the cradle? Do you think that when I left my husband I blamed it on some third party?'

The rain beat its irregular tattoo on the window. Dermot said in a low voice, 'Ah, but it was so public. Doyle gloated to her about it, and when she came into the hall my arm was draped about your shoulders. Dear God, she was right, about us soiling her world. Why did I not simply tell her, long ago, that we were making each other unhappy, and should separate? Then it would have been a clean break.'

He felt himself shuddering. He had come into that dark place where there were no moorings. How many times as a child had he listened at night to rain, breathed in a smell of damp stone, looked at his shadow on the wall? Where had he gone those rainy nights after his mother had looked at him with angry or indifferent eyes? There had been no solace for him then, those nights when he had felt himself dissolving into the watery darkness of the fields beyond his window. If she did not love him there was no grace. And he had known that the problem, the flaw, was in *himself*, not in his mother's hard nature, or his misbehaviour of the moment, but in himself, essentially. The time she had struck him across the face because his elbow had accidentally unsettled the milk jug onto a length of cloth she'd spread out to make a dress, the time when, surreptitiously, not knowing why but with a dark turbulence in his heart, he'd gone into the empty bedroom of his visiting cousin, and with the kitchen scissors had proceeded to fray the other boy's clothes till his mother had opened the door with a scream of rage.... What had he felt, those times and so many others? That he was bad, inferior to other children, deserved her contempt. And now he was back there, that place where there was no forgiveness. A spoiler, a destroyer, a wrecker of happiness, that was himself all right! There were no words to describe the nothingness he felt, so he stared at the ceiling, where a picture of Fiona, grieving, seemed to glow in the darkness.

Memories assaulted him, of how he had let her down. Just two years ago, Fiona had decided to journey out to Massachusetts, where he'd been teaching for a term in the Irish Studies department of a small private university. It had been a bleak winter, and his heart could not rejoice at the landscape — leafless boughs against a sky forever bitter with snow — but one of his graduate students, a rich girl with the haughty face and straight blonde hair of a WASP princess, had amused him. She'd scrawled a message underneath one of her papers: *Professor O'Duffy: I am just a pilgrim along the ancient love-roads, but you are a famous authority on love in Irish legends — you could initiate me into mysteries, maybe?* So he and this girl, called Antonia, had already embarked on a heavy flirtation by the time Fiona arrived, exhausted from the long flight, appalled by the snow and cold, and more than usually caustic. He had thought that taking her along to a faculty-student party might please her, but Fiona was no fool, and the moment she observed Antonia sidling up to him at the reception and placing a proprietary hand on his shoulder, her hackles had gone up. 'Who are you?' she had demanded, glaring at the girl.

Antonia (a terrible bitch, Dermot later admitted to himself) had replied, 'Why, I'm the professor's protégé. Who are *you*?'

Fiona, stiffening with resentment and misery, had whirled around and stalked out of the party, embarrassing Dermot before his colleagues, whose rapacious smiles above their stiff uniforms, tweed coats and perforated brogues, had convinced him that they were probably relishing the spectacle.

Fiona was unhappy that entire term, moving white-faced through the rooms of their small clapboard house, barely speaking to him. He and Antonia had an earnest talk during which they agreed there should be no affair, not only because Dermot had a wife on whom he would (of course) be loathe to inflict pain, but also because that wife just happened to be virtually (inconveniently) next door.

A few days after this, crunching to class through the snow, vapour pluming from his mouth, Dermot reflected that he truly disliked Antonia, with her spoilt, primly pretty face and complacent manner. He suspected that she would be vain and perfunctory in bed, and that she wasn't intelligent. Clutching his battered satchel of books, looking intently down at the

101

snow, he further thought that, really, he could have honoured his wife better. When all was said and done it shouldn't have been up to Fiona to reproach Antonia for her impertinence at that party; *he* should have made it plain to the gloating girl that she had violated something dear to him, that her behaviour had displeased not only his wife, but himself. And then there was that craven soul talk he and Antonia had indulged in, squeezing each other's hands, declaring, like brave, honourable, mythic lovers, that they must forfeit their dreams of each other so as not to hurt his dear wife. Whom of course he had already hurt, cruelly, by suffering Antonia to place her arrogant hand on his shoulder in Fiona's presence, after she had travelled all the way to America to be with him.

He was walking to his classroom through a small wood, and now he stopped, encircled by the black trees; the air was taut with cold, and in the stillness his own breath rasped in his ears. The truth was that lately his encounters with women had become more and more absurd: clumsy non-affairs with good, sober girls to whom he was only remotely attracted and with whom he could do no more than cuddle, or murky flings with sexy but unpleasant creatures like Antonia, which would leave him feeling impatient and angry. He was afraid that he was souring into a cynic, afraid that he would never be a loving man again, afraid that he was hurting Fiona deliberately, using his erotic conquests, bitter and unfulfilling though they were, to wound and embarrass her, using bitches like Antonia as instruments of humiliation, becoming, in other words, what Fiona had often accused him of being.

He looked up at the raw New England sky, blanched with impending snow. Oh, he missed the skies of Ireland, that great cloud theatre, he missed the Irish earth. What gods dwelled in this metallic air, this frozen earth? The other day he'd walked into the kitchen where Fiona, unaware of his presence, was baking bread, her cheek smeared with flour, a gauze of flour on the air, a beautiful woman, her eyebrows two thin fronds, the red hair curling on her white nape, her hands moulding yeast and flour: his wife, his wife. Suddenly she'd looked at him, and through the flour dust he'd seen the pain in her eyes, and without thinking he had extended his hand. But as in that Dublin restaurant after his reading (another place where he had failed her) the moment didn't last, they were not able to sustain it; looking alarmed, she'd bunched her floury hands in her apron and said something sharp to him, and he'd withdrawn from the kitchen, chilled as herself.

Beautiful, distant, hurt Fiona, idealised and betrayed first by Finn then by her husband. Brilliant Fiona, considered a prize in the Ireland of her youth, a Catholic girl, a country girl, but lovely and poised as any Anglo-Irish deb. Her father had polished her into a lady, young men had adored her, but no one had ever allowed her to be herself. Poor Fiona! But again his old plaint returned to him: *He had not wanted to be a libertine.* Doyle was right: he, Dermot, hadn't the proper style, or stomach, for a Don Juan. Despite the lure of the double life — doors opening soundlessly on underground passages, secret rooms where sirens beckoned — despite all those hackneyed thrills, the thing he had wanted when he married Fiona was not doubleness, but coherence, a coming together, a healing. That was why, after his marriage had begun to crumble, he had begun lavishing on his illicit affairs such an unseemly ardour, such a quality of yearning, such declarations of love. Now a kind of shame scalded his face as he realised that he had been looking for *love* in the pliant arms of all those girls, that he had ached with the desire not only to receive sweetness, but to give it; the phrases had been stored in his heart, growing old and ashen there for want of use, the things he had always wanted to say to the one beloved: *Come to me, there is easement here, you needn't be afraid, I love you....* The things he'd wanted to say, the things he'd wanted to hear said to him, they had mingled in his imagination, and he had moved restively from girl to girl looking in each one for that intimacy he'd thought his marriage would bring, but which had become impossible for Fiona and himself. But why? Had she been too riven by early blows to believe in him? Had he been too selfish for an adult love, too enamoured of the admiration his female students bestowed on him? Had she been too afraid? Had he been too childish, too cavalier? One thing he did believe: if she had only let him know how his profligate behaviour was hurting her, if she had only revealed *herself* to him instead of retreating into tears and frigid silences, he might have learnt to discipline himself. He had wanted to protect her, to understand how his bad patterns might wound her, so that he could change them. He had wanted them to be each other's charges, not each other's scourges!

Now Grania placed a tentative hand on his shoulder, and when he didn't spurn her she took him in her arms. Gratefully he embraced her, breathing a bit easier. She said, 'It *was* public, what Fiona saw. And I am sorry about that. We were so absorbed with Doyle that I suppose we forgot, briefly, that she would appear. It was terrible, really, to expose her to that.'

'Perhaps we did know, unconsciously, what it was we were doing. Anyway, Doyle didn't help, did he? One can imagine what he said to her!'

She said softly, 'Anyway, you shouldn't have accused me, before, of breaking up your marriage. It's hard enough for me, to be implicated in hurting another woman, to inflict loss and sorrow on her, things I'd hate to feel myself. In fact it's one of the most awful positions a person can be in....' She was silent a moment. 'Do you want to call on her at her hotel, make it up with her?'

He listened to the rain. 'No. From this point on, I cannot go back. What she did tonight was brave, and I must admire her decisiveness in the face of my passivity.' He paused, considering. 'It's strange, though. When she confronted us she was so deliberate and calm, as if she had rehearsed what she would say. Or else....'

'What?' Grania prompted.

'I don't know. It was as if her father had galvanised her. She has always admired him, even though he used her cruelly in the past, as an instrument to serve his own ambitions. But this evening it felt like he was fuelling her. She mightn't have been able to speak with such assurance if he hadn't been there to encourage her. Maybe old Finn is the only person whose approval she has ever really longed for. Or perhaps she thought that her courageous performance would shame me into returning to her. But I can't, you know. The marriage is over, and not a moment too soon, but all this is terribly painful.' He looked at Grania, this girl he'd known for such a short time, but who seemed to be implicated profoundly in his destiny. 'I am sorry for my outburst. Tell me, please, about your own life, your marriage. You must have gone through hard times, black periods?'

Chapter Eight

The rain sprayed against the window like a fistful of
pebbles. Grania said, 'He was the son of my father's best pal.'

'Was he another politician, your father's pal?'

'No, a real estate magnate. I don't know about over
here, but in America the urban landlord is quite a
phenomenon, the worst kind of wheeler and dealer, the
sort who allows babies and old people to die of expo-
sure in crumbling tenements while he and his family
live in luxury, you know?' She moved restively in the
bed. 'This fellow, Greeley, wasn't as notorious a mogul
as Donald Trump or anything, but he was a pretty big
deal in Connecticut, where I am from.'

'I know you are from Connecticut,' Dermot answered, smiling at her modesty. The MacCormacks of

Connecticut were nearly as famous as the Kennedys of Massachusetts, in Connecticut, anyway, and of course among Irish institutions ferreting about for grants, contributions, and general freebies.

'Oscar Greeley was a thug, really. Have you ever known people like that? Rich people who live in opulence, with houses and jewels and servants — the whole bazaar — but who are spiritual paupers? I have never liked any kind of class snobbery, because the class that people come from shouldn't matter a damn. The only things that should matter are the heart and the spirit. Greeley was like a Cro-Magnon man, hunkering down with a cudgel in his paw, ready to thwack anyone who ventured too close to his cave.' Grania's voice trembled with anger. 'But his cudgel was made of gold, as heavy as the rocks dangling from his wife's throat.'

'Rocks?' echoed Dermot, picturing an ageing woman with lumps of granite adorning her raddled chest and depending from her ears.

'A vulgar Americanism popular among vulgar Americans. Meaning diamonds.'

'I see,' he said slowly. 'But this fellow Greeley was your father's best friend, and you married his son?'

She sighed. 'Oscar was a keen gambler, and he and my father used to go to the races together, with their chequered coats and cigars, like two Damon Runyon characters. My father is a bit of thug, too, you know; I cannot excuse him. But he is an intelligent — no, a brilliant — man, and not entirely without compassion. Also he is handsome and gracious, while Greeley was an animal. There was nothing he could imagine beyond sly business deals, beyond chuckling brutally at the saps and suckers, beyond money and power. He couldn't *imagine* love, you see. Which my father could do, in a limited way, although he would never dedicate himself to it, or sacrifice too much for it.'

She continued talking, and Dermot pictured her life, the glittering society of Washington and Georgetown, the New England estate with its white house, and green lawns sloping down to the sea, the faces of her father and his cronies scarfed in aromatic smoke while they lingered after dinner over the port and cigars, plump, well-brandied men deciding how the nation should be managed (to their advantage, of course), their cheeks shining with the glow of privilege. Her mother was a brittle society matron from New York, her younger sister a ninny, interested in nothing but horses. Her family had always disapproved of Grania's desire to be a painter, despite her teachers' insistence that she was truly gifted and ought to be allowed to attend art college. It meant less than nothing to them, and perhaps they sensed a possible criticism of their own values. Both her mother and father were convinced that Art was by Old Masters whom you bought at auctions as business investments, and then displayed prominently on your walls. Paintings that hadn't been approved by experts were like newly minted money from some obscure banana republic which might collapse at any moment. Grania said, 'My father had collected a few very minor Italian and Flemish Old Masters, and once, on a holiday in Ireland, he plunged and bought a Seán Keating. I was always asking him to buy a Jack Yeats, but he said the guy couldn't paint. Yet they did let me go to art school. And it was while I was home from the art college, during a summer vacation, that I met Greeley's son, Thomas....'

She paused a moment. He caressed her hair, and she continued. 'I'd known Tom when we were children, but I hadn't seem him in ages. And now here he was, a tall young man, a year older than me, and so sweet and shy, so unlike his father. I must tell you that at that time, my late adolescence, I was much younger than my years, studious and chaste, much more alive in art than in the world.'

'I was chaste in my adolescence, as well,' said Dermot. 'In my day, in rural Ireland, there weren't many opportunities for lovemaking. Once, at sixteen, I tried to touch a girl's breasts, and she called me a scoundrel. Can you imagine? A little Irish girl using language straight out of the eighteenth century.'

'But you had chastity imposed on you by a repressive culture, while I imposed chastity on myself, in an age of permissiveness. I don't know why, except that I must have preferred my dreamy life of paintings and fantasies to my father's harsh world. Also, as I got older and saw how my sister and her friends were carrying on, I began to feel that their casual sex was sometimes *callous* sex, too easy and heartless, and I was afraid of that. And of course there was my father and his lady friends, so many, there were, or seemed to be. Sometimes, at dinner, my mother would suddenly throw her wine in his face, and one day I stumbled on her in a dark room, crouched in a chair with her head in her hands, like a statue depicting grief. Oh, I was afraid, all right, so I guess I just withdrew from the fray. I would float through the house in my long dresses like a creature from some other century while my poor father stared at me, completely baffled, or I'd do cnarcoal drawings all day long in my bedroom, or go to artists' supply stores because I loved just to look at the coloured pencils and thick paper and the paints. My father, who truly loved me, would throw up his hands and cry, "Grania, where are your suitors? I thought by now this house would be full of eligible young men instead of your sister's obnoxious adolescent boyfriends. Why aren't you having *fun*?" I didn't know why I wasn't having fun, or why I was alone most of the time. But then I met Tom, and he seemed to be like me, a bit childlike, and uneasy with Oscar and his gorgon of a mother, just as I was uneasy with my parents and Kate, my featherbrained sister. I think I believed I could counsel and protect him, and I also knew he wasn't like my father, or my sister and her friends, when it came to relationships; Tom wouldn't leave or betray me, and that was terribly important, because I was such a serious, frightened mouse.'

'When did you marry him?'

'Not for a number of years. He was entering graduate business school, at the insistence of Oscar, and I was going off to art school in Paris for two years, where I did manage a couple of clumsy love affairs. But something in me was still untouched when I came home and saw Tom again.'

Again she stopped talking. The rain had begun to soften. He sensed that she was telling him all this in an effort to distract him from his anguish, but also because her own memories were drawing her into new formulations of feeling.

'One day, not long after I'd come home from Paris, my father and I called on the Greeleys. Oscar and my father, and Oscar's dreadful wife Tippie, and Tom and I were drinking mimosas on their porch, when Tippie began telling us about this friend of hers who had killed himself by jumping out of a window in New York. I said, "How terrible!" And Tippie touched my shoulder and said, "Yes, my dear, how terrible. It was so embarrassing, his brains splattered all over the asphalt. He could have done it with more *style*, his poor wife was *mortified*." At that moment my eye met Tom's, and I thought, Here is a kindred spirit, as ill at ease among his people as I am among mine; we are a couple of changelings. And at that moment I believed I loved him. I looked at his face and — I know this will sound ridiculous — it was as if his face was *in* me. The mouldings of his cheek and jaw, his eyes, I felt them in my heart, somehow. So we got married — and I stopped painting.'

'Why?'

'I was asleep. Like a moth in a chrysalis. I had married him to retreat from the world, not to enter into it. And to retreat from myself, from my own unborn life, if you see what I mean. I suppose marriage can be a kind of initiation into maturity. But for me it was a means of avoiding becoming mature. I was a child, playing house.'

Chapter Eight

'And passion?' asked Dermot tentatively.

'Not much. We made love earnestly, awkwardly, and not very often. Sometimes Tom would giggle, because he was embarrassed by the intimacy. We were — undeveloped. And I moved through my days in a kind of fog, doing nothing, not even thinking about painting. Sometimes I would look around in a perplexed way, like I had stumbled into somebody else's dream. The too-luxurious New York apartment, financed by Oscar's dirty money, the fine plate bought for us as a marriage present — it wasn't the life I had wanted, when I'd been at art school in Paris, fired by the desire to draw, to paint, to live in foreign countries where I would take meals in cafés and raffish restaurants, and befriend artists and writers. A romantic dream, maybe, but at least it was my own. How had I become a New York matron, slouching around in this robber baron's apartment, dining in stuffy restaurants with people who bored me to death and whose political, ethical, and aesthetic views made me ill? At least my father was a Democrat, and some of his Washington parties were sort of bohemian. But these people were all like Tippie. They didn't care about anything except parties and clothes and making money at the expense of "the prolo masses", to borrow Oscar's delightful phrase.'

'And then you awoke? Like a D.H. Lawrence character? The female caterpillar becomes a butterfly and spreads her glistening virgin wings and sups at the sweet flower of love for the very first time?'

'Don't laugh,' she said, but it was true, she had been like a D.H. Lawrence character. She told him about the

113

inevitable affair with a man of greater experience and greater emotional and intellectual depth than Tom, how this had startled her out of her slumber and back into painting, how she'd reluctantly come to the conclusion that her husband was really not so unlike his parents after all. Despite his mild, brief rebellion, Tom had always coveted Oscar's position, embraced his values, allowed Tippie to tell him how to dress, whom to see, where to go. His diffidence in the face of his parents' excesses had convinced Grania that he was as restive as herself, but he was Oscar and Tippie's son.

'Which is not to say he wasn't a sweet boy. It's just that we shouldn't have married each other. It went on for four years. I'd have left earlier, but Oscar died.... The last two years were hell — I don't want to talk about it now. But when I decided to go through with the divorce, my father threatened to disinherit me, which he hasn't done, thanks to the entreaties of my mother and my sister, who came through for me, surprisingly, probably because my mother and Tippie detest each other. Anyway, my father agreed to give me a small allowance — *very* small — for two years. If I have no success as a painter within that time, no more support. That's the deal, as Oscar used to say. But the funny thing is, my father does love me deeply, as I've told you. He just doesn't understand. He didn't see why I had to divorce Tom, why it was necessary. He thought I should just revise the arrangement, take my own flat, and take lovers, if I was bored or unhappy. Why upset things unduly? And when I said I must leave because I would never be a painter if I remained married to Tom, that a door which had been sealed closed was now open, and I must walk through it, there was no going back — well, my poor dad looked at me as if I were a Martian with antennae sprouting out of my head. He just couldn't fathom it.' She placed her head on Dermot's shoulder. 'At least there were no children, thank God.'

'Thank God,' he repeated, thinking of Fiona's miscarriage. But better not dwell on that just now.

* * *

Next morning, a nasty surprise awaited Dermot in the breakfast room. He came down first; Grania was washing her hair. The big table was bare, and Mrs O'Malley, flushed and upset, was talking to Doyle.

'I simply will not have it,' Dermot heard her say. 'Comings and goings in the night, ladies smuggled into the rooms, guests moving from bed to bed. This is a home, a house, not a— a....' She faltered, her mouth trembling, and Dermot thought she mightn't even know the word *brothel*, much less permit herself to utter it.

Doyle, who hadn't noticed Dermot, said soothingly, 'Now, now, Mrs O'Malley, you mustn't be troubled. I assure you that I—'

'Professor Doyle, don't you be spinning wool over my eyes. I couldn't sleep last night and I was down here in the kitchen making a mug of Ovaltine when I saw you come in, stealthy as a tom cat, with a lady, a grey-haired lady. I don't know how you got her out this morning without disturbing me again, but that was the last straw, Professor Doyle, the last. First Professor

O'Duffy and the American girl are jumping like grass-
hoppers from room to room; then Mrs O'Duffy arrives
and settles in, only to leave the very same day, poor
lady, and now here you are, a respectable professor,
bringing strange women into my house in the middle
of the night!'

It must be Talon, Dermot thought, with a kind of
awe. He imagined trying to make love with that crusader, and decided it would be like a session with a
knife grinder, or an hour in the shark tank. Maybe
Doyle was not human, but a kind of bull seal with
rampaging hormones who would hump a rock if it
were soft with seaweed. He had a momentary vision,
or nightmare, of Doyle and Talon flailing in bed, bundled together like barnacles, emitting hoots and hisses
of steamy marine pleasure. It was probably such un-
earthly sea sounds that had alerted Mrs O'Malley to
Doyle's riotous goings on. Mrs O'Malley herself had
probably made love with her husband by remote control in their early days, after saying the rosary, of
course, to speed their fruitful congress. To his surprise,
despite the events of yesterday and his sombre discussion with Grania, he was actually smiling, and enjoying
Doyle's discomfiture. As for old busybiddy O'Malley, it
served her right to be roused from her sleep-of-the-just
by murmurings of love and longing from Grania's
room, and yodels of lust from Doyle's. If she had frol-
icked a bit more herself when she was a lass (although
he couldn't imagine Mrs O'Malley gambolling in a
coquettish nightie, barefooted and brazen in the marriage bed), she mightn't look so long in the tooth now.

Chapter Eight

But his vengeful chuckles began to wane as she swung her tiny howitzer round towards him.

'And what are *you* looking at, Professor O'Duffy?' Mrs O'Malley cried. 'You're as bad as him, if not worse. Not only disturbing everyone's sleep, skulking along corridors like a criminal, but now listening in like a naughty schoolboy. The pair of you should be taken out and sunk in the Claddagh! You are not professors, but a couple of scamps gone dead daft on petticoats. God be with the old days,' (she glanced piously up at the inflamed heart of her 3-D Jesus), 'when there was respect for the holy sacrament of marriage, and supposedly educated men didn't behave like dogs in heat.'

Dermot could see from Doyle's face that, chagrined as he was, he was still impressed by the old-fashioned fury of Mrs O'Malley's invective — maybe he was hearing echoes of his own mother. Mrs O'M might not know personally what forbidden pleasures her two rascally professors had been up to under her welcoming wing, but years of listening to sermons about the flesh she had probably never enjoyed herself, plus the prurient knowledge of human behaviour she had gleaned from her years as a landlady, were coming together in a fine flourish of antique rhetoric.

'You are a disgrace to Ireland, the both of you. In the old days, I'd have had you read from the altar.' Her cheeks reddened and the whites of her eyes misted pink as she warmed to her subject. 'I'd have had you denounced from the pulpit. I'd have—' she began to stammer '—I'd have had your names printed in the papers, like stray bulls that have wandered from their pastures and gone on the long acre, a danger to every poor heifer. No decent, self-respecting neighbour would have ever spoken to you again! But now that foreign immorality has engulfed even Ireland, all I can do...' She paused, and the two culprits exchanged guilty glances, like accomplices; '...is to telephone your wives, and make sure they know the details of your shameless behaviour! And now collect your luggage and get out, the pair of you! As for that American trollop, she's as bad as the worst of you. And her with a good Irish Catholic name like MacCormack, the same as our great tenor, the Papal Count, who sang in the Phoenix Park for the Pope himself. Only 'twas not after him she was named, oh no, but that big machine which used to tear down the fields, the MacCormack Reaper and Binder. Ah, but that hussy will bind and reap no more here! If I have anything to say about it, then my-self and that fine Mr O'Reilly whom I met yesterday (such a noble and upstanding gentleman!) will blacken her name from one corner of Ireland to the other, till she'll have to sleep in a stable. And her middle-aged fooleen of a boyfriend with her.' She glared at Dermot, twisting her apron in her hands. 'May you and your strumpet be denied a bed in all respectable houses, may you be forced to sleep in a byre in Donegal, or some outhouse in Kerry, or a slab of stone in Clare, for you have jointly disgraced the holy name of Ireland!'

Then she turned again towards Doyle, who was trying hard to control himself. 'As for you, my boy, don't think you can get away with it either, with that smirk you have on your face like a cat with its whiskers dripping cream. *His* wife knows the kind of scoundrel he is, but yours is going to learn, or my name is not Philomena O'Malley! You thought you were canny, but I heard every creak last night, and I was in two minds to ask the parish priest himself if he wouldn't come over to chasten you.' Dermot thought, And she accuses *me* of listening in like a naughty schoolboy. 'But I shall leave that to your good woman, and if I have any say in it, you too will soon be stravaging the roads, like what they now call the travelling people, and laying your head on a bed of stone instead of my decent pillows!'

She swept from the room. Doyle looked dejectedly at the naked table. 'Not even breakfast?' He managed a watery replica of his lupine smile. 'One gets hungry, after a night of bliss.'

Dermot, consumed by curiosity, couldn't but ask, 'Was it Professor Talon you brought here? She seems so forbidding, Doyle.'

'Yes, it was Beatrice Talon, though I don't suppose she much resembles Dante's lady. And yes, dear boy, I suppose she can be forbidding, but also quite passionate. As I've told you once before, you mightn't be as sensitive a judge of female pulchritude as you think you are. Beatrice's lively intelligence renders her quite alluring. Point is, she happens to be resigning as president of the Sheela-na-Gigs.'

'And you are applying for the job?' asked Dermot, laughing.

'Don't snigger, O'Duffy. I am indeed applying, and I intend to apply myself to all the lovely Sheelas, if you see what I mean. Only...' He fumbled for his handkerchief and smoothed it across his brow, '...do you think that woman will really ring my wife? Blow my cover, as they say?'

'I don't know, but she certainly was impressive, our Mrs O'Malley. What happened to the mild little woman who served us all those delicious breakfasts and clucked over us so maternally? How did she transform herself into a dragon?'

Doyle laughed grimly. 'My dear man, you are a Gaelic scholar. Surely you know that whenever one offends a female O'Malley, up surges a pirate queen? Give any O'Malley lady the slightest push, and old Grace erupts. But what am I to do?' Again he looked mournfully at the shorn table. 'The breakfasts here were so *big*, and the accommodation so *cheap*. I intended to use this place as my centre of operations, so to speak. I suppose I shall have to take a room in Beatrice's hotel. The Sheelas will be in Galway another week, you know, for their own conference. And I am determined to be a prominent presence among them, as their future president and token manikin.' He paused, and that cute Monaghan look sharpened his features for a moment. 'Maybe I could even share Beatrice's room, and save the shekels for better things.' He chuckled, but then his face tumbled again. 'Only, Jesus, what about Pamela?' Pamela was Doyle's English wife. 'D'you think the O'Malley will really telephone her? Perhaps she'll stalk me here, and give me a public tongue-scourging, just as you were given. I suppose it would serve me right.' He smiled apologetically, and Dermot found himself smiling back. Only last night they'd been intent on drawing each other's blood, and now here they were exchanging sheepish grins.

'Seems we're all three in disgrace,' said Dermot. 'Poor Grania. She was quite settled here, with her paints and things in her room. She and I will have to look for another place as well, and we haven't enough money for an expensive hotel.'

Doyle produced a piece of paper from his coat pocket. 'Here is the name of a guesthouse in Salthill, given me by Cordelia Callaghan. You know, the lady with the rather unbalanced face. It's supposed to be a bit classy, this house, but very good, and not too expensive. Why not give them a ring?'

* * *

Further bad news: Grania telephoned her painter friend in town, who glumly informed her that he hadn't enough money for a holiday, after all, and would therefore remain in his flat and studio throughout the spring and summer.

'So we've lost that prospect also? Well, we'll just have to look at this B & B in Salthill and see whether it's a place we'd be comfortable living and working in for a while, till we think of a better solution,' said Dermot firmly, trying to be sensible. He had a gnawing suspicion that Big Finn was responsible for their expulsion from Mrs O'Malley's little Eden — no doubt he'd spoken to Mrs O'Malley about his dear daughter's perfidious husband. At least he and Fiona were driving back home to Dublin now, Dermot thought, with a mixture of relief and rue.

Chapter Nine

The façade was austere, even grim, three storeys of rough grey stone in a style less neo-classical than stern, and without even the smallest of gardens to soften the leaden impression. Dermot expected the proprietress, a Mrs Rabitte, to be equally severe, but the door was opened by a young woman with bright green eyes in a slender, smiling face. Her hair, heavy and dark, was coiled up on her head in a rather exotic style, and she was wearing a vaguely exotic-looking blue tunic. A paperback collection of short stories by a fashionable new writer dangled from her hand.

She gave a short laugh, as though of delight at seeing old friends, and beckoned them into a cool entrance hall. Dermot immediately registered the absence of carpets, unusual in an Irish house, and the presence, along the walls, of jewel-bright Indian pictures, land-scapes, and sari-draped women with oblique, liquid eyes. To the woman, who had introduced herself as Cressida, Dermot said, 'Your house looks quite different from our last B & B. That place was all religious icons and Belleek trinkets.'

She gave another laugh. 'Oh, I know. And carpets, I shouldn't wonder, with patterns all over of big blowsy roses and things. There are no carpets or Christs in this house. I wouldn't let one of them in.'

Experiencing a sudden desire to defend Mrs O'Malley's gentle kitsch against this ultra-stylish Cressida, Dermot said mildly, 'But it was charming in its peculiar way. I see you have been to India.'

'No, actually. Only in the mind. I think I am a reincarnation.' They looked at her exotic hairdo. 'I feel such an affinity with the great Indian beauties.' She tilted her head to display her profile. 'I much prefer them to that silly girl, the Blessed Virgin.' Producing a cigarette from the pocket of her tunic, she flourished it at Dermot, who wondered if she wanted him to light it for her, but she swept up a black lighter from the hall table, and let out another laugh. 'Imagine getting pregnant by a bird! I much prefer the real thing. Let me introduce you to my husband.'

They followed her into a large room dominated by an immense abstract painting, black dolmen-like squares floating on a wash of aquamarine. There were oyster-coloured sofas and lacquered blue chairs, and, arranged with apparent artlessness on small blue tables, an array of *au courant* novels and volumes of poetry. A youngish, blond man was slouched in one of the sofas, reading a book called *What's In, What's Out, In the 'Nineties.*

'Owen,' called Cressida, 'Say hello to our new guests. This is Dermot O'Duffy, the famous *scholar*, you know. And — em — Grania.' She gave Grania a smile of supreme condescension. 'From America.'

Dermot said, 'Grania is a gifted painter.'

'You have never seen my paintings,' Grania whispered, but he could tell she was touched.

'Good for you,' cried Cressida, squeezing Grania's shoulders. 'Would you like tea, or real coffee?'

She served them the coffee, and a plate of delicious cakes. Dermot, talking with her and the friendly husband, began to relax. It would be all right, living for a bit in this large cool house with these cordial people. It was true that their aggressive trendiness was somewhat oppressive; he supposed they were what people now called yuppies, eager to accrue the best of everything, except that they probably regarded the 'best', whether paintings, books, music, or even this fine strong coffee, as little more than merchandise, plunder, to be prized for its *chic* more than any inherent qualities. But Owen seemed kind, and Cressida was discreetly incurious. Dermot supposed this couple might know what had happened to himself and Grania the night before, since they were the type who would keep a finger on the local pulse, and there was no underestimating the swiftness of the Irish grapevine, but they asked nothing, and presently Cressida brought them up to a pleasant room decorated with another

Chapter Nine

Indian picture, a capering blue god with an entourage of ladies under a flowering tree, Krishna among the cowgirls.

'There are linen sheets on the bed,' cried Cressida, waving her cigarette. 'Only the finest for my guests. I hate those nylon things. So *slimy*. Toodle-loo.'

She flashed a smile and was gone, leaving a cloud of spicy perfume behind her.

* * *

An hour or so later, after they'd broken in the linen sheets and got dressed again, and were placing their things in the handsome oak cupboard, Dermot said, 'Grania, will you let me see some of your work?'

She hesitated. 'I have only drawings here, some of the best of the things I was expected to do at school.' But she produced a black portfolio, and opened it on the bed. 'They were still pretty backwards in the American art school, so we had to begin with life studies, and then portraits. I used to practise on my family, which developed my skills a bit.'

Dermot took up the thick sheets. Why, she's all right, he thought, and was startled to realise how relieved he felt. What if she'd been awful, and had eagerly asked him to praise her, and the compliments had clogged in his throat? But she's all right, he said again to himself, looking at the portraits she'd done, of her family mostly. She seemed to have captured something of their spirits in the mouldings of their heads, their smiles, their eyes. And technically they were quite fine, as far as he could tell, although perhaps a bit derivative of old-fashioned American portrait artists like Sargent. He examined one of a girl looking up at the viewer through her lashes, half shyly, half slyly, embodying the self-absorption of adolescence. She was a prettier version of Grania, with dimples and flaring cheekbones, clearly an apprentice charmer, future man meat. Then, a man, almost too vigorously handsome, with smooth, pampered skin and cash-register eyes. And a woman, also handsome, her slender head on its slender stalk of a throat tilted imperiously, her nose and mouth too strong, her eyes a bit like Fiona's, narrow and tapering, nearly Asiatic. Letting this sheet fall from his hand, he remembered how Fiona had looked when he'd first known her, that nimbus of red hair surrounding the lovely face, so bright, that hair, it was as if it had drawn all the colour out of her skin, which was dead white. And those light, elongated eyes! Later on in their life together, when she'd become so aloof, so despondent and silent, her eyes had sometimes looked to him as chill and pale as quicksilver. For the thousandth time, he asked himself, What did I do to contribute to her pain? Am I as much to blame as she says? Should I have tried harder to woo her away from her simian-yet-reptilian rapacious old lummox of a father? Then he roused himself and returned to Grania's pictures.

But he was interrupted by a vaguely familiar voice, female and trilling, in the corridor. 'Professor O'Duffy, *do* let me in!'

He and Grania stared at each other: What next? Then he went to open the door, and there, chuckling on the threshold, was Cordelia Callaghan. Of course, he thought, she'd recommended the place to Doyle; she must be a guest here.

'You poor lad,' she cried. 'That horrid drubbing you received last night, and then to be denounced again this morning, and by a little old lady on the warpath! I know all about it; Professor Doyle told me. You silly thing, to have *such* bad luck with the women. Our Professor Doyle has gone to Beatrice Talon's hotel, but this place is much pleasanter, don't you think? And Cressida cooks like a dream. I'm so pleased you're here.'

'Come in,' said Dermot reluctantly; he could hardly close the door in her face. She swept into the room, her listing eyes aglow, but when she saw Grania, encircled by her drawings on the bed (the sheets still tousled from their lovemaking) she was clearly less than pleased.

'Oh! Hello, my dear. You are visiting Professor O'Duffy, also?' Before Grania could reply, she cried, 'How nice for you, Dermot. May I call you Dermot? Despite your wicked lecture, the girls still pursue you. And *this* one,' she smiled remotely at Grania, 'was the cause of your marital turmoil last night. Naughty boy.' She waggled her finger at him. 'And now that I am finally talking with you, I must ask you to please forgive my overly passionate response to your presentation the other night. I *am* a passionate woman, but I certainly had no desire to insult you. It's merely that your views are absolutely benighted!' She threw back her head and gave a gurgling laugh, like a toilet being flushed. 'What you need is a kind woman to teach you a lesson, wouldn't you agree?' She glanced at Grania. 'A fellow *scholar*, who could explain to you how feminist theory and Early Irish literature can be *warmly* brought together. Perhaps you and I might have dinner soon, to discuss the connection?'

Dermot, whose head was a collage of Cordelia images — Cordelia shrieking at him after his talk, Cordelia cornering him in the Gents, Cordelia listening while Fiona reviled him — felt overcome with confusion, and gave her a noncommittal smile.

From her seat on the bed, in a low voice, Grania said, 'I am not *visiting* Dermot. I'm living with him here. We are *together*.'

'How nice,' answered Cordelia brightly, scarcely missing a beat. 'Then you will have to come out to dinner as well. I love loving couples. Anyway, I must be off now. Bye!'

Dermot turned back towards Grania. 'What a to-do!' He smiled, but she looked grimly at him, and demanded, 'Why didn't *you* tell her?'

'Tell her what?' Once again he had that dropping sensation of having put his big foot in his mouth. Maybe pretending to be mute would be the best strategy in all future dealings with females, although that approach would hardly serve for a lecturer.

'She was horrible. Why did you let her go on, gloating and gushing and insulting me?'

'What would you have liked me to d-do?' He was thinking, Women! They're altogether too much. He was beginning to feel like a ping-pong ball ricocheting amongst ferocious paddles.

'I'd have liked you to affirm *us*. It's true we have known each other only briefly, but over just a couple of days we've weathered at least two crises together, and have become deeply close in many ways, and have realised that we are not just a you and a me, but an *us*.'

'Why, of course we are,' said Dermot, astounded. 'I haven't denied to anybody that we are an — er — *us*.'

'Then why didn't you respect me enough to introduce me to her, which might have silenced or at least subdued her? She's so smarmy and catty! And you *disavowed* me. You could have corrected her when she said all those demeaning things about me, but you chose not to, which probably gave her the message that you are still available, still an academic Don Juan just like your pal oily Doyle. Finally *I* had to speak up, like a minor character from the wings.'

'Grania,' he said, genuinely surprised, 'I did not *disavow* you. What are you talking about?'

'It hurt me, the way that predatory woman was coveting you, for your stature or your charm or whatever, and the way she was presuming that I was nobody to you. She was making the most idiotic passes at you *in my presence*, and either ignoring or insulting me!' She began to gather up her pictures and to stuff them back rather roughly into the portfolio. 'It was an important moment for me, you looking at my portraits, and then she came in and blasted it. And you could have diffused her, but you didn't. You liked it, I bet. You'd probably *like* to see her for dinner, just the two of you. Too bad I was here, making it difficult for you to play the field. Perhaps I should leave, and then you and that insufferable, calculating, egghead bitch could have a marvellous talk about Early Irish love poetry!'

Women, he thought again, wearily. The idea of dinner with Cordelia Callaghan, those haphazard eyes gazing moistly at him over the wineglasses, made his flesh prickle with displeasure, but it would be no good telling that to Grania, who had apparently decided he wanted to keep his options open with the Sheelas, like Doyle.

'Darling,' he said firmly, 'Last night, my wife of many years denounced me in public and threw me out of her life. I haven't thought about the legal implications, or even about how I am to collect my clothes and books from Dublin, and arrange to have my letters forwarded. My entire, orderly world was dismantled yesterday. Do you think I want to complicate my life further, especially with someone like Cordelia Callaghan? I am lucky you are here with me. I don't know why you are here, or why we seem to love each other. The whole business is absurd and impossible, I suppose, but there it is. I was thrown out of my old life, we were both thrown out of Mrs O'Malley's, but we have each other.' He paused over this last sentence. Was it possible that he was sounding like a windbag, sermonising with the awful pomposity of the seasoned lecturer, the rhetorical snare they all got tangled in after years of handling bright and volatile students? He registered the self-criticism, but then realised it couldn't be true, for, if so, why was he near crying?

Grania's cheeks reddened. 'You do love me?'

He went back to the bed and buried his head in her hair, pressing his face against her throat. Her arms came round him, and they remained like that for a little while.

Chapter Ten

Dermot thought, And now the problem of engaging some solicitor (certain to be a gnarled crustacean in sumptuous chambers, washing his hands drily at the prospect of skinning his poor client alive, a Dickens character more than a human) and attaining a legal separation, surely an awkward and distasteful business at best. But trifling details compared to the matter of emotional separation! That night Dermot was sleepless again, trembling as though with fever, remembering how their two cats had drowsed at his feet while he worked in his study, remembering how that room had quickened with a gold light each evening, remembering the sweet things about Fiona, her lively mind, her beauty. He was like a man who has lived in a barren, stony field and who, forsaking it for a place far more lush and promising, nevertheless sees the loveliness of his old field, sees all the things that have grown familiar over the years, sees it blaze with memory, just as he is saying goodbye to it. It is always so, he thought, always when one makes a choice, a door is closed, something vanishes.

Next morning, after Cressida's delicious breakfast, he rang Fiona from the telephone in the entrance hall, to discuss the legal arrangements, but there was no reply. 'That's peculiar,' he said to Grania, 'Where could she have gone?'

She opened her mouth to answer, but just then Cordelia Callaghan walked in, looking quite pretty with her unruly hair clouding round her head, and her cheeks flushed from the sea air. He saw that her right eye really was positioned higher than the left, and that it sloped up while the other drooped slightly. Had she been American, she would doubtless have had plastic surgery, but, as it was, they gave her a kind of lopsided charm, those eyes of hers listing to starboard like a couple of sailors on shore leave.

'Dermot,' she cried, 'How fortunate to see you! I must talk to you *straight away*.' She placed a hand on his arm. '*Alone*.'

More sensitive, this morning, to Grania's feelings, he answered firmly, 'Anything you would like to tell me, you can say before my friend.'

'All right. It was only that my news might upset you both, so I thought I ought to break it to you gently.' She said this without archness, and he sensed that her request for a private talk had been empty of guile; she was truly agitated about something. 'I was up early, and I decided to stroll along the promenade and then into town. So good for the figure, a walk before breakfast. And who do you think I saw, *striding* down Shop Street?'

Uh oh, Dermot thought. With heavy irony he answered, 'Give me one guess.'

'Exactly. They haven't left town. I didn't speak to them, of course. *She* looked resolute, a woman with a purpose. But *he* was *blazing*. I must say, when I saw him pushing past the people in the road, with that grim and florid face on him, I felt a bit weak at the knees myself. He was like some kind of ferocious bird getting ready for flight and attack.' She gave them a pitying smile. 'You poor things. I wouldn't like to have that man as an enemy, though it's difficult to understand why he is *so* consumed with rage at you, Dermot. After all, countless fathers learn every day that their daughter's marriage has failed, and they all don't go *stalking* the poor husband. Could it be that he considers your very existence, as a scholar and writer, an affront to his values, and now he's got an excuse to try and crush you?' She paused, sighing. 'I don't know what the two of you believed you were doing, but it seems that you did handle your affair rather gauchely, if you don't mind me saying so. Anyway, whatever you thought you were up to, I reckon Mrs O'Duffy and her father won't be satisfied till you are both pelted in the public stocks for adultery.' She grimaced, then, newly excited, placed her hand on Dermot's arm again.

'And I nearly forgot! It's been a busy morning, let

me tell you. As I was walking past the station, I thought I saw Professor Doyle's wife! I recognised her from the Fair and Dark Women and Short and Tall Men in Early Irish Mythology Conference, in Cork last year. She had accompanied her husband there, you see, and I remembered her red hair and English accent. Pamela, is it? Anyway, I was *sure* I saw her this morning, and she was looking scarcely less determined than *your* spouse, my dear. Are she and Mrs O'Duffy intending to form The Angry Wives Association? If so, then I tremble for you, *and* for poor Doily. I know he is an able fellow, but I imagine that those two redheads in combination, with your wife's dad behind them, could scalp the bollocks off a Cuchulain!' She gave Dermot's arm a friendly squeeze. 'Nice to press the old limbs while they're still intact. Sorry, that wasn't funny. I'm off to breakfast. See you later, and the best of Old Irish luck. You had better discover a charm against castration in one of the lesser known testicles — I mean, texts! Sorry again. Couldn't resist. *Bon chance.*'

Grania said, 'Fiona doesn't know where we are, does she?'

'That prurient little O'Malley woman might have told her. She heard me telephoning here, to ask had they a room. Oh, God, what does Fiona want? She was talking about leaving me to my own life, and embarking on a life, a truer life, for herself. She did declare something like that, didn't she?'

'She mightn't have meant it, as you suspected the other night. She might have thought that if she told you to leave you would crumple, and ask her to forgive you

134

and take you back, as if you were a naughty child pleading for mercy. She might have thought you were dependent on her, and would quickly realise it when left to your own resources, or the care of some incompetent flibbertygibbet like me.'

Well, if she did presume he would be penitent, she had reason, thought Dermot. He recalled a party they had gone to about ten years ago, when she was in her early forties and still beautiful, though already cold and disapproving most of the time. *Don't lose your temper*, Dermot had often counselled himself during that period, remembering how desolate he had felt in his mother's house, and that he had promised himself never to inflict a similar grief on Fiona if he could help it (sometimes, of course, he couldn't help it, and despite himself had begun to cultivate a talent for divining the places where she was vulnerable, a talent for psychological bloodsport that he loathed in himself, yet couldn't resist exploiting now and again — anything to provoke a response from her!). Still, as a child he had noticed on his walks through the fields that the pleats and fissures in stone were often clogged with moss and minute white flowers delicate as tissue. Surely we, too, can blossom from the cracks in our psyches, he would tell himself, but their house had grown so arid and sad, that even then, ten years ago, he had begun to despair.

The party they had attended that summer night (at the large house of a powerful newspaper editor) was a *chic* affair, so *chic* that the glassy prattle, laughter, witticisms, and gossip spilling through the perfumed rooms had made the air in them seem nearly friable. Their hostess, the editor's rich American wife, disliked Fiona, and, ostentatiously, in her presence, introduced Dermot to a pretty blonde, saying, 'My dear, you absolutely must meet Orla. Isn't she lovely? She has just told me that she would adore an intimate discussion with you, about your work.'

The girl knew next to nothing about his work, but he talked to her a bit (she was an 'actress-model', she informed him, throwing her flaxen hair first over one shoulder, then the other) and presently she nestled a piece of paper with her address on it into his palm. He and Fiona left soon after, and during the drive home she criticised him for getting drunk (he had drunk one gin-and-tonic and two glasses of wine, and was feeling uncomfortably lucid) and for 'flirting with every morsel of girl-flesh in that horrible *nouveau riche* house' (this, unfortunately, was true).

At home, she refused to talk to him. Well, why should she talk to him? Even Dermot could concede that her disappointment in him was justified. Tonight she'd had to endure the malign manoeuvrings of Mrs Editor, who had behaved like a bawd, foisting that young woman on Dermot with his wife looking on. And his responses, as usual, had been less than gallant. But now she was so wintry, so silent, that finally he walked out into the dark road, and, after wavering briefly, took a taxi to Orla's address.

She smiled serenely when she opened the door, and brought him immediately to her bed, but it was no good. She lived with a pal, another blonde, and this other girl was clunking about in the kitchen, cooking something incendiary like curry which soon engulfed the whole flat in an oppressive, sooty odour. And he could summon forth no passion for the inert girl beside him on her lumpy bed; his hands moved mechanically over her body, his mouth fumbled for hers — but who was she, what was she to him, and why in heaven's name was he here? Finally he left, his last glimpse of Orla being her scowling face as she closed the door abruptly on him.

When he let himself in, Fiona was in bed, weeping. 'You were with that woman, weren't you?' she asked in a low voice.

'Of course not,' he answered, trying to sound indignant. 'You were so disapproving, I thought it best that I should leave for a time. I walked through the streets for hours, and saw nobody. Why should I passively endure your coldness and your silent censure of me, Fiona? Why shouldn't I leave, when you won't even talk to me?'

But, hearing the pomposity and self-righteousness in his lying voice, he faltered, and took her in his arms, and cried, and asked her to forgive him, he would try never to betray her again. And she caressed his head and did forgive him, until a number of days later, when she discovered that he had bought the wrong kind of lamb chops, too thick or too old, and smiling frigidly had left the house without telling him where she was going. She had returned hours later, with new lamb chops, which they had eaten in silence since he could hardly reproach her for vanishing mysteriously when he'd done the same only a week or so before.

Of course such incidents were not the whole story, but like a *chiaroscuro* painting where light, spilling into a dark room, pools on a corner table at which two men are drinking, or a young girl is smiling, or a woman plucking a hen. Memories were panels of light in a darkness thick with other stories: the merry times with Fiona, their happy years before she lost the baby, and other love affairs, some frivolous, others serious enough to imperil his marriage for a time. But always he had gone back, even after Kitty, a fellow academic whom he had truly loved some five or so years ago. No, nobody before Grania had broken the tether which had kept him bound to Fiona over the years, though Dermot knew that this final break could not possibly be due to Grania alone. Certainly she had startled him into an awareness of what he had been living without, but, by God, he was fifty-eight years old, and probably would have decided soon enough that the autumn of his life should be happier than the preceding seasons, Grania or no Grania.

On the other hand, given his record, he supposed he should not be surprised if Fiona had indeed expected him to trudge remorsefully through the rain to their hotel after her father's public tirade, to implore her for forgiveness. It disappointed him to think that her eloquent announcement of the night before last, her declared desire for a life unclouded by lies and deviousness, might have been nothing more than a performance. Anyway, her strategy, if that was what it had been, hadn't worked; he hadn't been shamed and penitent, had not tottered back to her — and now? Cordelia had described Big Finn as *blazing*, and apparently Pamela Doyle, fresh from Dublin, was also in high dudgeon. Surly Finn and two imperious redheads, stalking himself and Grania and poor old Doyle! An imminent showdown at the Hibernian Corral! But what was Finn really up to, Dermot asked himself, echoing Cordelia's puzzlement. The possible answers made him queasy.

Finn must know, on some subterranean level, that a great deal of Fiona's unhappiness was due to himself. He had worshipped her beauty, used her unabashedly to vault himself into society, but he had never tutored her in affection, or introduced her to sweetness. The chill that Dermot had always felt in her was an absence in her character, a rent in the web of her psyche, and it was Finn, along with his alcoholic wife, who had done this, and so he must be feeling guilty now, Dermot reasoned, and that might be why he'd decided to champion his daughter in such an excessive way.

Also, Dermot admitted, Finn had always hated him, had been boorish and truculent towards him and Fiona ever since their wedding. Not that Dermot had been excessively fond of Big Finn. In fact he'd been astonished that his beautiful fiancée could have such a bellicose, mercenary, bullet-headed, ham-handed, cattle-smuggling philistine for a father. Anyway, at this point Finn was probably exultant: his daughter had insulted him by marrying a man so different from himself, had flouted his values and spurned his choices for her — but now she had finally learnt her lesson!

And he, Finn, would make sure that Dermot, the Rival, the Other, the Interloper, would be trounced forever. And in public, for good measure.

Trying to analyse further, Dermot doubted that Finn had ever violated Fiona in any physical or sexual way. She maintained that once he had brandished a riding crop at her, before flushing with embarrassment and muttering an apology, but she had been clear that he'd never actually struck her. Yet what Dermot did not doubt was that Finn had indeed violated her, invaded her, in a spiritual way. He had behaved as though Fiona were his property, had rendered her into a *thing*, and to some degree she had submitted to this, had become in fact his creature. Dermot sensed that she was gratified now, in ways she'd never been with himself. Finally, 'Daddy', the love of her life, was pleased with her, was devoting all his attention to her! Finn had sulked at Fiona's wedding, barely speaking to anyone. No doubt he had known that Dermot's accomplishments, university degrees and monographs, were considered impressive, that they impressed Fiona, but it was plain that he could not understand why, and so he'd growled and blundered about all that day like a sullen, uncomprehending animal, cherishing his own woundedness. Yet now that was all changed; fire had finally been breathed into Fiona the cold mannequin, and it was dear old Daddy who had done it!

Anyway, Dermot prayed that his wife and her father would not discover his and Grania's new whereabouts, but, considering how eagerly that ferret O'Malley would supply them with information, this new address

remaining a secret seemed about as likely as Fiona
baking him a cake today.

* * *

Grania had been keeping her paintings and supplies
with her Galwegian friend, but since he wasn't leaving
town after all, she decided to collect the canvases,
paints, and brushes from his studio, and bring them to
Cressida Rabitte's guesthouse. Dermot, interested in
looking at her current work, encouraged but didn't
accompany her; he wanted to call on Doyle, to alert
him that his fiery spouse had arrived in Galway, if he
didn't already know.

Walking towards town, he feared stumbling into
Fiona, but the woman who called out to him, an angu-
lar brunette, was a stranger, he thought. He was at the
bottom of the promenade when he heard her strong
voice crying, 'Dermot! Dermot O'Duffy! Is that you?'

He smiled warily. Was she yet another fractious
Sheela-na-Gig? A former student? A former lover
awash with grievances? She was a tall woman, about
forty, and quite attractive. Her hair, short and buoy-
antly curly, was very dark, but her eyes were light blue.
Something about her slow smile as she extended her
hand to him, and her soft laugh, suggested she was an
actress, something not affected, exactly, but conscious, a
conscious poise, as though she had for years been
called on to analyse her own 'presence'. Baffled, he
took her hand.

'Don't you remember me?' she asked pleasantly.
'Last year, at Tony Flynn's party? You are a beast for not

remembering! We had a lovely talk, and you kept trying to *grovel* before my knees. You said they were the
most exquisite knees you had ever seen, and deserved
the homage of every man in the room. So full of mischief you were — you did manage to prevail on all the
men, and they did all genuflect before my poor, embarrassed knees, every single gentleman at that party,
including a government minister and an American
diplomat!' She gave her low laugh again, and it was
that laugh, and not the silly anecdote about her knees,
which kindled his memory: she was Laura Murphy, an
accomplished actress, just as he had suspected. He
couldn't for the life of him remember offering obeisance to her knees, but he did, now, recall the long and
lively conversation he had managed to sustain with her
during Tony Flynn's riotous party just under a year
ago. That summer evening, she had thrown back her
boyishly cropped head and laughed this same low,
throaty laugh, and whether he'd admired her knees or
not, he had indeed registered such laughter, rough but
strangely sweet, and he had registered as well that
while her hair was a rich black, her eyes, encircled by
lashes equally black, were exceedingly light and clear.
He and Laura Murphy had talked about the theatre,
about books, and about themselves, her convent
schooling and his days on the farm. And then? He had
had complicated feelings about her — a slight but
emphatic surge of desire, to be sure, as he'd regarded
her in her white summer dress (long throat, smooth
brown arms, high breasts, though surely her *knees* had
not arrested him) but he had also sensed that she

would make a better pal than a lover, that whenever they happened to meet they would always be at ease with each other, just talking, or walking, or seeing a film together. He'd come alone to Tony's party; Fiona had been away, visiting family in Cavan, and Laura was unattached, so they could have made love that night, and he was nearly certain that they had indeed exchanged a long, cool kiss at the door of her house. But then hadn't she given him an amused, sidelong look from those pale eyes with their heavy black lashes, as though to ask, Why spoil such a sweet and uncomplicated night? Anyway, they hadn't slept together, and he hadn't seen her since, till today.

'Laura Murphy,' he said. 'Sure, I do remember you, though your knees are covered by your mac today. What are you doing in Galway?'

'I live here now. My mother has a house in town, and she is ill. So I came back. I look after her, when I can. I mean, when I'm not touring in anything.'

'You are living with your mother, then?'

'Oh, no,' she said with another laugh, and then again, 'Oh, no,' giving him the sidelong look he remembered. 'I could never live with anyone, Dermot. I am a bachelor girl, too independent for domestic intimacy. And I have seen too many of my married friends sour over the years! The women have nearly all become fat and dull and matronly, or thin and dull and petulant, and the men are either fat and lecherous, or thin and dispirited. Oh, no! I live alone, and have my adventures if I please, and my privacy, just as you men have been able to do since the dawn of time.' She gave his shoulder a conciliatory touch. 'Not that I would be so arrogant as to condemn all marriages as thankless. I know you are married, though I have never met your wife. People tell me she is beautiful?'

'Indeed she is. And since you ask about her, I might as well inform you that my wife and I have just separated, under fairly melodramatic circumstances, right here in Galway. Up until this morning we believed she had returned to Dublin, but it seems that she is still in town, probably in order to stalk me.'

'You're not *serious*? How thrilling! Who is "we"? Oh, you rascal, don't tell me! There is *another woman*?'

'I am afraid there is. But I am not sure I approve of your facetious attitude towards all this, Laura Murphy. My personal drama was not designed to give you a cheap thrill, you know.' But he was smiling.

'I do know, and I am sorry for making light of your crisis. But, dear Dermot, one must laugh, mustn't one? Life is just too absurd.' She rummaged in the pockets of her elegant mac and produced a pencil and a square of paper. 'Here is my phone number. If you and your new lady intend to stop in Galway for a few more days, you must come to my little flat for dinner.'

They said goodbye, and he couldn't help thinking, as he walked along the damp roads (the perpetual, soft Galway rain had commenced, and a whitish fog was mantling the low Claddagh houses) that really Laura Murphy was much prettier than Grania. An ungallant observation, he supposed, but one he made with amused affection. He did not know why little Grania with her mouse face and doe eyes had captured his

144

heart and spirit, but there it was. And even now, reflecting that women like the striking Laura Murphy did, unfortunately, throw Grania's physical disadvantages into sharp relief, still, what he felt for her was desire. He wanted to hurry back right now to the guesthouse, to smile into Grania's face, kiss her, make love to her. As a young man he had been as brutish as most youths, he supposed, when it came to female beauty. Only the prettiest girls deserved notice; the plain ones, the 'others', were thought to be nervous, frantic, and too clever (it was agreed that nothing could be more mortifying than to appear in public with a girl who was cleverer than you, and whose deft witticisms would expose you as the imbecile you doubtless were). And if you were mutinous enough to defy the conventional wisdom, and cultivate a girl who was too fat, too scrawny, too blonde, too dark, too freckled, too anything, your friends would deride you pitilessly: *Surely you can do better than that!*

What idiots young men were, Dermot thought as he walked into the small hotel — and young women, too, he supposed, with their dreams of film stars. Beauty appeared in such myriad and unexpected guises, and surely beauty was simply the power to disturb. The celluloid faces and faultless bodies he had coveted in his youth were without siren-power for him now. It was the solemn and nondescript face of Grania that had the power to disturb him, in his psyche, his spirit, and his body.

* * *

'Would you please tell me the number of Professor Doyle's room?' Dermot asked the hotel receptionist, a chubby young woman.

'He's with Miss Talon. Number fifteen,' she said indifferently, barely looking up from her fashion magazine. She was, he deduced, the opposite of Mrs O'Malley, oblivious to the odour of scandal, bored by everything except advice on hairstyles.

He hastened up to the room, where Doyle was alone, pruning his negligible beard with a tiny silver scissors.

'Hello, O'Duffy. Come in. Beatrice has gone out to the Sheela-na-Gig Festival Committee meeting. Care for a wee snort?' He indicated a half-empty bottle of Powers by the bed. 'Fighting's hard work, but not as hard as pillow sport!'

'Good God, Doyle, it's a bit early.'

'I know, Dermot my boy, but I am under pressure. From Beatrice.' Sighing heavily, he lowered his neat body into the room's only chair. 'She seems to be presuming that she and I are — well — a *couple*, now, if you see what I am getting at.'

'I suppose you and she *are* something of a couple,' answered Dermot, settling on a corner of the unmade bed. 'I mean, the two of you have made love, and you are *living* with her, Doyle.'

'Yes,' conceded Doyle mournfully, producing a smeared water glass from the floor and pouring an ample measure of whiskey into it. 'But, old man, the other night, after my lecture, I was presented with a veritable *bouquet* of Sheelas. You must admit that they were all practically drooling with lust for me, except for the members of the Sheelas of Sappho Club, or the SSC, of course.' He gave another doleful sigh. 'I cannot possibly *commit* (what an ugly word!) myself to Beatrice, fine sturdy woman though she be. There are too many other succulent prospects out there, and I certainly did not agree to become President of the Sheelana-Gigs in order to *shackle* myself to Professor Talon, even if she does have a fine mind and an extremely healthy libido. For instance, I expect Miss Cordelia Callaghan is ripe for the plucking at the moment, and those startling eyes of hers do encourage one to conclude that she must be quite appealingly lewd, wouldn't you say? Point is, my intention is to make the rounds, so to speak, and the one thing I *don't* want is to become someone's muse figure. After all, I've a perfectly good wife at home, and my humble desire here is simply to be monarch of all I survey, not to *entangle* myself in a *love* affair.' Shuddering at the word 'love', he took a loud slurp of whiskey.

Dermot sighed. 'I cannot say whether your desire to be lord of the Sheelas is humble or not, but one thing I can tell you is that you've a bigger problem on your hands at this moment than Beatrice Talon. Your wife is not at home, Doyle, but here, in Galway. And so, I am dismayed to inform you, is mine.'

Surprisingly calm, Doyle splashed more whiskey into his glass and took a contemplative swallow. Then he mumbled, 'Ah. Pamela. Fiona. Grania. Beatrice.' He smiled wryly. 'Such sweet names. A quartet of heroines.'

'It's no good for you to loll there guzzling spirits and

cataloguing the names of the people involved,' said Dermot irritably. 'I am telling you that Mrs O'Malley has apparently spoken to your wife, and she is in town, along with my wife and her father, who did not, it seems, return to Dublin after their display of affection for me the other night. What do you propose to do, Doyle?'

It seemed that even great armchair and bedroom generals had their moments of weakness. Smiling beatifically, Doyle lifted his small hands helplessly in the air, and, with a sigh, slumped abruptly over in a sleep of sensual, drunken exhaustion. Clearly a couple of nights with Talon were equivalent to a year's hard labour, the Munster hurling final, or a championship boxing bout. Victory over that blustery Sheela was sweet, but apparently it siphoned away the energy essential for a different kind of campaign. Dermot would have to do the thinking for both himself and Doyle.

Chapter Eleven

After leaving Doyle to his whiskey-soaked slumbers, Dermot went into a quiet café, where he drank a pot of tea, ate two thickly buttered scones, and thought deeply. At first his thoughts wandered; the café overlooked a small garden, where the grass was swathed in gleaming spiders' webs. Suddenly, while he was polishing off the last crumb of his second scone, the rain stopped, the web-draped garden flared with sunlight, and Dermot, looking at this through Grania's eyes, said to himself, Ireland is a cup of light — sweet, clear, watered light — especially in summer. *Summer!* And the Gaelic equivalent of *Eureka* curved like a rainbow across his punch-drunk psyche.

* * *

If his wife felt compelled to throw him out, Dermot reflected, at least it could not have come at a better time. While the whole world was furiously attempting to simplify its calendar, Ireland was furiously attempting to complicate hers. From early summer on, a motley procession of festivals and *fleadhs* would stagger across the country, with the venerable established summer schools, like Yeats or Merriman, grumpily moving over to accommodate newer celebrations all the time, literary, historical, archaeological, musical, every kind of fun-for-all, from chamber music in stately houses to séances at the Writers Museum.

For writers were fair game. Even poor Gerard Manley Hopkins, so despondent in Ireland, had become as lauded a national hero as a soccer mercenary, with a summer school in his honour, for people to do what he had almost never done himself: have fun. Wicklow and the Aran Islands were squabbling over which should have the rights to the Synge Summer Festival. There was George Moore madness in Mayo, and if Belfast would only calm down and learn to behave, the Northern Summer School Committee (NSSC) intended to launch a week on Brian Moore, a Northern Irishman who happened also to be Canadian and Catholic, a crisis of identity seminar formidable enough to rival John Hewitt's colonial confusions in County Antrim. Exiled and censored writers who had loathed their native land were quickly elevated to the status of saints: visitors to Cork were shepherded from O'Faolain's birthplace to the orphanage of Little Nelly of Holy God, via a reception at Beamish and Crawford at which an abundance of stout and whiskey was consumed by all, thereby addling the general sense of values.

Not to be eclipsed, the historians threw themselves into the cauldron of summer jollity, raucously competing for attention. Since Parnell's private life no longer excluded him from national favour, his birthplace in Avondale had become a gathering place, and the Historical Summer Schools Organising Committee (HSSOC) was concocting a scheme for a Smuggler's Irish Cup at Derrynane, with Spanish wine, of course, and no cannabis. The HSSOC agreed that it was not easy to celebrate gloomy de Valera, but the hierarchy had promised a seminar on austerity and family life at Maynooth. In West Cork, a French frigate was to glide into Bantry, successfully this time, and then curve round to north Mayo. The two ultimate objectives of the HSSOC were: 1) to establish a Saints and Scholars Theme Park close to Dublin; and 2) to move the Twelfth of July south, and conduct a big, garish Orange parade on the Boyne — ecumenism being a large factor in tourism.

But, alas, these last two ambitions still seemed more a dream than a reality, as did the Sheela-na-Gig Festival. The Sheela-na-Gig Festival Committee (Shee-Fest) was determined to establish three days of gynophile celebrations throughout Ireland, climaxing with the enthronement of a queen on the Paps of Áine between Cork and Kerry, in defiance of the great-testicled goat elevated at Puck Fair, but so far the Sheelas had been thwarted by clerical intervention. In ironical contrast, last summer's attempt to launch a Gae Bolga competition at the Carlingford Peninsula, in honour of Cuchulain, had been foiled by the local gay community, who had declared that Kinsella's translation established beyond doubt that the great hero was (at the very least) bisexual. On the subject of Irish alternative sexuality, the burgeoning Oscar Wilde Society was considering venues for an All-Ireland Gay and Lesbian Hooley. And not to be outdone in the scandalmongering department, the Irish Association for the Legalisation of Cannabis (IALC) intended to conduct its summer festival on Tara, where its slogan would be 'Get High with the High Kings'. Other mythical characters were shining in the cosmogony of summer congresses: the Mad Sweeny Bicycle Marathon around Ireland, and the Deirdre Beauty Pageant, to name only two....

* * *

'Doyle! Open those eyes! C'mon, old fellow. Up!'

Doyle, still crumpled in the chair, muttered, 'Sausages and bacon!' Then his whiskey-dimmed eyes slowly opened, and he looked bemusedly up at Dermot. 'O'Duffy? Christ, I was having the most unpleasant dream, that you came here to tell me *Pamela* was in town—'

'That was no dream, you idiot. Now get up, and I'll take you out for a coffee. We have important matters to discuss!'

'I don't want a coffee. I want a *drink*,' said Doyle sulkily, but he straightened his clothes and followed Dermot out of the room.

Chapter Eleven

* * *

'Doyle,' said Dermot, back in the small café, 'What season is fast approaching?'

'Summer, I imagine, though every season is so rain-sodden on this delightful island that one can scarcely distinguish summer from any other time of year. Why do you ask such an inane question, O'Duffy?'

'I thought you loved the Irish climate, Doyle. I have heard you talk to your foreign students about how dreamy and soft it is, and how good for the complexion. Anyway, it is actually easy to distinguish Ireland's summer from her other seasons.'

'How? In summer the air is still wet and chilly. The earth is still insufferably green. Nothing changes, really, except that the whole country erupts with tourists and summer schools.'

'Summer schools. Exactly. And what do summer schools require?'

Doyle stirred his coffee impatiently. 'What are you getting at, Dermot? Summer schools require a proper venue, which means good pubs and decent restaurants. And there should be a fair amount of pleasant female company.'

'And what else?'

'What else is there of importance in this life besides booze, food and women? Oh, I suppose summer schools require scholars, to provide an excuse for the general merriment.'

'Precisely, old bean. They require disgusting degenerates like yourself, to convince poor gobshites from around the globe that the Ireland of saints and scholars is still extant. Don't you see?' He tilted towards his erstwhile foe, now transformed into a comrade-in-arms. 'Summer schools! Meal tickets! Free accommodations! Even a modest fee! *That's* how we can evade Spouses on the Rampage, Squawks in Pursuit, Warrior Wives! It shouldn't be difficult for us, esteemed scholars that we are.'

Doyle said slowly, 'You mean we get ourselves booked into summer schools, as speakers, and we move from one school to another, till Pamela and Fiona cool down, or fuck off, or what have you?'

'I am dazzled by the lightning speed of your comprehension.'

'Well, it *is* still early in the morning for a sybarite like myself. It takes at least two hours to clear the cobwebs out of the old brain, and to flush the poisons out of the old body. But this is not a bad idea, Dermot, not bad at all.' He gulped down the lees of his coffee. 'Tell me more.'

Dermot began to explain. 'I don't know your Pamela, so I can't speculate about her motives in coming here. But I think I do understand Fiona's. She doesn't really want to let me go, and she would like to sabotage my relationship with Grania. And while I suspect she would have misgivings on her own, with her father fuelling her she is quite emboldened. I imagine those two would have no qualms about pursuing us from guesthouse to guesthouse, prevailing on the proprietors as they did on the O'Malley woman, convincing them, through tears, threats, moral exhortations, whatever, to throw Grania and me out. You see, Fiona has never truly understood how unhappy I was in the marriage; she thinks I was just incorrigible. So now, with her father's help, she will try to *teach me a lesson*. They think they can harrow and humiliate me until I return home, cowed, to be controlled by Fiona, and by Finn through her. Why, they have probably already called on Cressida Rabitte!'

'But mightn't they do the same at the summer schools? Follow you there, and try to make trouble, heckle your lectures and so forth?'

'They could do, but colleagues may be more sympathetic than B & B people. Anyway, at least I would be *earning* money, instead of lavishing it on hostelries. And perhaps Fiona would eventually calm down.'

Doyle thoughtfully lit a cigarillo. 'My objective, in the domestic sense, is different from yours, old man. You would like to sunder your marriage to Mrs O'Duffy, but I certainly do not want to lose my spouse. Despite her faults, the home she maintains for me is a welcoming harbour after my long and turbulent voyages. Such graciousness! Such good cooking! Such civilised comforts! I must say, I fail to fathom you, Dermot. For some lunatic reason, you seem not to mind the prospect of an extended life on the road, and with a little American, no less, who probably cannot cook or iron your collars properly.' He grimaced; then exclaimed, 'Good God, man! I would never sacrifice my Pamela for something as cloying, smarmy, and embarrassing as *love*. She can be rather haughty, mind you, but she is an excellent cook, and the very notion of giving up her superb *saumon en croûte*, giving it up *forever*, and for a clumsy *American*....' He smoothed his hankie over his brow, as though the very idea of relinquishing his wife's cuisine had drenched him in a sweat of despair.

'I believe you must be out of your mind, O'Duffy, but I also believe your summer school idea might be rather brilliant for me as well. After all, Pamela might have come to town in order to throw me out, banish me, exile me forever from her impeccable housekeeping and her *confit de canard*. Why, she might even present me with something as vulgar as an ultimatum! She might insist that I give up *women*! And if that is indeed her intention, she must be defused. If I eluded her by travelling from summer school to summer school, an academic vagabond ... it might just work.' His eyes suddenly glinted, and he gave a sly laugh. 'Also, I must escape from the talons of Beatrice; she's *exhausting* me. And there will always be a spare Sheela about. When the younger women of Ireland declared their freedom to fornicate, they forgot that the activity requires a small supply of able-bodied men, unless, of course, they fall back on themselves and become members of the SSC, or the Sheelas of Sappho Club.' He made a moue of disgust. 'Sappho, indeed! How absurd! I know that substitutes are available, but surely there is still a lot to be said for the male sceptre. Anyway, which summer schools should we tackle?'

Dermot quickly explained why they should avoid applying to the same schools. First of all, it was already late in the season, and at this point few conferences would still be in the market for lecturers; no, most summer schools had assembled their full corral of illustrious guests months ago, and both he and Doyle would have to accept what terms the organisers might extend with regard to themes, schedules, and fees, and surely no school would be able to accommodate *two* last-minute speakers. Furthermore, if their wives were indeed determined to dog them all over Ireland, it would be rather appalling if both those ladies, plus Big Finn, arrived in the same lecture hall at the same time, since the convergence of their wrath could result in a kind of spontaneous combustion, as well as enabling them to collaborate on a strategy of pursuit.

'We must scatter our forces,' Dermot concluded. 'I thought that Grania and I might head south, to the new summer school in Allihies and then to Cork, and then perhaps to the Honey Plain School in Clare, if they'll have me. While you could travel north, Doyle, to the Drumlin School in Cavan, and then on from there.'

Doyle placed a thick black phone book on the table, and announced, 'In here, O'Duffy, are the names of every summer school organiser in the whole country plus Northern Ireland. I presume that we recognise no border in *any* of our activities, the amorously aeronautical, as in hang-gliding, or the quiet drink at close of day, which usually extends till the rosy fingered dawn. Or scholarly. There are a few new topics I should like to pursue in light of my new and eminent position in the Sheela-na-Gig Society, such as: A Comparison Between Sappho and the Early Irish Female Poets; The Sexuality of the Medieval Irish Nun as Glimpsed in the Land of

Cockaigne; and From Eve to Great-Bladdered Emer to the Sheela-na-Gig: Woman as All-Engulfing Vulva. Although I had better be careful with that last topic; trying to purloin your thunder, I might stumble into the same bog-pool as yourself.' He placed his hand carressingly on the phone book. 'Anyway, I suggest we repair immediately to the public telephones in Jury's Hotel, and ring up these precious numbers. Our destiny is in our dialling fingers, my boy!'

* * *

After two or so hours of telephone toil, while Dermot was hurrying back to the guesthouse, he reflected on just how unfair it had been of Talon and the Sheelas to bludgeon *him* the other night, when really it was Doyle who regarded women as less than human. As far as the enlightened Doyle was concerned, women were either culinary paragons like Pamela, beneath his notice like the dowdy Maeve, or else sex kittens! And the man simply couldn't imagine a woman having any sort of vigorous, important life which didn't include looking after him, the glorious Doyle, in one way or another. But Dermot supposed he shouldn't excuse his own blunders in the area of love. Throughout his life, all promise of solace and sweetness seemed to flow from Her, from his idea of Woman, Woman as Siren, as Inspiration and Mystery, but he was only just now learning about real relations with a real woman. Fiona might be determined to teach him a lesson, but he was absorbing a different one. Yet he was genuinely sorry that it should be learnt at her expense, that he and Finn and other men should have imposed their own inchoate yearnings, their own desires for completion and perfection, on poor Fiona, whose heart was as sore, and need for love as great, as any of the needs visited on her, but who had always remained invisible even to her own husband, except as the brief and radiant image of his dreams.

* * *

At the guesthouse, Cressida Rabitte, wearing a blue sari, was grimly waiting. 'Dermot, a man called Finn O'Reilly has been *screaming* at me on the phone all morning. And then he and your wife came *pounding* at the door, which absolutely *flattened* my broccoli soufflé. I will not have your domestic crises disrupting my discreet house and *ruining* my cooking! I'm sorry, but you and Grania will have to leave—'

'I know, I know. We'll leave straightaway,' answered Dermot brusquely, bounding up to their room, where a pale and melodramatic Grania cried, 'Dermot, thank God you're back! Fiona and her father were here. Cressida tried to placate them—'

'Never mind,' said Dermot, taking her in his arms. 'We're off to West Cork, to the Hag of Beare School, in beautiful Allihies! Get your things together as quickly as possible. A new adventure is about to begin.'

Chapter Twelve

Summer seemed to arrive in earnest while they were travelling by bus from Cork to Allihies. There was no rain in the low sky, only a rich, interior light, and the lush fields, the brilliant fuchsia, foxglove and heather, the green-shadowed stone walls, all were charged with this glow, a silent chorus of light and colour: deep green; watered green; fuchsia bright as blood; heather vividly purple on the slopes. Grania, her face nearly plastered to the coach window, seemed to forget their troubles in an ecstasy of gazing.

It was evening by the time they came to Bantry, but the bay was still limpid, and the Chaha mountains looked shadowy as vapour on the radiant horizon. After they drew out of Castletownbere the sky was clothed in lilac clouds, but the new, rough landscape,

mountains and great stones, glowed still with the un-
canny, silver brightness that had suffused the air all day.

They arrived in Allihies exhausted and famished.
What a small, curious place it was, a dream-hamlet
with its tidy parade of houses curving up to a green,
stony wilderness. The village's single road, encircled by
mountains and the sea, was unpeopled in the darkness,
except for Shay McCarthy, the summer school organiser, who had come out of a large white house to
welcome them. He shepherded them into an airy
dining-room, and, apparently without effort, served
them a splendid meal: a pork curry which was in-
tensely hot and marvellously delicious, a dish of thick
cool yoghurt, salads of lentils, potatoes, and pickled
vegetables, and a great platter of sautéed aubergines.
Both Dermot and Grania ate two enormous servings of
everything, while this extraordinary man, so easy and
quiet, poured what seemed like torrents of strong red
wine into their glasses, and smoked his pipe, and
serenely drank a whiskey. Then, also effortlessly as far
as they could see, he took all the plates into the kitchen,
and returned with a green salad and a board of local
cheeses.

'This is beautiful, Shay,' said Dermot, 'but you
needn't have gone to so much trouble.'

The man smiled. 'No trouble. I enjoy cooking for
people. I'm only sorry I can't introduce you to the other
guests, and to the students. They're all in bed now, I
imagine, as the pubs are closed. But you'll meet them
tomorrow. Not everybody is sleeping here.'

He indicated the big room with its ample hearth,

and, beyond, the long corridors and the other rooms of this old village schoolhouse, renovated by Shay himself to accommodate a number of festivals, including the Hag of Beare Summer School, which was a summer programme for American university students. 'Most of the students and guests are living with local families. The only people in this house, other than yourselves, are me, an American professor called Carter Lewis, and Patrick O'Driscoll, the poet.'

Up in their small, simple bedroom, Grania said, 'You know, in all the tumult of leaving, I didn't really ask you what this place is all about. What do they expect you to do tomorrow?' She was taking three small canvases out of a portfolio for him to look at; she had left her larger paintings with her friend in Galway. She was half undressed, and in the lamplight her hair, flowing over her naked breasts, had a smoky glint like chestnuts.

He felt a tremor of desire, but answered levelly, 'The Hag of Beare School gives these young Americans a chance to study Celtic civilisation and Irish history and so on, in Ireland itself, which, theoretically at least, should enrich their experience of these things. It's a kind of pilgrimage to the source, and Pat O'Driscoll, who conducts a writing workshop with them, is a genuine Irish bard, and something of a druid, I suppose. So these kids can glory in the real thing for a time. Their American teacher, Carter Lewis, is thought by Irish scholars to be something of an egomaniac, though I couldn't give you my own impression as I have never met him.' He laughed. 'As for myself, I'll give them one of my standard lectures on love in Early Irish Literature, and read from my own translations. It should be money for jam.'

She came over to the bed, on which he was reclining, with her paintings in her arms, like a harvest goddess. Again he stared at her white skin and gleaming hair, but, obligingly, postponing carnal joy for art, he refrained from touching her and looked down at the pictures instead.

They were oils of Connemara, where she had gone with her Galway friend before Dermot met her, just after she had come to Ireland. And if she had wanted to capture some essence of the ever-changing Irish light, she had done, he thought, a fairly good job. The first painting depicted a landscape seen from the Sky Road at dusk. A gold light, thick as pollen, flushed the fields, and the sky glowed pewter, silver, blue, and lambent gold. The second, done in a rather different style, with looser strokes, nearly abstract, was of a blue road, a white house in a wet green field, and violet mountains under a sky swollen with rain. But it was the third canvas which made Dermot pause, and stare. It was more highly detailed than the others, and the small details of the Irish landscape were what he loved best: a wall furred with moss, or a whitewashed byre, or a milk churn on a flagstone floor, or a fuchsia bush thick with bees. Grania's painting was of the wall of a house to which ivy clung, with, beside it, a path curving into a wood, all under a low, luminous sky. He liked this picture for how it conveyed the lushness of Ireland, the tussocks of grass, the stone house so dense with ivy and leaves it seemed natural as the living earth, not man-made at all. But what arrested him most about the scene was the figure of a man in the foreground, an old farmer by the looks of him, bowed but still strong, as though he were all sinew and cable, sleeves bunched above corded forearms, face lean, with a craggy nose and shining blue eyes. The light in this painting was well done, the clouds washed with a delicate glow, but Dermot had to admit that Grania's skies, at least in these three landscapes, were nothing special, that quite a few other painters of his acquaintance, both abstract and figurative, were able to render the Irish light in a more original, mysterious, and sometimes joyous way. No, Grania was competent enough at what she was trying to do, but it seemed to him that her true gift, perhaps unsuspected by her, was the figure. Just as her family portraits had intrigued him, so was he moved by her Connemara farmer, his bony face and hard-worked body, the laughter in his old eyes. It seemed to Dermot that gifts were a kind of visitation — he had wanted to be a novelist in his youth, and Doyle had dreamt of becoming an engineer! But Dermot had come to believe that our talents were given to us, and were often utterly at variance with our expectations, or our desires for ourselves. He presumed that Grania, in wanting to convey the magical Irish light, was eager to move into the province of the abstract, but he suspected that her talent was firmly moored in the representational, that the magic she could best express was housed in the lineaments of the faces she chose as her subjects. But he wasn't sure, and so he praised the paintings; then drew her into his arms, having earned, he thought, a measure of bliss after such intellectual labours.

* * *

Next morning, they ate a superb breakfast prepared by the ever-tranquil Shay. And they met their fellow guests, Pat O'Driscoll, the poet, and Carter Lewis, the American Irish Studies professor. Pat was a broad, sturdy fellow, with a thick beard and large, childlike eyes. Dermot had never seen him before, but had heard much about him. He was a kind of local bard, enthralling the people of Allihies with his verses, delivered extemporaneously in the pubs late at night (although he himself did not drink). He was also a farmer, and a modest sort of mystic. This morning he was going to give the students a lesson in water divining. Dermot immediately liked him. There was, he thought, a great deal of sweetness in Pat's guileless eyes, and he was a fount of local lore. Carter Lewis, however, was another story.

Dermot supposed he was what the psychologists would call a narcissist, self-important and pompous. A rather small man in his mid-to-late forties, he had an annoying way of bridling when he talked, moving his shoulders this way and that, throwing his head back, and frowning or smiling in an exaggerated fashion, as though he were admiring himself in a mirror.

Dermot's strong distaste for this Lewis fellow upset him. He disliked meanness in himself, and usually tried to cultivate tolerance. So what if Carter Lewis was

a bit of a *poseur*, or what his countrymen would doubtless call a jerk? We all have our faults, Dermot
reminded himself. But Lewis seemed so grossly self-
satisfied, and his gloating manner was in such contrast
to the sweet Pat and nourishing Shay, that Dermot felt
his nape prickle with dislike as the man talked at
length about his own accomplishments, his numerous
articles and books, his illustrious teaching career, his
famous friends.

After breakfast the twenty students appeared, each
clutching a bifurcated hazel rod. 'They do look American, don't they?' commented Grania ruefully.

It was true, Dermot considered, observing the young
men and women with their hazel boughs — there was
an old-fashioned American wholesomeness about their
fresh, robust faces. They must have been upper middle-
class kids, or their parents could not, probably, have
afforded this junket to Ireland, and significantly, he
thought, there were no blacks amongst them. The
modern, multi-racial, multi-lingual America was not
being represented in Allihies by this group with their
earnest, charming, clumsy politeness, a kind of cour-
tesy that was somehow uniquely American. And their
scrubbed faces and meat-fed bodies evoked for Dermot
not the America of troubled cities and ethnic discord,
but the mythical America of all-white, suburban happiness which he had seen in innumerable 1950s
television programmes. The girls were mostly blonde,
and some were quite pretty, while the fellows were
uniformly tall and healthy looking. They all had those
vigorously white American teeth. They said good

morning to Pat with great enthusiasm, but Dermot noticed that their hellos to Carter Lewis were cooler; was his fatuous self-regard annoying the kids, too?

After the students left, following Pat in a ragged procession, divining rods poised in pursuit of secret streams, a drizzle began.

'Poor girls, poor lads,' sighed Shay. 'If they wanted water, they'll have got it now. They'll come home drenched, I imagine.' And he excused himself to prepare great pots of cocoa, coffee, and tea, saying, 'I'm sure they weren't prepared for the cocoon of Mother Machree's shawl after their torrid American summer. It's very nice to be swathed in the romantic Irish fog, but they'll all have colds before the week is out, spluttering up phlegm to be doctored with plenty of hot whiskies! I'll have to buy lemons, and cloves.' And as he began to heat the water they heard him singing:

> 'It's my old Irish womb,
> I'll be in there soon.
> It's warm and damp as a postage stamp,
> And shawled it is like an old oil lamp.
> It's a soft day today, there'll be fuck-all hay.
> Wrapped in this mist, I'll have to get pissed....'

In the afternoon, Dermot and Grania wandered through the tiny village; then up along rough paths surrounded by immense stones under a pelt of grass and flowers, to the ruined copper mines. Despite Shay's fears, the rain remained gauze-light, and the air was balmy. Although Dermot was happy, he felt, now and again, a flutter of apprehension; since he had told no one except Doyle of his acceptance by the H of B School, it was unlikely that Fiona and Finn would discover his whereabouts, but 'Daddy' was cunning and determined, and so Dermot was tense, though he tried to conceal it from Grania.

He spread his Burberry on the grass by a stream where the water, tinctured by copper, was the colour of rust, and they lay down. It was too damp to take off clothes, but they caressed and kissed each other. The mizzling rain felt cool on his skin, and the air was full of the metal-smell of water. Presently they slept, and he dreamt that he stumbled on two lovely small animals, playing together in the ferny corner of some green wood.

* * *

Dermot, Grania, Pat O'Driscoll, and Carter Lewis were served dinner by Shay at half past seven; Dermot was to speak to the students at nine. Throughout the meal (a salad of mussels and avocado; then *spaghetti puttanesca*, with plenty of rough red wine) Pat told stories about his water divining class, how, as he and his apprentice druids had scoured a field with their magic wands, one young man, famous for his prowess with the girls, had bellowed, 'Pat, Pat, my rod is jumping!' and how one young woman had been pursued by an affectionate bull. Carter Lewis, eclipsed by the droll and ebullient Pat, slurped his spaghetti and sulked, while Shay and Grania ate abundantly and laughed. Dermot, on the other hand, drank too much and was nervous: Would Fiona contrive to appear during his lecture, in order to embarrass him yet again? Would he strew *faux pas* about him like petals, as he had done in Galway, managing to offend everybody in one way or another? American academies were the most politically correct of the whole pedantic lot, and he would simply have to approach tonight's talk as though words were a mine field — utter the wrong one, and it blows up in your face.

* * *

A large cool room, the students' flushed and open faces, Grania towards the back, smiling at him: a good atmosphere, though he was slightly tiddly. He imagined he could actually feel Shay's wine surging through his veins. Plus the spaghetti they had eaten, redolent of garlic and powerfully flavoured with anchovies, was doing curious things to his stomach. Oh, shit, he thought, looks like I'll bomb again.

But miraculously he was fine. Doyle's Galway talk had taught him something, he had to suppose. Plunging straight into his standard lecture, love in Early Ireland, he changed the emphasis slightly, to focus on the sweetness that the Early Irish had seemed to long for between men and women, how in their myths and poetry they had conjured up a land, a magical plain, of total love and easement, and equality between the sexes, a pagan Eden where male and female honour each other as aspects of the great mystery of love, are made whole through love, are able to make love in fragrant groves, drink beer and mead from the streams: an Irish version of the Golden Age or the paradise of the Koran, where men and women eat and drink with abandon but are never made sick from excess, and then recline to mingle their bodies in love, naked and without shame. He recited from *The Voyage of Bran* and described the Land of Women, or Honey Plain, in entertaining detail, quoting also from *The Wooing of Etain*. The students, he could feel, were rapt, and even Carter Lewis was listening intently.

Sighing inwardly with relief, he was still discussing the old Irish vision of paradise as a realm where the sexes were equal and physical love was celebrated, so different from the modern world in which men and women circled each other warily, or embarked on campaigns against each other, when, from the corner of his eye, he saw a journalist he vaguely knew, a Margaret Something-or-other, come softly into the room. His stomach seethed with *spaghetti puttanesca*. A journalist! How could he and Doyle have forgotten that journalists clung like barnacles to the summer schools? Indeed, all of Ireland's newspapers seemed to operate under the foolish impression that gatherings of intellectuals and artists were good copy, but if this Margaret woman, who worked for a particularly hysterical tabloid, wrote about Dermot's talk at Allihies, Fiona might come roaring down after all. Well, he and Grania would be gone by then. The day after tomorrow they were leaving for the Glee by the Lee School in Cork.

He closed with a summary of women's freedom under the Brehon Laws: you could divorce your husband if he became too fat, too stingy with the housekeeping funds, could no longer function properly as a man, or spent too much time with the boys on hunting or beer-guzzling expeditions. He emphasised that there were serious textual problems concerning the Brehon Laws which were beyond the limits of this present discussion (although he used not 'limits' but the fashionable cant word 'parameters', since he was talking to Americans) and some scholars argued that they had never been seriously practised. But *The Book of Invasions*, a summary of Early Irish history, contained an account of Ireland's first law case, in which Partholan's wife countered his accusations of adultery by declaring that he had left her too long alone with his handsome servant, so what had he expected? She was human after all, like himself. Anyway, Dermot concluded, remembering how fulsomely Doyle had flattered the Sheelas, he himself was certain that the Brehon Laws had indeed been practised, and in his opinion the most significant of all of them were the laws establishing economic freedom for women. For instance, women in ancient Ireland were entitled to own property (in contrast to more 'modern' societies, where women *were* property) and could take back their lands and goods if their marriages were sundered. Imagine that! A land where women had the same force in the world, and the same liberties, as their brethren, a society in which the province of commerce and power, as well as the realm of the heart and hearth, belonged to both sexes!

The audience applauded vigorously. Dermot, wondering what would happen to his own property, and Fiona's, once the solicitors began meddling in their lives, saw that Margaret Something was not the only special visitor; he recognised a well-known artist who lived in the area, and a few other men and women too old to be members of the student group. He was glad that the artist, a sturdy, smiling man of about forty, had come tonight — he painted landscapes and would therefore be of interest to Grania. Grania, in her pretty green dress, was grinning at him, obviously proud, and the students were eager to ask questions. Again, he sighed with relief. He had finally managed to redeem himself on the lecture circuit, the garlic and anchovies were settling nicely, and his faint, unpleasant tipsiness had eased. He was lucid and confident — why, he was Dermot O'Duffy, scholar and gentleman, and the pretty girls, to whom he had just talked about love, were looking at him with glowing eyes.

'Questions?' he asked, cupping the audience, so to speak, in his palm.

Chapter Thirteen

Carter Lewis, his brow furrowed earnestly, came up to congratulate Dermot. Then Shay and Pat, and a shy, pleased Grania, approached to offer more heartfelt praise. Finally the students surged forward, clutching his books and monographs, and displacing Grania, who looked slightly perturbed.

Shay suggested that they all repair to the pub, and off they went, Dermot seizing Grania's hand and kissing her, since he could tell she felt flustered by the admiring students, this sudden plunge from their intimate time together into the soup of public life.

At the pub, someone thrust a large whiskey into his hand, and he took a relieved gulp, the night's work being over, and managed successfully as well. Of course, if he'd made a mess of his lecture, he'd still have wanted to swallow great draughts of whiskey, for consolation, but, as it was, he could enjoy a celebratory drink (or two) to savour his modest but morale-enhancing triumph. Dermot O'Duffy was back in the ring!

Grania began talking to the local painter, Fergus Sweeney, about her preference for oils over acrylics; Sweeney, surprisingly, used tempera to create the small, luminous canvases for which he was moderately renowned. Dermot, listening to them, realised he was a bit in awe of Grania. Where did her gift come from, and what would she make of it? And here she was, conducting a lively conversation with an established artist, who appeared to be enjoying both her comments, and the fact that she was favouring him with that intense, gazelle-eyed gaze of hers. Dermot, feeling a slight tug of jealousy, surely the most fruitless and bitter of all the passions, and one he tried not to foster in himself, polished off his whiskey, and requested another.

Suddenly Pat O'Driscoll, who had been talking to Shay up at the bar, let out an animal cry. The clamorous pub fell silent. 'What's going on?' whispered Dermot to the artist, who murmured, 'He's going to recite. It comes on him like that.'

Pat clenched his fists and threw back his head in a kind of paroxysm. Then he relaxed, gazed levelly into the middle distance, and launched into a poem:

> *'From the rugged crags of Allihies*
> *Soar the bleak copper mines,*
> *Where Cornishmen and Englishmen*

Came, to plunder our dear earth's prize.
Beside brave Dunboy, the Puxley family's
Monstrous mansion grew,
But now all is lost as that star-shaped fort
Laid siege to by Sir George Carew.
Desolate and ruined is Hungry Hill,
And fled, the Sassenach crew.
Our stone goddess, the Hag of Beare
Chants her song as the waves crash in:
"My body has welcomed many men
But beware: this rocky coast is my lair."'

'A sonnet, composed on the spot,' he announced; then returned to his glass of mineral water, grinning modestly while applause and shouts of 'Hooray, Pat!' thundered about him like the waves on the rocks outside.

'An amusing fellow,' smirked Carter Lewis, strolling up beside Dermot. 'Though rather *rustic*, wouldn't you say?' And he gave a cackling laugh.

Dermot replied blandly, 'The tradition of the local bard is ancient and highly esteemed in Ireland. A poet who chronicles the lore of his or her region in spontaneous verse — quite profound and marvellous, really, wouldn't *you* say?'

Lewis laughed again, but uneasily this time, as though beginning to wonder whether Dermot was a fellow sophisticate after all. Then, swallowing the lees of his pint (he was a bit unsteady on his feet, and there was a drunken glitter in his eyes), he murmured, 'Have you noticed the number of able-bodied young things among these students?' He glanced at a table in the back, at which some of the young Americans were gathered. 'Why don't you help yourself? After all, it comes with the territory, a fringe benefit, so to speak. I mean, Jesus, I don't have to remind you that academic salaries are pretty low, compared to jobs in business and the like. But one advantage we do have is an inexhaustible supply of adoring young creatures. Besides, it's good for them. Basic instruction in the arts, know what I'm saying?' He sniggered, and made his way to the bar to call officiously for another drink.

Dermot was gazing incredulously after him when Margaret Something, the journalist, materialised at his elbow, proffering a glass. 'I took the liberty of buying you a whiskey, Dermot, to congratulate you on your splendid talk.'

'Thanks,' he said warily. His head was spinning a bit, but he would have to remain alert; this woman with her sly whippet's face and insinuating smile was a famous scandalmonger. Against his better judgment, however, he helped himself to an ample swallow of her whiskey.

She sidled closer to him. 'Your companion seems charming. I was talking to her briefly, just before. Miss MacCormack, did she say her name was? One of the American MacCormacks, perhaps?'

'She is American, certainly.' Dermot tried to back away, but the place was too crowded to allow for much movement. It seemed that the whole village as well as all the immediate country folk had poured into this pub tonight. A large farmer with a fragile glass balanced in immense red fingers was pressing against his right side, and a tiny, yellow-haired little girl kept scampering between his legs. Where was Grania? Was she still talking to that artist fellow about how to make paint from egg whites or whatever it was that he did? The air was bleared with cigarette smoke and dense with bodies, and he could barely hear Margaret Something above the laughter and clatter of glasses. The little child jostled him; Margaret, her shrewd eyes narrowed against the smoke, took his empty glass, fed him another, full one, and asked, 'How is Mrs O'Duffy? How does she feel about you appearing in public with another woman? Is your marriage "on the rocks" as the Americans say?'

The tiny girl, screeching with laughter, was clutching onto his trousers like a monkey. Crouching to disengage her, he shouted up, 'It's nice to see you again, Margaret. And thanks for the drinks. But I really must go now, I'm afraid.' He straightened, and, with the little girl still clinging to his legs, lurched through the crowd.

He discovered himself in a sort of clearing at the back. 'Haven't you any parents?' he asked the child, giving his leg a vigorous shake. She tumbled off. 'Sorry, kid,' he said hastily, but she glared at him in a disconcertingly adult way, and flounced off. He straightened his clothes and looked about him for Grania, but noticed instead the table full of students which Carter Lewis had pointed out to him earlier. They cried out with delight upon seeing him; they were all girls, and before them on the table was what appeared to be an extra pint of stout. A black, malty, luscious pint of stout, untouched, waiting for him, meant for him. After all those searing whiskies, what could be nicer? He looked round again, and finally saw Grania, a little bit away from him, on her feet, on her own in the crush, a glass of red wine in her hand. She smiled beckoningly, but he gestured to the table of students and tried to give her a resigned duty-calls-so-what-can-I-do? look. Unfortunately, he was a bit too pickled to control his facial muscles properly, so that the look he gave her was probably more clownish than resigned. Anyway, he decided, he was sick of trying to please people. He would please himself for a bit. He went over to the crowded, waiting table.

How sweet they were, the young girls! They were honoured, charmingly flustered, to have the great professor in their midst, and he had a dim impression, in the dim and lighted room, of birds, a disturbed dovecote, warm creatures ruffled and palpitating; their hair falling like feathers over his cheek as they inclined their heads to listen or talk to him. He finished the pint and one of the laughing girls brought him another. Why, he had forgotten that this was such a pleasant way to live!

Poor Fiona, he thought foggily, she was actually a complicated and intelligent woman, but something in her past had so disappointed her, so chilled her, that she'd become blunted, reduced, or, more simply, depressed. But he had married her anyway, and finally when they had hurt each other enough he began to do what he had always done before: look for solace from girls and women. He began, again, to harvest women, to follow up every advantage, to never let a woman go by, to make certain that he would never be without one, would never travel alone, never be bereft, unloved and unlovable. His mother and Fiona would not thrust him back onto that scorched, windy, empty plain where there was no love. And it had been so pleasant, had made up for his monkish youth, made up for his wife's unconquerable melancholy. How nice it had been, to travel the world, an authority on love, loved by women, a succession of women like these young ones here: blue eyes, brown eyes, grey eyes; pink, brown, and freckled cheeks; glossy blonde hair, ink-black hair, springy ginger hair; young smooth healthy torsos breathing under soft jerseys. How could he live without it? Why should he live without it? How lovely women were, and how lovely of them to love him, comfort him when he lectured badly, reward him when he performed well, soothe him when he was lonely, assure him with their sweet voices and soft bodies that he would never have to be alone.

Ah, he had forgotten how sweet it was to be in love, infatuated (especially if one knew that the object of one's attentions was not the love of one's life), how sweet to be taken over by this siren or that one, to drown oneself in a woman for a time. A girl across the table was talking excitedly to him. Why not her? She had beautiful dull-gold hair and a pretty smile. Why not her, tonight? The room dipped and spun; he tilted forward to answer her, steadying himself by draping his arm unconsciously over the shoulders of another girl, beside him. She was pretty, too, and smelled delicious. He abstractedly caressed her long black hair. She was laughing. Why not laugh? He laughed, also. A blonde and a brunette! How marvellous! If one let him down, there would always be the other, countless others. Why had he ever contemplated placing all his love-eggs in one basket? What happened when the basket crashed on the shoals of life? *Is your marriage on the rocks?* Ah, no, he would never again depend on one woman. And he didn't have to! He was Dermot O'Duffy! Doyle and that Lewis man were right, although Doyle liked the older, more established ladies, and Lewis seemed to prefer greener apples. Well he, Dermot, would be less discriminating, open to the charms of all women. The sweet raven-haired girl beside him murmured something in his ear. He didn't quite hear it, but was sure it was amusing, so he threw back his head and laughed.

And Grania? What of Grania? Her face suddenly appeared before him, either conjured up in his imagination, or actually there, he couldn't say. Something, some uneasiness, stirred in him, but then a coarse old farmer's saying jumped into his mind: *Why should I buy a cow, when I can get a haporth of milk?* Indeed, and why should he repeat with Grania the mistake he had made in his marriage? How could he be certain she would not betray and disappoint him, as Fiona had done? And Margaret Something knew who Grania was; her family name was notorious. Why should he encumber himself with a member of a bothersomely famous American family? No, no, it was unsuitable, wrong!

Besides, she should know who he was, how weak and fickle and heartless. He loved the double life too much, he was not good for her. A strange bitter flavour flooded his mouth, but he drowned it in a swallow of stout from the fresh pint on the table. At least drink was always there, and didn't let you down, or answer back. He would enjoy himself.

Chapter Fourteen

A woman is on her knees in a bare stone room with curving walls, like a turret chamber in a castle. She is weeping into her cupped hands; her ragged hair flows over her face, concealing it, but he knows who she is, or does he? He feels she is in great distress, inconsolable, feels her heartache in his own heart; her grief in his own belly. He believes he has the means to comfort her, but something restrains him, keeps him silent in a corner of the ancient room. And then he realises that the weeping woman is himself, and a sob of terror and confusion bursts from him....

Dermot's eyes opened. He was filmed in sweat, and trembling. He looked at the illuminated clock beside him on the table: four in the morning. Grania was huddled away from him, her back to him, clutching her pillow, deeply asleep. He must have drunk too much last night, he reasoned, since he was still a bit drunk. The room was pitching slightly, and his mouth felt parched. He pressed his tongue up against his palate, which produced an unpleasant, thick, crackling noise, as though his saliva had turned to paste. He sighed, irritated with himself, his poor self-control. Stupid, at fifty-eight, to poison oneself with drink. He returned to a murky sleep.

But an hour later he was awake again, and rigid with horror and remorse. What had he done in that pub? What kind of mad fool had he made of himself? He could remember last night only dimly, but knew in his bones that he had disgraced himself, damaged something, hurt someone — hurt Grania! His body, toxic with whiskey, scourged with dismay and doubt, had begun to shudder alarmingly. In the wan grey light he looked at Grania, still drawn away from him, her hair a dark tangle on the white pillow. And she was wearing pyjamas, a very bad sign.

'Grania,' he said softly, touching her shoulder.

Immediately, as though she hadn't been asleep at all, she turned round and stared at him. Her eyes were black with emotion, and the skin around them was bright pink. She said loudly, 'Don't *touch* me! I *hate* you! Don't *touch* me!'

'Sh-hh!' He made vague consoling gestures. 'Shhh, child! You'll rouse the whole house.'

'I'm not a child! And I *told* you, don't *touch* me!' She clenched her small hands into fists and proceeded to pummel his chest rapidly. Since his whole body was already throbbing with post-whiskey tenderness, these blows were more unwelcome, and painful, than they might ordinarily have been. He seized her wrists but she writhed like a cat until he had to release her. She didn't try to strike him again, only glared, and said passionately, 'I remember you telling Doyle that his facetiousness was despicable, that it was people's *lives* he was playing with. Well, what sport do *you* believe you are engaging in, Professor O'Duffy? Do you think women are *baubles*? Expert on love! You desecrate love, you trivialise it and destroy it! It was my life, my heart, that you were playing with!' She gave his chest another punch. 'You *bastard*! I *hate* you!'

He reflected (quite sensibly, he thought) that he was unable to respond properly to her accusations because he could not remember what he had actually done last night, what cruel, drunken, capricious thing, to cause her such anguish. He was aware that he had gloated excessively over his performance, and that he had flirted, probably rather childishly, with a tableful of American undergraduates. But it occurred to him now that during these last emotion-charged days he had been under much more pressure than he'd understood. He realised that he had feared, in some shadowy place in himself, that Fiona and Finn would blight him with their anger, that a new inability to perform well would be their revenge for his treachery. So his aplomb last night, his clear and (he had, in all modesty, to admit) rather riveting talk, had reassured him more than he could have expected. He was all right, after all, still sound, still himself: they had not destroyed him with their derision, and perhaps he was not really so wicked, perhaps he had done nothing so terribly wrong, in choosing, finally, to love. And the attentions of the girls had been further reassurance; the young women were not abandoning him, even though he was fifty-eight, even though his wife and her prehistoric father had seemed to want to wreck his confidence. Couldn't Grania see that it was only reassurance he had been looking for, last night in the pub, only his desire to touch, once again, the magic stone? Surely he hadn't done anything too awful — or had he? Even in his cups, surely, he wouldn't have *kissed* one of those little girls, or, God forbid, *slept* with one? He said nervously, 'Grania, what did I do, to make you behave like this?'

She stared at him for a few moments, breathing heavily, pale, her eyes so dark they were like ink spilled on a white page. Then she began to speak in a low, urgent voice.

'Your problem, if you don't mind me saying so, is that you have conducted a double life for too long. It has created a schism in your spirit. Oh, I am all for the double life, myself. To travel in a foreign country, where nobody knows me or my family, to drink in smoky pubs and eat in odd restaurants with people my mother and father would consider unsuitable, in a town where the streets are strange to me. I am all for that, for the secret place, the separate place, where I am islanded from the "me" most people know, that special freedom. But what you do is different. You have lived so long with deceit you don't know how to be whole. When you are in public with me, I, who am implicated in your life, you deny me. Yes, you do! It is as though there has to be something clandestine in everything you do, as though you must always be deceiving somebody, Fiona or me or somebody, as though you do not want to be your entire self, living a truth which is entire, which encompasses your heart and your spirit, which endures and to which you bring your whole life, your public and private life. Love, I am talking about! But you don't want love, you want sport, you want to pretend, in public, that I do not exist, so that you can have every fucking girl in the room. Then you want to come back to me and say, Oh, it was only a bit of mild flirtation. You know what scamps we boys are! Do you think it's daring and amusing to be naughty in public, with me in the same room, deceiving me, defying me, as though I were that Fiona of yours, or some beastly mother figure? Or maybe it's that you just want to keep every door open. You might like me, but that blonde in the corner looks tempting. Why not have her, too? Why close yourself off to that one, just because you've got this one? After all, your mother let you down and so did Fiona. Why should you give your heart away? Or maybe it's just that you are a conceited, vain bastard who doesn't mind trampling on the heart of the woman he says he loves, because suggesting to other girls that he might be available to them is simply too much fun for him to give it up. Cheap thrills, I suppose. And then they can whisper to themselves about me: *Well, he mustn't love her very much; see how he flirts with all the other women.* If you behave like a bastard you turn women into bitches!'

Dermot sighed, trying to summon up last night, but all he could remember was feeling vaguely jealous of Grania's rapport with the painter Fergus Sweeney, and feeling beleaguered by that relentless Margaret Something (who had apparently fed him cataracts of whiskey) and being fastened onto by a limpet of a child, and then being eased by the attentions of the American girls. But he couldn't remember any single one of those girls, only that they were all young and pleasant.

Falteringly, he said, 'But, Grania, don't you see? Those girls, they were so young, and had such lovely skin, all warm and downy, like peaches. They were just human *peaches*, don't you understand?' He knew he was expressing himself badly. His post-alcohol gloom was making him dull and stilted, and he was so exhausted his eyes kept closing. He wanted Grania to understand that they had meant nothing, the girls in the pub, weren't even individual human beings to him, but, as soon as he finished speaking, he realised that praising their twenty-year-old complexions might not be the right move at the moment.

Grania said, with a break in her voice, 'Well, you seem to enjoy your fresh fruit. You were touching their arms and hair, and kissing their cheeks, and I did overhear one, a terrible freckle-faced girl, say about me, "Oh, yes, that's the woman he came with, but he doesn't seem to care much for her." And why shouldn't she have come to that conclusion? Supposedly I was your girlfriend, but you were indifferent to me, and behaving towards them with real ardour. After all, you could have included me in that group at the table, called me over, but you didn't want me there. You hurt me, Dermot. And all you did the whole night long was say "I".'

'"I"?'

Grania jumped out of bed and stood there glaring, her hands on her hips. 'Yes, "I". You never said "we" or "us", never! When Fergus Sweeney asked you, "And where will you go after Allihies?" you replied, "I am going to Cork, to the Glee by the Lee School, and then I am travelling up to Clare." It was like that with everyone, all night. Nobody would have thought you had a companion, not by the way you were talking. Why, a young man, one of the students, even came over to me and asked, "What will you do, Miss MacCormack, when Professor O'Duffy goes to Cork?" You can imagine what a splendid time I had in that pub last night, Dermot. Our love has been very delicate, and very private, but like all profound things it must have its public expression, too. And there I was, last night, all by myself in that thronged place, being jostled by people I didn't know, trying to drink my wine and smile and be civil to everybody, with you in a corner publicly making love to other women. Once I glanced over, and saw a dark-haired girl whispering in your ear, and then you and she exchanged this warm, long look, and you kissed her....' Tears shone in Grania's eyes. 'Why, Dermot, did you have to humiliate me? And for no reason, that I could see. We should have been celebrating together! Your talk was marvellous, and it was about love. Love!' She sobbed, and he extended his arms to her, but she gave him another clout on the shoulder, and said, in the broadest American accent he had ever heard her use, 'This is the late twentieth century, buddy. And that kind of stuff doesn't wash any more. Being a devil-may-care, glamorous, lothario professor who romances his students, and plucks whatever peach happens to be dangling before his eyes. Well, that stuff *isn't* glamorous, not anymore. All those sexual high jinks you and Doyle and that slimefoot Carter Lewis indulge in! They are not about romance or love, they're just about old-fashioned sexist notions of prowess and power, and about exploiting vulnerable or lonely people, and they are all just so *stupid*!'

'Slimefoot?' asked Dermot, delightedly picturing Carter Lewis walking through the groves of academe with seaweed squelching out of his shoes.

'Yes, that's just what he is, a fucking slimefoot. And that insufferable, pathetic little peacock Doyle is a slimefoot, too. And you are no better.' She stopped talking suddenly, as though spent after her eloquent diatribe. Dermot regarded her, and registered for the first time that she was wearing pyjamas with a pattern of small Minnie Mouses on them, a plethora of Minnie Mouses with big red ribbons between their ears, and flaring saucy dresses, and enormous shoes, each Minnie Mouse smiling and capering across Grania's body and down along her legs. And the combination of her rumpled hair, grim expression, and Minnie Mouses, moved him not to laughter but to a sensation of ferocious and tender love. He said, 'But I love you,

Grania. And you are right, and I was terribly wrong. All my old bad habits! I can't even promise it will be the last time. But I do love you, my dear. And I will try. Only you must tell me, wherever did you get those elegant pyjamas?'

Distracted, she glanced down. 'These? Oh, in a second-hand shop, in New York. The East Village. I used to buy a lot of my things in vintage clothing shops. And I couldn't resist these.'

'Neither can I,' said he, opening his arms again, and this time she came into them.

* * *

They slept, Grania being, if not mollified, at least exhausted. She was still asleep at nine o'clock when Dermot's eyes opened and wandered up to the room's single high window, glinting with sunlight: it would be a fine day.

His skin still felt raw from last night's excesses, but his spirit was calmer. He lay there with Grania's head on his shoulder, and considered what she had said to him earlier. Some of her words had echoed Fiona's familiar refrain: *Why must you humiliate me in public? Why must you lure every girl in every room over to you?* Despite Fiona's apparent inability to consider how *she* might have contributed to the wrecking of their marriage, he had to admit that there must be some truth in her accusations, since Grania's were so similar. He would have to confront the fact that, after all these years, he seemed still to be a collector of women, that he used them still to buttress his teetering confidence, poultice his absurd old heart, that, sometimes, in an attempt to ease his fear of having *no* woman, he campaigned, still, to have *every* woman. Staring at the light-filmed window, he caressed Grania's head, and thought about the blows we all are dealt; so early, they come, and so out of the blue, we haven't the means to give them a name; our cries are wordless and extreme, and then we conduct our whole lives informed by a pain we cannot articulate or remember. Buried, it is, buried in the mystery that is ourselves, lost in the dawn of our lives — his pain, Fiona's, Grania's. Love, he thought, only love and nothing else can save us. And then he must have slept again, for he had another dream, a familiar dream, this time, one that had been visiting him for many years, repeatedly, with small variations:

He has resolved not to be wicked, to let no girl tempt him, but a siren appears, a girl with witchy eyes in a thin face (this time she is blonde, but in other dreams she has been a brunette or a vivid redhead — it doesn't matter; she is the same girl). He is appalled by her, knows she is rapacious, callous, brutally ambitious, and yet he cannot resist her. *I don't like you*, he thinks, *You are a decidedly unpleasant creature*, but she has unbuttoned her blouse and is drawing it slowly off, exposing first her white, sloping shoulders, and then her heavy breasts, also white, with delicate blue veins and crimson nipples. He caresses them, but she laughs disdainfully and says it isn't enough, he must do more for her. Her eyes shining malevolently, she taunts him, says she knows he is ineffectual, but still he must try,

191

touching her breasts is not enough, he must satisfy her more deeply. And then before he can absorb her words she has adopted the posture of a sheela-na-gig, her legs spread wide, her fingers opening the lips of her vagina. He stares in dread and desire as her vulva flares open, layer after layer, like ink burgeoning in water, like a rose opening, like umbrellas unfurling within other umbrellas. Blood-rich, shining, she opens, and, in revulsion, knowing he will be spent in her but not fulfilled, knowing that she is not the fertile but the barren place, knowing that even so he *will* return there, to where all is barren, as though compelled to look for solace from the very source of pain, he embraces her.

* * *

It was ten o'clock, and Grania was still sleeping. He passed a hand over his face, as though to clear cobwebs from it. What a cliché of a dream! What Freudian fuckology! Why an intelligent man should be embarrassed to dream a dream like that dream! And pronouncedly politically incorrect it was, too. Woman as Chamber of Horrors was not a popular theme these days. If Talon and her cronies could peer with their mental torches into his unconscious, into all the dust and spiders there, they wouldn't like it one bit, would probably declare that he was the most fucked-up, woman-loathing, castration-obsessed gynophobe they had ever glimpsed, and, if it were possible, a regiment of Sheelas would trudge into his psyche clutching cloths, brushes, and disinfectants, and scrub away his mother, Fiona, and all those capricious sirens, so that he would have only sexually wholesome, woman-respecting dreams from now on.

His thoughts returned to the still-vivid dream. Who was that girl with the face of a vixen? She had appeared to him on numerous occasions, and not only in dreams. Throughout his amorous career that kind of girl had often been able to throw a net over him and drag him in, thrash and flail though he might. Antonia, the haughty New England blonde, was one of the more recent examples, along with Orla the 'actress-model', and a dark girl called, ridiculously, Melody, whom he had known in Dublin six years ago. Unkind, shrewd rather than intelligent, coquettish, feckless, that was what he had thought of Melody at first, before he had come into her thrall, enchanted by her forthright love of sex, her azure-black hair, her vivacity. Ah, but he hadn't liked himself for liking such a shallow creature, and, predictably, their affair hadn't come to much. But, anyway, who was *she*, the woman who visited him like a succubus in dreams, and whom he had glimpsed in Melody, in Orla and Antonia?

Of course he knew who she was, the woman who haunted his dreams. He was being coy with himself, pretending he did not know. And indeed she was the barren place, for him. How many times will a man return to the desert, his breath harsh with thirst, his flasks and wineskins empty, looking in that dry region for water, for honey, for nectar? When he was a boy, his mother made him feel that he was terrible, but he had thought that if he could ease her sorrow, replace her scowls with smiles, then she would smile on *him*, and ease *his* sorrow. It was grace he was looking for, but there had been no grace in that house. And over how many years had he kept returning there? Had he now, finally, ceased to make that unprofitable pilgrimage? Had he learnt, finally, that the voyage one must make is to a different place? Did he now know where he could divine the source of grace? He closed his eyes. If he could talk to Fiona at this moment he would tell her this, that they had not been able to soothe each other, that they must now journey on, both of them, separately. It was their responsibility to do so. They had hurt each other too much, over too long a time, and now they must let go, and he would give her his benediction, if she would receive it.

Grania stirred in his arms, and he kissed her head, thinking, Ah, Fiona, can we live without bitterness?

Chapter Fifteen

Their last day in Allihies was so beautiful, Dermot
and Grania borrowed togs from Shay, and bathed
in the Atlantic. The mountains, their hollows full of
light, their slopes clothed in heather and grass thick as
fur, glimmered above them, and the water, so chilly and
exhilarating, seemed to draw the poisons out of Dermot's body.

He was embarrassed to appear before the students
— would they now regard him as nothing but a boozy
philanderer, a lubricious, whiskey-guzzling bag of
Gaelic wind? But the kids, who had the day off and
were frolicking through the village, eating lunch in the
pubs, walking up to the mountain, were friendly and
unselfconscious as ever to both himself and Grania.
Good boys and girls they were, no doubt simply

amused by his ebullience last night, except for the freckled girl mentioned by Grania, whom they saw in the pub nibbling at a sandwich and whose smile was indeed wintry. Dermot realised uncomfortably that she reminded him of Fiona, though without Fiona's style.

The Allihies Summer Festival commenced that afternoon, and they were fortunate enough to witness the Turnip Relays, where the children of Allihies rolled turnips up the road in a fierce competition. Many were afraid that the older children, who were more spry and whose legs were longer, would trounce the toddlers. But the older kids began to squabble among themselves, enabling a five-year-old girl to ferry her turnip quietly past the bickering groups and come in an easy First; she was awarded two packets of sweets and all the battered turnips for her mother to boil. Then they saw the Adult Wheelbarrow Heat, during which townsmen (in drag) were trundled through the village in barrows. The trundlers halted at every pub, where they pitched their wheelbarrows forward, spilling forth the bedizened cargo, who were required to drink down a bottle of beer before returning to their chariots and proceeding up the road. The victor here was the man who arrived first at the final pub, located just before the village dwindled up the mountain, and this year that man was none other than a grinning and spiflicated Shay, wearing a lot of bright rouge, and a purple dress over false breasts. His prize was six bottles of stout, which at that point were rather redundant, there being five pubs in the small village of Allihies, meaning that five bottles of beer had just cascaded down between his garishly painted lips. His 'Acceptance of First Prize Speech' was less than coherent, but everyone applauded wildly anyway, and Pat (himself dressed in a yellow, sequin-spangled gown) recited a poem called 'The Lovely Ladies of Allihies':

> *'Oh, the lovely ladies of Allihies!*
> *Such scanty breasts, and bony knees.*
> *On a winter night in Allihies,*
> *Our ladies cause your blood to freeze....'*

By afternoon, Dermot was finally convinced that Grania was no longer angry with him; indeed, he felt that the tenderness between them had deepened. He knew that after lovers' quarrels the air is often rinsed clean, as after a squall, and that in this new sweet air couples become more delicate with each other, grateful to have made it through the storm, and because their hearts are convalescing. But this deeper tenderness between himself and Grania seemed to be a more profound thing, as though they had broken through together into a new and unexpected place.

* * *

Next morning they departed for the Glee by the Lee. While the bus jostled them past the boulders and moors of the Beare Peninsula, back into Bantry, and then east through gentle farm country, Dermot began to feel an increasing sense of foreboding. What could such a feeling mean, except that Fiona was in town?

Grania was drowsing, her head on his shoulder. He

remembered the fondness with which Shay had seen them off, thrusting into Grania's hands a thermos flask of his delicious coffee. It was just like Shay to deprive himself of a perfectly good flask merely so his guests could be sustained by a bit of hot coffee on their journey to Cork. And the students, with their endearing, gauche politeness, had clustered in the road, not minding that the morning was blustery, to say goodbye. It seemed that no one had been offended by his flirtatiousness, except Grania, of course. He looked down at her sable-shadowed, gold-glinting hair, her eyes closed in sleep. While agreeing with her that he had behaved badly the other night, and while he felt, now, genuinely contrite, he considered the possibility that her own insecurity might have contributed to her distress at his roguishness. Despite, or perhaps because of, the wealth and fame that had always surrounded her, she seemed deeply insecure, and he wondered was it a legacy from her father, this too-fragile belief in herself. In his experience, women with strong fathers were either quite bold, as though a kind of manly aplomb, a confidence in the world, were a girl's natural patrimony from such a man, or else their self-confidence was dealt a ferocious blow, as with Fiona, daughter of antediluvian Finn. He tried to picture Grania's father, the cavalier, arrogant, and handsome Senator MacCormack, but his imagination faltered, understandably, since he'd had little experience of American robber baron families. But one thing Dermot did know was that Grania had no intention of being anything other than his equal in love. Whether she achieved success as a painter or not, and despite the doubts and insecurities that assailed her at times, she was not about to recede into the shadows. Fiona had seemed content to establish herself as a kind of stern mother figure in his life, like Doyle's Pamela, and his girlfriends had mainly been biddable creatures, content as himself to keep things light. But Grania would bring him into deeper places, throw him up against himself, open her passionate heart to him. Of this he was sure, and he was glad for it, or at least so he felt on this bright morning.

Carefully, so as not to disturb her, he opened Shay's flask and took a swallow of the steaming coffee, then grinned. Shay had laced it amply with some splendid brandy. He helped himself to another scalding gulp, reasoning that if Fiona were indeed in Cork, a bit of Dutch courage mightn't go amiss.

* * *

And indeed there she was, in the foyer of the hotel, erect and composed on a small green sofa, looking away from them.

'Dermot,' Grania said in an urgent whisper just as they entered through the revolving door, 'Fiona is over there, *waiting*.'

Dermot, who had already seen her (those narrow eyes in that fine-boned face, the long throat and square shoulders; all so familiar, and so strange) answered calmly as he could, 'She hasn't noticed us yet. Leave the bags here for now, and go up to our room. It's better that I should speak to her alone.'

'Of course.' Grania gave his hand a squeeze and hurried to reception.

Dermot walked across the foyer and lowered himself into the chair opposite Fiona. Sensing his presence, she turned her head and regarded him silently. Deciding that she was probably as little inclined to engage in small talk as himself, he asked bluntly, 'How did you know I would be here?'

She answered calmly, 'Margaret Keogh.' (Keogh, yes, that was Margaret Something's name.) Fiona tilted her head, regarding Dermot mildly. 'She rang me yesterday, from Allihies. She is a women's rights activist, you know, and was incensed when Daddy told her about your behaviour. Anyway, she's covering the summer schools for her paper, and when she learnt that Doyle would be at the Drumlin in Cavan, she alerted Pamela and me. We hastened up there, and Pamela was able to confront her husband. I, however, was thwarted, till now.' She sighed regretfully, but Dermot noticed that she was looking mildly radiant, cheeks flushed, lips curving in an involuntary smile. It was Finn, he realised, who had done this for her, who had been her Pygmalion, breathing life into that waxen face, kindling her as Dermot had never done. Regarding her, he was sure that, despite her distress, she was overjoyed that Finn was proud of her, since she looked so animated, so vivid, more so, in fact, than he, Dermot, had ever seen her. Even when he'd adored her he had registered the cold, pale, almost inert quality of her beauty. But she was glowing now.

Chapter Fifteen

'I'm sorry, Dermot, that you've had to skulk about the country like a fugitive. But then again, you've given no thought to me, none at all.' Her face suddenly changed, in the disconcerting way such changes took place in her, the lovely eyes dulling with pain, the cheeks seeming to grow hollow. She spoke softly. 'Not only do you humiliate me in public yet again, but you also don't seem to care about the distress I must be in, at a time like this. My whole life feels barren, and lonely, and broken, because of what you have done to me. Daddy says—'

'Oh, please, Fiona, give us both and all Ireland a break. The *last* thing I'm interested in is what "Daddy" says. Can't you speak for yourself?'

His tongue fairly prickled with the desire to go on: did she really believe that she and her father would *expose* him, indeed that his own friends would censure him when they learnt that he had finally left a marriage freighted with bitterness, and parched for want of love? Furthermore, did she truly think that she and Big Finn would break his spirit, cow him into some kind of submission? What on earth did she think she was doing? He looked at her chill face. Why, she was not grieving, not bereft at the loss of him; she was merely insulted, a mother confronting a mutinous child, a keeper whose charge had dared to flout her commands. He wanted to answer back, to chastise her, but a compunction stilled his tongue. *My whole life feels barren, and lonely, and broken....* How terrible to suffer the death of love, how grim her nights must be. Ah, and how could he presume to know what she was feeling? It was fine for him to decide that she was merely cold, but no doubt her steely composure had always concealed more turbulence, passion, and sorrow than he'd ever understood. Fiona, he thought, I wanted to love you, but I did let you down; I returned to our bed still warm from the arms of other women; I got drunk; I hurt you; I *did* humiliate you. He looked at her, and could not speak.

She sighed, and glanced about her. 'This is hardly a luxurious hotel. Is that unpleasant for you?'

No, it was not a luxurious hotel; it was a just a comfortable place, with a friendly bar; he often came here when travelling alone to Cork. And he loved hotels anyway, for their hectic, anonymous glamour, for how travellers, converging in them, in the bar or tea-room or restaurant, become (briefly, glancingly) intimate, like passengers on a ship. What need had he for luxury? And why, oh why, had Finn done this to his daughter, why had he terrorised her with his lust for social success, engulfed her with his own overweening ambition, made her esteem herself too much, and love herself too little? Dermot had a plummeting glimpse into her psyche, the quality of her anguish, how her *hauteur* was born of a simple need for love which had hardened into a husk around her heart.

'Whatever are you intending to do now?' he asked softly.

Her head lifted; he saw the taut blue cords in her white throat. 'Daddy says I mustn't let you get away with this. He says that you are not entitled to forsake, with impunity, the woman who sacrificed her whole life for you.' She paused, as if to relish the effect of her threat.

'Jesus Christ, Fee! Of course I am *entitled* to leave. Marriage is not a bloody prison. Surely it is not only our right, but our *responsibility*, to embrace love, or at least the possibility of love, instead of sacrificing our lives to a blighted marriage. Why, there must be few things in life more terrible than meaningless sacrifice! Yes, it was *both* of us who sacrificed our best years, who punished and poisoned each other. Surely it is our responsibility to stop doing so, now, before we are too exhausted and embittered ever to love again!'

'You are *shouting*,' she hissed. 'And you are deceiving yourself, Dermot. It *was* I who sacrificed, while you indulged yourself. You could never forego illicit pleasures, those girls, you had to have them all. While I spent my youth, my good looks, my dreams, on you. You! A cruel child—'

'I worked hard, while you savoured your grievances as though they were joy, and never hesitated to throw your reproaches at me, when I came home tired in the evening. Or else you just cried, and retreated into your silences, leaving me frustrated and lonely. What did you expect me to do?'

'You always went mad for any girl who happened to be nice to you, as though love were just a trinket in Woolworth's, some shallow thing to distract yourself with, before moving on to the next pretty object. You married me because you liked my looks, because I was your dream girl. You couldn't bear that I should become real, that your selfish dream might shatter. And then when I ceased to be your dream, you simply moved on to the next dream girl, and the next. And has it never occurred to you that you were able to accomplish so much, to write your articles and studies, because I protected you, took care of you, tolerated your insults to me, your excesses—'

'Without ever asking me *why* I might be drinking too much, or fastening compulsively on women, what despair might have compelled me, what solace I might have been looking for. You say I wanted you to be a dream but you never let me close to you!'

Oblivious, she cried, 'I *spent* myself on you, and now that I am old you have discarded me, for a woman who is still young, who might yet give you children—' Her voice broke, but immediately she composed herself again, and resumed. '*You* have possibility before you, and promise. All my promise was fed into you, and now there is nothing, I am nothing, only an old, ex-hausted, childless, hollowed-out *thing*.'

He answered gently, 'But you are not old, Fee. You are young, still, and beautiful, and accomplished.' He paused. 'And we could have had a child, after the miscarriage, but you didn't want to.'

She spoke in a low voice, 'You didn't want to try again, I could feel it. You were already moving away from me. And then I decided it would be awful to impose a father like you, a womaniser and a drunk, on my baby.'

He sighed. 'All right. We made a sorry mess of our marriage. But does that mean we haven't the right to some happiness now? Are we obliged to cling to our double misery forever? I am not betraying you, Fiona, by making a new life for myself, and leaving you free to do the same.'

She seemed to hesitate, to falter. The lashes dropped over her eyes which had been two pale flames, and she began to pluck confusedly at the sleeve of her jumper. A moment before he'd been impressed by the vitriol scalding her vocabulary. *Insulted, humiliated....* Good God, he had thought, if Fiona is pursuing me like this because she still loves me, why does she not cry, *My love, my heart is breaking, why have you left me all alone?* as he, as anyone, would cry, who felt forsaken? He had been dismayed to think that she might be experiencing their separation merely as an injury to her pride. But her obvious confusion now, her bowed head, the loss of her repose, told him a different story. As so often before, he did not really know what she was thinking; she had delivered Daddy's condemnations with some style, but he could vaguely sense other currents. Regarding how her head dipped like a swan, how her pale fingers kept touching the woollen sleeve of her jumper as if for comfort, he tried to appeal to her, again.

'Fiona,' he cried, extending his hands, 'Don't forget! *You* forced a confrontation in Galway, and asked me, publicly, to leave. Don't you see? You must have been longing for freedom as much, or more than me, because you were braver than me in Galway. It was you who defied our uneasy silence, you who tore away the veil and revealed the truth. And what you said remains true, and Grania has little or nothing to do with it. Our marriage has been over for a long, long time.

Only the two of us are here now; there is no audience. Surely you will not look at me, now, and tell me that what I say is a lie? Fiona! Come to your senses. Don't falsify the rift between us.'

Her mouth hardened, and she looked away. 'I'm afraid that *you* will falsify it. You will tell people how miserable I made you, and everyone will believe you because you are so *charming*, Dermot, with your candid eyes and your curls.'

'Don't be silly,' he said uncomfortably; she had always been able to expose his foibles with a merciless accuracy. 'I have no intention of saying anything derogatory about you, to anyone. And I've never contended that you made me miserable. Only that over the years, when you were in pain or lonely, you never confided in me how you were feeling.'

'How could I tell you anything? I didn't *know* what I was feeling, when we married. I was too young, and nobody had ever taught me to be introspective. And I was dazzled by you, how handsome and intelligent you were. You certainly weren't what Daddy wanted, but you were a bohemian, and an intellectual, and much less boring than those future judges and company presidents he kept foisting on me. Oh, I suppose I idealised you. Until you revealed your true nature, and my hopes crumbled.'

'Ah, Fee, everybody's hopes crumble. It's only after you stop idealising people that you can really begin to love them.'

She looked at him silently for a moment, colour flaring along her high cheekbones. Then she said, 'But you idealised *me*, Dermot. You thought I was marvellous and defiant and brave. You never understood the things I needed for myself.'

They stared at each other, and Dermot believed that she must be thinking the same thoughts as himself, remembering the same things, their early days in Dublin, the Dublin of that time, grey and grim enough, but also emerging from a kind of chrysalis, as Catholic boys and girls attended university, graduated with honours, prospered, became politicians and barristers and artists, entered society, attended the horse shows and balls, made bundles of money, ignited the city with something brash and bright, supplanted the creaking old Anglo-Irish gentry. This was Big Finn's dream for his daughter, but she had liked the looks of the slightly shy, slightly threadbare, very romantic Dermot O'Duffy, who was, after all, prospering in his own way, as a writer and academic, not that Finn had understood such things. And what had Dermot sought, in the still, chill Fiona O'Reilly? He pictured her as she had looked at twenty-five or so, proud, pale, carelessly elegant in cashmere scarf and loose raincoat, those fine eyes with their somewhat haunted expression gazing at him over thin glasses of sherry in the pub where they had gone then. She'd been so alluring, so beautiful, so tall, like the heroines he was reading and writing about....

'I suppose you are right,' he said. 'I suppose we did idealise each other. And you have a point about my immaturity.' He paused, a thought occurring to him for the first time. 'But, Fee, where is your father, anyway? I presume he's with you here in Cork?'

Again she looked away, and he sensed another change in her, something a bit abashed, nearly sheepish, in her manner. 'No. I — I sent him away, back home, from the Drumlin School. I thought I could— manage on my own.'

'Really? What do you mean by "manage"? What is there to manage, Fiona?' All at once it occurred to him that this banishing of Big Finn really was quite dramatic and unexpected. Picturing the old bore snorting and fuming all the way back home, he ventured, 'Incidentally, how did the ole cattle rustler feel about being dismissed by you, sent back to the hacienda?'

She actually grinned. 'Daddy didn't mind. He was — you see, certain changes took place in *my* life, as well. At the Drumlin. And I realised I didn't need the — er — old cattle rustler to ride shotgun for me anymore.'

He couldn't help grinning back, and for a moment they were pals. Then she resumed. 'I'm in the process of making certain decisions myself, just now. And I must confess that I don't really know what I mean by "manage". I have spoken to members of the summer school committee, here in Cork, about your — about you. I thought they should know about your behaviour....'

He stared at her. 'Surely you're not serious? You mean you discussed our private life with the Glee by the Lee committee? What business is it of theirs?'

She gazed fixedly at some point above his head, her face wearing the remote expression he had come to know, and dread, over the years. But he was glad to register that she was also squirming slightly, and that once again her hand had begun to tug at the sleeve of her jersey.

'Daddy said they should know who they were harbouring, that I should encourage them to entertain second thoughts about having someone like you lecture at their school. Only I — I myself have had second thoughts, since speaking with the committee. And honestly I am not quite certain of what I will do now.'

He felt his cheeks burning. 'Jesus Christ, Fee!' he cried for the second time. 'How could you consider even for a moment doing such a daft thing as speaking to the summer school? Do you think people care that you and I are separating? That they would presume to judge? All you have accomplished is to embarrass me. But I suppose that was the point.'

She suddenly rose. 'I don't know what the point is. I must — I must decide how to — what to do now.'

'I don't understand. You are being so cryptic. *What the hell are you doing, Fiona?'* He tried to formulate something more to say, but before he could open his mouth she had murmured, 'Good bye, Dermot, we will speak later,' and walked stiffly out through the hotel's glass doors. If she had earlier dismissed Daddy, she had now dismissed Dermot, as well.

Chapter Sixteen

He was trembling when he came into their room, and Grania, blessedly, said nothing, only embraced him. He had thought he'd want to talk to her, but the moment she took him in her arms he was overcome by something more than lassitude, a terrible aching weariness, and as though she had intuited this Grania drew him onto the bed and lay quietly down beside him.

Immediately he slept, and dreamt he was a child again, walking into the farmhouse kitchen where his mother is drinking tea, her hands curved loosely round the cooling cup, her head straight and handsome in profile; he feels suddenly clumsy with his dirty hands, and grass-smudged shoes dragging over the flagstones. *Mother, I've a present for you.* The shy palm extended with its offering, a blanched, blue-veined stone. His mother's blue eyes gaze with mild indifference. *Now, what would I be wanting a stone for, Dermot, with a hundred just like it out in my own garden....* Then he is his current age, with Fiona: they are the only two passengers in a Dublin bus that has gone suddenly out of control and is careering along Baggot Street. He is terrified, but Fiona, wearing a bizarre futuristic dress made of aluminium foil, is completely unruffled.

'Dermot, speak to the driver,' she admonishes calmly while they pitch past the canal. Her dress is shining into his eyes so that he can barely see, but he staggers up to appeal to the man at the wheel, only to realise no one is there....

His eyes opened. The din of a city, klaxons and shouts, floated up from the street, and a panel of white sunlight, fuming with motes, sloped in through the great Georgian window. Grania was asleep; he touched her hair, which the strong light had bleached to a fawn colour, like toffee. Sighing, he reflected that no matter what disruption Fiona might devise, he would have to press on here in Cork. After all, he had a job to do. But her strange behaviour continued to trouble him. On the one hand, she had actually gone so far as to speak to the summer school committee of his low morals and corrupt character, but on the other, she had certainly waffled during their exchange today, indeed had seemed to be questioning not only her own actions, but even those of Daddy, her paragon, as well. And he couldn't make sense of her oblique references to something that had happened at the Drumlin School.

Whatever it was, it had unsettled her, or at least given her pause, since in the course of their brief interview she had hurtled back and forth between being his baleful nemesis, and expressing real self-doubt, and even something close to affection.

Grania moved beside him; he kissed her, and immediately, surprisingly, a white-hot desire coursed through him. He pressed her to him, rousing her from sleep with urgent kisses, determined to make love to her.

Could it be that his troubles had released a turbulence in him, which now, without thought or effort, he was translating into passion? He didn't know, but suddenly it was as if a crush of images, fantasies, dreams, was moving out from the corners of the room, breathing along his spine, bearing down on him. Childish fantasies, wicked fantasies, silly fantasies (are all sexual fantasies, he wondered, cargoed with clichés, and potentially hilarious?) but terribly potent; he tilted Grania's head back and kissed her again, greedily....

He is a cruel pasha, sampling the new harem girl; the transparent veils which clothe her, and the gold bracelets on her wrists and ankles, make her seem even more naked; he beats her first as is his wont; her tears, the marks on her thighs, make him shudder with possessive joy....

Grania cried out. She was sweating, clutching him. He looked through her tangled hair into her enormous, glittering eyes.

'Go on,' she whispered, 'Go on.'

He is a labourer, a big, loutish fellow, working on

some grand estate. The lady of the manor beckons and he comes shambling into the house, bony wrists dangling stupidly from grubby sleeves. She takes off her dressing gown, sprawls on a sofa, and orders him to make love to her; he is awkward and shy and she taunts him, squeezes his poor privates in her cruel beringed hand....

'Not so hard,' he murmured. They were both glossed with sweat and breathing heavily. He was half laughing at his fantasies and half wild with lust. Ah, yes, it was lust, now, not passion, or tenderness, but only this ferocious heat. Now he is Monsignor O'Duffy, serene in his cassock, until a horrible American girl presses her warm body against his, caresses him, croons to him in a voice of terrible sweetness; he tries to resist but she has insinuated an obscene hand underneath his holy vestments, looking, no doubt, for a rub of the relic....

They both burst out laughing at this use of an Irishism he had casually explained to her a few days before. Then they embraced and were quiet. He looked at the gauzy sunlight and wondered at the marvellous thing going on between Grania and himself. It seemed that in her he had discovered someone with whom he could explore all the dark regions, those places in himself and in her which reminded him of the secret paths, wooded, smelling of loam, that he had explored as a boy, the deepest regions of the psyche, of the body, the place where there was no shame.

He kissed the top of her head, then closed his eyes against the light, and they slept a bit more. Then they rose, showered, and went down to meet Liam Cahill, director of the Glee by the Lee. Dermot had never seen or talked to the man, whose minions and student volunteers had arranged Dermot's visit. But last night, on the phone, one such assistant had told Dermot that Professor Cahill would like to have a pint of Murphy's with him at six o'clock, in the hotel bar.

The moment they entered the bar, like a small forest with its wooden counters gleaming in a perpetual dusk, Dermot finally felt that he was indeed in Cork. They were surrounded by murmurous voices that dipped and lilted in the peculiar Cork fashion, at once melodious and petulant, with those strange quaverings at the close of each sentence, like querulous doves. And there was for Dermot the sensation he had every time he visited this city, of sedateness, gentility, a comfort that was wholly material and nearly self-satisfied; ample burghers relaxing over amber whiskies, tilting towards each other to gossip in the undulating accents of their city, self-contained, content. He had just ordered a pint for himself and a sherry for Grania when a voice cried, 'Doctor O'Duffy! What a felicitous occasion! My world-weary orbs take an untrammelled pleasure in alighting on your good and august self. Liam Cahill here. And if I might be so churlish as to venture so bold a query, who is the bright jewel at your right hand?'

Dermot regarded Professor Cahill, a short, rotund fellow, beaming at Grania and himself through thick round spectacles. 'Uh,' he said after a moment, 'This is Grania. Grania MacCormack.'

Chapter Sixteen

'An unalloyed delight, Ms MacCormack. Now, may I salve your throats with a libation? Oh, good heavens, I observe that you have tankards already before you. Well, you must quaff them with haste so that I may replenish them anon.'

Dermot, dazzled by such verbal opulence, such archaic scrolls and curlicues, was rendered mute, but Grania exclaimed, 'Goodness, Professor Cahill, you speak in such a vivid way.'

Cahill smiled bashfully. 'Yes, I am compelled to admit that my diction is to some degree flamboyant. In truth, I cannot help it.' He sighed. 'I suppose that one could maintain with no small measure of veracity that I am simply a hoor for the rococo.'

Dermot nearly laughed, till he observed that Liam's broad and shiny brow was furrowed in consternation. 'Professor O'Duffy, Ms MacCormack, would you perhaps not contend, in all honesty, that my idiom is a *soupçon* old-fashioned? There are times when I am convinced that my vocabulary is just a bit too enamoured of the eighteenth century. What do you think?'

Grania answered promptly, 'Oh, no, sir, not at all. We are enchanted by the splendour of your verbiage.'

He chortled. 'Marvellous, Ms MacCormack, marvellous. You are without doubt a kindred spirit. Another sherry, mayhap?'

After a second round of drinks, Liam offered to take them to dinner at a good restaurant. The hotel was above the city, and Dermot was glad, when they walked out onto Sydney Place, that Grania could look down and see Cork at its most lovely, on a summer evening, with a brumous glow still flushing the distant slopes, but the streetlamps already creating a scattered, firefly brightness along the darkening roads. Saint Finbarr's spires seemed to float in the powdery dusk, and below them the Lee gleamed dull silver. When Grania exclaimed at the river's beauty, with its doubled course, and its ducks and swans, Liam said, 'Our Lee is indeed lovely in the crepuscular glow of twilight; however, in harsher daylight one is often dismayed by its turbid and greenish aspect. Here we are.' They had been strolling down the terraced roads and then along St Patrick's Street, and now he gestured them into the restaurant, an airy place painted ochre and gold, like a house in the south of France.

While they read the menu he declared that he had brought them to 'one of the most superb dining establishments in our modest city,' and, indeed, the fine food and good wine seemed to make Liam even more expansive than before — and more candid — for over the cheese he suddenly tilted forward, clutching his napkin in both hands, and murmured solemnly, 'Professor, you are doubtless aware that your lady wife is in town?'

Dermot and Grania looked at each other. Dermot said gruffly, 'I am indeed aware. She welcomed me with threats today, the moment we arrived at the hotel.'

Liam helped himself to some cheese and bread, and took a slurp of wine. 'I am reluctant to serve as a harbinger of unsavoury tidings. However, at present, Mrs O'Duffy appears to be in a condition of high perturbation.' He gave Grania an abashed smile. 'I do not relish the prospect of blundering into your personal

lives. Yet with sorrow I must inform you that Mrs
O'Duffy seems determined that I should do precisely
that. What I am attempting to express is that her
insistence on thrusting private concerns into a public
assembly has compelled me to address such issues
now, no matter how unseemly I might consider them.
The Glee by the Lee is an academic congress, not a
forum for personal grievances, but, since her arrival in
Cork Mrs O'Duffy has demanded a private audience
with every member of the organising committee, and
when we honoured her plea, impressed as we were by
her tenacity, she chronicled — to each of us, singly —
the same story of woe and weal. Her complaints
centred on — er — you, Professor, and Ms
MacCormack, and whilst we appreciated that the
dissolution of a marriage is a painful and sad business,
we were not prepared to countenance her request that
you be ousted from the Glee by the Lee. After all, your
spouse's grief and dismay — strong emotions, without
doubt — might be urgent, and central, to her good self,
but they are not central to us.' He spread his hands.
'How could they be? How could we possibly allow
personal issues to encroach on scholarly endeavours?
Why, we academics are notorious for spawning
scandal! Some of us are ungovernably salacious, others
engage in eccentric behaviour, whilst still others are
acidulous with envy. And some of us are veritable
beakers overflowing with extravagant speech. And
nearly all of us are lamentably immature. Good
heavens, if we indulged in self-righteousness, and
condemned our colleagues for their private crises, if we

thwarted their scholarly efforts because their spouses disapproved of them, if, in short, we permitted the personal to intrude on the professional, then every university in Ireland would collapse in a day!' He took another, agitated gulp of wine. 'Professor O'Duffy, we did not consider even for a moment exiling an eminence such as yourself from our summer confabulation merely because of a personal vendetta against you, but then *something else happened!'*

Dermot swallowed a bit of cheese, which seemed to have transformed itself into dust on his tongue. 'What else happened, Liam?' he asked as levelly as he could.

'Well, Mrs O'Duffy had been speaking to one of our organisers, Professor Cordelia Callaghan, an ardent feminist and champion of wronged women.'

'Cordelia Callaghan? With the Picasso eyes? What is she doing here? I thought she was up at the Sheela-na-Gig thing, in Galway.'

Liam said, 'Dear me, you haven't heard about the split? There was a rift amongst the Sheelas, having to do with policy as regards the lesbian members. I am not aware of all the details, but Professor Callaghan and her followers defied the greater group, and established a splinter organisation of their own, called, I believe, Daughters of the Gig. Anyway, Professor Callaghan, and three other Dees of the Gees, all in fine and angry fettle, journeyed down here, and offered to help us prepare for our summer festival. She is a splendid organiser, and, if I might venture an opinion, quite attractive despite the facial peculiarity to which you referred. There is a deep attraction, at times, in the asymmetrical.

It can transcend the norms of pulchritude.'

Inconsequentially, Dermot remembered Doyle making a similar observation about Beatrice Talon, something about how her passion and fiery intelligence endowed her with a beauty that only unimaginative oafs like himself could not see. He supposed that this lesson, in the real nature of beauty, was one advantage of his current ordeal.

Grania said, 'I can scarcely believe that Cordelia Callaghan would embrace Fiona's crusade. She was so sympathetic to our plight, in Galway.'

Dermot sighed. 'But remember how wrathful she was, how she shrieked at me along with those other Sheelas, after my talk? Perhaps her character is like her eyes, tilting this way; then that.'

'But she *is* sympathetic to you,' cried Liam. 'Without doubt our dear Cordelia did offer consoling murmurs to Mrs O'Duffy. Who, confronted with such distress, would not experience sympathy?' He clasped his hands in a near prayerful attitude. 'We are all brokenhearted creatures, fearful of rejection. And we are, all of us, woven into humanity's star-crossed web. How could Cordelia not weep for her, a fellow human being in anguish?' He gave a wry smile. 'But her compassion for your separated spouse did not convince Professor Callaghan to denounce *you*, Professor O'Duffy. After all, separations do take place, distressing though they be. And I would hazard that most such sunderings are no one's fault.' Nibbling a sliver of Coolea, he continued.

'I suppose it is rather splendid that here in Ireland

we still consider marriage a profound union; we are not cavalier, or casual, about separations, as perhaps the Americans are, if you will forgive me, Ms MacCormack. However, in this day and age, even we Irish must concede that it is wrong to exact from unhappy men and women the futile sacrifice we demanded of them in the past, wrong to expect them to live without love. God Himself, after all, has exhorted us to love one another.' He thrust a didactic finger in the air. 'Therefore, Cordelia, whilst not impervious to Mrs O'Duffy's dolour and worry, refused to embark with her on a campaign of denigration.' He drank down his wine and replenished all their glasses. 'But then a most curious permutation took place. Mrs O'Duffy herself seemed to revise her position, in a most dramatic fashion. Cordelia has informed me that your estranged spouse called on her just the other day, in quite an altered humour.'

Liam paused, and Dermot passed a weary hand over his face. He was deeply angry with Fiona for imposing her concerns on his relations with other people, as if she were determined to be an acrid presence in this very room, breathing a gunsmoke of bitterness into the air, forcing him to speak about private matters to someone who hadn't the right to know about them. But then Liam continued, 'Cordelia revealed to me that Mrs O'Duffy expressed regret, even chagrin, about her previous actions. She told Cordelia that she hoped her complaints to the committee had not inflicted harm on you. She apologised quite genuinely, according to Cordelia, who was baffled and intrigued. Especially since Mrs O'Duffy continued to fluctuate, even after her apologies. One moment she declared that she had been immoderate in her behaviour and was therefore contrite, but the next moment she embraced her former position again, describing you as a reprobate and deserving of her wrath. But there *was* a change in her. Even when she tried to denounce you she seemed unconvinced, completely unlike the Mrs O'Duffy of even a day or two before. So Cordelia pressed and pressed her until finally she revealed that it was her father, Mr Finn O'Reilly, who was insisting that she continue to censure you, but that her own heart was no longer in it. Imagine! What do you think might have changed her mind so completely, and so suddenly?'

'I have no idea,' Dermot answered bluntly. 'None at all. I'm as baffled as yourself and Ms Callaghan.'

Liam sighed. 'Perhaps it was merely time that prevailed on Mrs O'Duffy to behave in a more reasonable manner? After all, time has a way of soothing even the most ruffled breast. Anyway, I should be deeply upset if any of this were to sully your visit to our conclave, Professor. Would you and Ms MacCormack care to partake of this establishment's exquisite apple pie?'

'No, thank you,' answered Dermot and Grania in unison. Dermot imagined that Grania, like himself, wanted only to walk back to their hotel room, where they could discuss how to handle whatever further surprises might await them tomorrow.

Chapter Seventeen

Next morning, gazing from the lectern at a smiling Grania, the plump and rosy Liam, and the typical summer school throng of students, journalists, acolytes, and academics (including Cordelia Callaghan, looking, as usual, thin, tousled, awry-eyed, and rather lovely), Dermot thought, *Here we go again.* So as not to be thrown off form, he was reluctant to examine the audience too closely; yet, like those horror film characters who can never resist exploring the shadowy corridor, the derelict house, the menacing wood, he was overcome with curiosity, unable, despite himself, to keep from scouring the crowd for his former spouse's red hair and white face.

She was not there.

He felt peculiarly disappointed, but reasoned that he

had worked himself up to a raw pitch of expectation, so Fiona's absence now was bound to be a bit deflating. He even half-missed the ponderous presence of Big Stupid Finn, who at least would have been a lively antagonist. Sighing at life's ironies, he arranged his papers, and launched into his talk.

Love, love, love, commented a disdainful voice in his head, while he expounded on the theme which for some mad reason had become his province of expertise. *How you do babble on, O'Duffy; whatever could have persuaded you, absurd bumbler that you are, that you're an authority on, of all things, love?* Shut up, he told the voice sternly, then concluded a bit too hurriedly, since he was apprehensive about the question and answer period. He was afraid there might be a Margaret Keogh type in the crowd, who would jump to her feet the moment questions were called for, and shrill: *Professor, since we are discussing love, how do you feel about geriatric scholars who abandon devoted spouses in order to kindle their decaying gonads with inappropriate trollops?*

But he needn't have feared such a presence — this was a thoughtful group, composed mainly of university people, and their queries were scholarly. Even *la* Callaghan, so incendiary when last a member of his audience, asked a mild, intelligent question this time, about professional female poets like Liadan and the bardic tradition in ancient Ireland, and her sister Daughters of the Gig were equally gentle. What had he done right to deserve this dispensation? Had he perhaps attracted the violence of the Sheelas just as he had fostered the glacial disapproval of his spouse? Had those Galway crusaders been responding to some need in him to be thrashed, reviled, chastened? If so, then perhaps Grania's influence was defusing his victim-hood! Anyway, he thought, thank God, or Goddess, for this more tranquil air.

At the post-talk reception, Cordelia cornered himself and Grania. Her hair seemed to be swirling in excite-ment about her head, and she was wringing her hands agitatedly. 'Hello, you two. I have heaps of stories to tell. Isn't our darling Liam the most splendid creature, a living lexicon! You know,' she placed a confidential hand on Dermot's arm, and lowered her voice, 'as he says himself, he's just a hoor for the rococo. Anyway, let's have lunch, and I'll explain everything.'

They walked through the lovely, leafy university grounds, then along the bustling roads to a quiet res-taurant, where Cordelia began talking in a highly animated, almost hectic way.

'First of all,' she cried, fastening her crooked and glistering eyes on them, like a female Ancient Mariner, '*everything* erupted in Galway the day after you left. Gender politics! I won't go into detail; the theoretical thickets are just too brambly. Point is, before departing for Cavan, our new president, your pal Doyle, declared his desire to oust the Sheelas of Sappho from our or-ganisation! He said they were too extremist, especially after he learnt that they were co-ordinating a Woman Warrior Festival for next summer, which will include a brigade of courageous lesbians parading bare-breasted along Galway's major roads, to protest the fact that men are allowed to show their naked chests in public, while women are forbidden this right.

'Anyway,' she continued, 'Beatrice supported Doyle, predictably, since she was besotted with him — even though she is bisexual herself — but I and most of the others refused to tolerate such a masculinist, reactionary, homophobic position. However, the ensuing political tempest did not bode well for our Sheela-na-Gig Festival. The whole thing collapsed, in fact. A delegation of us pursued Doyle up to the Drumlin School, to confront him there, but he and his misled followers, including that traitor Talon, refused to relent. So here I am, mustering support for the Daughters of the Gig from dear Liam.'

She paused to take a forkful of her lunch; then continued at rollicking speed. 'Anyway, who did I stumble on up at the Drumlin School but your wife, Dermot, along with her blunderbuss of a father, who I must say reminded me of some kind of dogged, mad *bull* or something. He was very angry, and very *thick*, if you know what I mean. And do you know who *else* I saw at the Drumlin? Mrs Doyle! Well, *she* was looking for Doyle, and *your* missus was looking for you, it goes without saying, but,' she swallowed some wine, 'but the funny thing is, Doyle and *your wife* became pals. Yes, Doyle, and Fiona! Just a couple of nights ago, while I was having a solitary evening meal at a hotel in Cavan, I glimpsed them across the room, your wife and Doyle, talking earnestly over a bottle of Gevrey Chambertin. And very cosy they seemed, too. You see, my eyes might look a bit wonky, but I have excellent vision, which is how I could read the label on their wine bottle from a distance. Why, I even saw him place a comforting hand over hers on the table! I was a bit amused, as well as flabbergasted, you can imagine. Anyway, after my dinner, I walked back to my own hotel, thinking mournfully that the Sheela-na-Gig movement had begun to founder on shoals of discord (sorry, I have been listening too much to the loquacious Liam) and wondering if Doyle was hostile to our lesbian members for the simple reason that their indifference to *his* member had galled him to distraction. But while I was brooding about these things I glimpsed, along the road—' she took a deep breath '— Pamela Doyle, and Beatrice, walking arm in arm!' She smiled, rather triumphantly. 'Can you believe all this? I certainly couldn't. Still can't, really.' She beamed at them with the satisfied look of someone who has delivered a truly juicy and unexpected story. 'Do you think that Mrs Doyle and Beatrice, and Mrs O'Duffy and Doyle, are, as they say, having it off, an unholy quadrumvirate? Not all of them together, of course; one's imagination does boggle a bit. But things are happening that make the two of you begin to look quite simpleminded. You must be the last couple in the world to go voyaging round the country hand in hand, like old-fashioned true loves from a children's storybook.'

Dermot said, 'And it seems Fiona descended on you, here in Cork?'

'*Yes.*' Cordelia tilted forward, wringing her napkin in a gesture curiously reminiscent of Liam's the night before. 'A number of days ago she came to my hotel room, and spoke to me for half an hour. At that time she was rigid and controlled, but I thought I detected something doubtful, something *faltering,* in her eyes, even then. She wanted me to insist that you and Grania be expelled from the Glee by the Lee.'

'She must be mad with misery,' said Grania dejectedly. 'And she must hate me. If I were her, I would hate me.' She gave Cordelia a dry little smile. 'Of course I know I didn't break up their marriage. It was in shards when I met Dermot, and he was so marooned and lonely. But sometimes I see it all from her perspective.'

'Nonsense,' Cordelia answered briskly, lighting a cigarette. 'Nobody should remain in a marriage which damages them, although Mrs O'Duffy's pain at this time is understandable. If you don't mind my temerity, Dermot, it does seem to me that you should have spoken to your wife about separating a long time ago, instead of taking lovers and being duplicitous, which she was bound to learn about, and be hurt by. Anyway, all three of you are quite tender now, but that will change. Nobody need hate anybody.'

At these words Dermot felt a surge of relief. After all, he did not want to hate Fiona. He was sick of resentment, the dark flavour of it, sick at how the two of them had fed on it so greedily during the later years of their marriage; he did not want to do it anymore. He wanted to be free of hate and rancour and pain, wanted to love Fiona in a comradely way, since they had been through the wars together, as well as the few blessed truces.

As though she had read his mind Cordelia said, 'No reason to hate your Fiona. What an astonishing

The Honey Plain

creature she is! Such style, and beauty, as well. And such an astringent intelligence, though I imagine she was not well-served by that father of hers. One senses that he made her lonely, and melancholy. Anyway, now she will be free to form a happier alliance, with a more suitable partner. Which is not meant as a criticism of you, Dermot, only an observation, that the two of you were obviously not suited to each other.'

'Are she and Doyle well-suited, perhaps?' offered Dermot, grinning. He had actually forgotten that, according to Cordelia, Fiona and Doyle had quite recently drunk a bottle of burgundy together in a Cavan hotel. He pictured them, his aloof and handsome wife at a restaurant table beside Doyle, who had doubtless tumbled all over himself with concern for the poor, beleaguered Mrs O'Duffy. That conniving hypocrite! Dermot, laughing to himself, realised that he was not at all jealous, which both startled and pleased him. But Doyle, of all contenders! On the other hand, he could be suave and courteous with the ladies, virtues which Fiona might appreciate, since she had so often accused her husband of being a drunken and indecorous lout, grappling girls while guzzling pints like some kind of mythical creature with numerous, flaring arms, a Celtic Shiva.

Cordelia continued. 'You *must* let me complete my tale. As I gather you know, Fiona has done a *volte face*. She called on me again the day before yesterday, to declare that she'd decided her pursuit of you was actually quite ridiculous, not to say exhausting. I was once again startled by her — what sense can one make of such extreme fluctuations? She was looking beautiful and rather serene that day, with a smile playing about her lips, as though she were relieved, even amused. Her formidable dad had gone home, so it seemed to me that she might be emerging from under his influence, and gradually beginning to think for herself. Or else that Doyle had persuaded her to relent. She *did* waver a bit, saying at one point that that she must not, after all, weaken in her resolve to stalk you across Ireland, but I had the impression then that she was merely speaking in her father's voice, saying the words he would like to hear, but that she herself was not convinced by them.'

'Where is Fiona now, I wonder?' asked Grania. 'We thought she might come to Dermot's talk this morning, but we haven't seen her.'

Smiling ruefully through her cigarette smoke, Cordelia said, 'I hate to tell you this, but she might already be travelling up to Clare. Apparently she approached a member of the Glee by the Lee Organising Committee (or GEE-LOCK) who did not recognise her, and innocently told her that you would be speaking tomorrow at the Honey Plain School. Whether she has gone there to continue to harrow you, or to make peace, or simply to meet up with Doyle again, we shall have to wait and see.'

'Anyway,' Dermot said firmly, 'I will not be intimidated by her.'

'Have another glass of wine,' suggested Cordelia, 'or perhaps a bottle.'

* * *

When they emerged from the restaurant the air shone with a strange, scalding brightness; the day had grown hot, nearly as hot, observed Grania, as a summer day in Connecticut.

Slightly stupefied by the heat, the harsh sun, the people jostling along with sunglasses and bare arms as though, suddenly, while they were eating, Cork had been miraculously transformed into a Mediterranean town, Dermot and Grania walked back to their hotel room. There, she unfurled some pastels she had done in Allihies, lovely semi-abstracts or something, Dermot thought, knowing too little about art to define them properly: washes of pearly colour, green tendrils, lapis lazuli pools — plus *figures*. It seemed that, by instinct, or through the insistence of her gift, Grania had come, or was in the process of coming, to the same conclusion as Dermot, that her real subject might be the human face and form. He examined one picture, of a man — Pat O'Driscoll, he thought, by the sturdy shoulders — looking into a churning stream; another of a naked couple reclining on grass, their limbs intermingled; another of a woman with streaming hair and eyes like lamps walking along a dark road under an opalescent sky.

'Oh, dear,' he said, meaning it. 'My dear, these are good.'

Grania said she wanted to sleep a bit, and, looking at her more closely than he had done recently, so preoccupied had he been these last two days, he saw that she did seem exhausted; her small face was very white, with a curious grainy pallor, like talc, and her eyes seemed heavy with fatigue. Remorse flooded through him; he hadn't considered seriously enough how their tumultuous flight, and Fiona's grim pursuit of them, must be affecting her. This kind of adventure was not what she had bargained for, when she'd come to Ireland to paint! Just today, at lunch with Cordelia, she had alluded to her own dismay, but he had not even acknowledged her words.

'Oh, my Grania,' he said, 'I do ask a great deal, don't I?'

'You ask for love, and so do I,' she said with determination, clambering into bed. But almost immediately she was asleep.

* * *

Restive, he went out again. A walk, he thought, might help him prepare his lecture for the Honey Plain School.

The sun was so hot, he was again reminded of towns in southern Europe, as though if he were to walk now into a pub he would see not carpets, mirrors, and pints of stout on an oak bar, but café tables, and dark women drinking dark wine and minute cups of ink-black coffee, while men with black moustaches slouched at a counter, their eyes lingering on the women.

On St Patrick Street he saw Laura Murphy, looking brown and splendid in a white linen dress. '*You* again,' he cried.

She gave her delightful laugh. 'I was shopping. I am in a play here, at the Opera House. *The Merchant of Venice*.'

They walked through a small park in sunlight so strong, it made the trees seem to fume with a golden smoke, and their leaves to glint like smoked glass. A bee blundered against Laura's cheek; she brushed it away indifferently, and he noticed how cool she looked. He had begun to sweat, and to feel clammy and rumpled, but her linen dress was crisp as new snow, and her fine head, graceful throat, the honey skin of her arms, all were smooth and cool. Her lips would also be cool, he thought. To tilt her head back, to kiss her deeply, would be like drinking iced coffee, dark and chill.

She was chattering in that way all actors had, slightly arch, histrionic, eyes widening with disingenuous astonishment at this director's churlishness, that fellow actor's lubricity. But he so liked her throaty voice, and she was terribly attractive. Perhaps because his life lately had been so hot, with Finn's anger blasting him, Grania's sometimes feverish insecurity pressing on him, he couldn't stop thinking now about Laura Murphy's coolness, her airy laugh, her cool silky skin. He imagined that even to enter her body would be a coolness, a splash into a cool lake. This thought made him laugh; she looked at him quizzically; then resumed her stories of greasepaint and gossip. But he couldn't attend to them. He was imagining her light fingers brushing his spine, her hair springing under his hand, her body opening to him, but only coolly, lightly, since she was, she had said, a 'bachelor girl'. And that, he realised, was what was appealing to him now, what was suddenly beckoning to him out of the welter of emotions he had been swirling in lately, to the point of near drowning.

Laura suggested they halt for tea; she needed replenishment, she said, after her foray through the shops, though she had bought nothing. They went into a dim restaurant where they were served hot scones, and tea in a heavy green pot. Looking at her pale mouth, glossy with butter, he reflected that, had he only taken up with some sophisticated creature like Laura Murphy, he could have avoided all this current appalling mess: Fiona steaming after him, Grania expecting a grand love, lawyers hovering in the shadows like carrion birds. Self-contained, poised, she would have welcomed him into the cool vault of her body, cooked him delicious meals, conversed with him about art and the theatre and politics. But she would not have wanted him to disrupt his life for her, and he would not have been tempted to do so. What a rash fool he had been!

Laura continued, 'And then I realised he had made up his mind, and it would be up to me to break things off first, before he delivered the blow.'

'What blow?' Dermot asked. He had no idea what she was talking about.

'*You* know. And I was a bit in love with him, although I hadn't wanted to be. Christ, it was so ironical. He liked me for what he called my independent spirit, how I never drew people into any kind of stickiness. He thought displays of emotion were vulgar, and when girls wept or implored him to love them, that sort of thing, he would absolutely shudder, like someone who has just discovered a bug in his salad. And there I was, self-sufficient me, beginning to *care*. It was too awful. Anyway, the play has rescued me, thank God, though I must say I don't know if I have what it takes to be a really good Portia, you know? The quality of mercy has been a bit strained lately.' She paused, and her light blue eyes with their sooty lashes gleamed at him. 'So, Declan, Sunday is my night off. Are you alone, here in Cork? I think a little distraction might hasten my cure. And you could tell me all about love. Aren't you supposed to be a specialist? Theoretically, I mean, though I would not object to a practical demonstration. Only no fuss, please. I should die if things got messy again, so soon after my ordeal with Christopher.'

He laughed, feeling, suddenly, outrageously lighthearted. 'My dear, my name is *Dermot*.'

She gave a melodramatic gasp. 'Oh, heavens! What a *faux pas*. *Do* forgive me! I suppose I am just too addled these days, and I am afraid I have always been hopeless with names. Besides, Dermot and Declan *are* so similar, aren't they? Oh, dear, what an absolute idiot I am.'

He regarded her, the lovely cropped head, the fine eyes wide with exaggerated dismay, the high breasts sheathed in crisp linen. Echoing her own misgivings, he wondered did she indeed have it in her to depict Portia, that advocate of sweetness, mercy, and amplitude in love. He laughed again. Good old Laura Murphy, blatantly offering what he had just imagined he might desire. But even she was not impervious to strong emotion; this Christopher, whoever he was, had apparently breathed some disconcerting heat into the cool chambers of her life. And now, in flight from him, she wanted to return to the world of light affairs, where she might draw back from an intimate embrace and look bemusedly at her companion, unable to recall his name, which didn't matter that much, anyway. And here was himself, thinking he desired someone cool and unruffled, after he'd lived years and years with frost and chill!

'You needn't laugh at me,' she scolded, affecting a petulance which her grin belied. 'I feel awful enough, calling you Donal or Denis or something. At least I didn't call you Delia, or Doris! You needn't laugh, and make me feel even worse.'

'I think I am laughing at myself. You asked was I free. I suppose in a way I have never felt more free in my life. I am in love, you see, or perhaps that isn't exactly true. I am not *in* love, I simply love someone, which is actually much more complicated than being in love, and has been making my life extremely awkward lately.'

She tilted her head and considered him as though, he thought, she were a naturalist and he some rare bird. 'Really! Yes, you spoke about all this when last we met, in Galway. And your new friend is in town with you? Pity. I could have used a nice civilised frolic, and you were such an appealing candidate. Still, I must say that you are looking happy. Anyway, if you ever *are* travelling alone, and we happen to discover ourselves in the same town? A little limb-play now and then is relished by the wisest men, to adapt the old song.' She laughed, but a bit unsteadily; then swallowed painfully, as though there were some dry, stubborn thing in her throat.

He answered gently. 'You flatter me, Laura Murphy. But I imagine that I shall not be travelling alone much in the future.'

Again she gave an embarrassed laugh, not looking at him. 'Anyway, *c'est la vie*. She must be an awfully nice girl. Perhaps I shall meet her, one day.'

Finally looking up, she smiled rather wearily. *La vie*, indeed, he thought. She was certainly forty, if not older; soon she would be past Portia and all the other ardent young girls. Even the best actors had one day to forfeit *jeune première* roles, those brash, youthful, stylish characters in which one saw oneself so gladly, only to realise by and by that life insisted one abandon them: Pegeen Mike, if she's lucky, finishes up as a good Widow Quinn, Ophelia becomes Gertrude, Hamlet the prince is transformed into King Lear, still raging against the world, still mad, but exhausted, gaunt, and in tatters.

For the women it was probably harder, because an unenlightened public still seemed to demand that they should be talented *and* lovely in a youthful way. Considering the plucky but perhaps secretly lonely woman before him, he thought she might never manage the middle-aged rancour of a Lady Macbeth; Big Finn, on the other hand, would be brilliant in the part, and should perhaps contemplate a stage career, in drag!

'Why are you laughing again, and so *wryly*?' Laura asked.

He gave her hand a friendly squeeze. 'Because it's better than crying.'

'My,' she said, grinning, and seeming, finally, to relax, 'you *have* changed since Galway.'

Chapter Eighteen

'Quite surprisingly, considering the conservative, even puritan, attitudes which inform contemporary Irish Catholicism, virtually no moralistic harshness trammels Early Irish literature and history. Asceticism does exist, but it resembles the asceticism of the desert fathers, who sought to subdue the flesh by retiring to rocks and mountains. Many beautiful Early Irish lyrics portray the monk, the anchorite, in his stone cubicle overlooking the turbulent Atlantic or some lush river valley, delighting in nature and composing a small poem in its praise.

'But these lyrics emerge from a relatively late period in Irish history. What existed before are what Lady Gregory called "Gods and fighting men." These heroes and warriors do not dream of the Christian paradise, but of a blissful home whose sweetness far surpasses any vision described in the Koran. They are dreaming of what is called the Great Plain, or, more lusciously, the Plain or Land of Honey. Many place-names in Ireland still resonate with that dream, for instance, Clonmel, or Honey Harbour. It is alternatively known as the Plain or Land of Women, and that is the paradise which the old Irish longed for, even in this life, since not far from Clonmel, the Honey Harbour, soars Slievenamon, or the Hill of Women.

'Before the monks, you had the valorous Fianna, and the Red Branch Knights. And before even them? There is ample evidence that Ireland, a land usually personified as a woman, was once indeed a matriarchy, her most powerful deity being Áine, goddess of the river Boyne, whose breasts are the mountains on the border of Kerry and Cork. The Hag of Beare herself is really a survivor from those matriarchal days. She, like Oisín, lived long enough to discover herself in the early Christian era, and was bemused as he by the stern climate which this new Roman religion had breathed into the sweet air of her green island.

'From the early *Voyage of Bran* to the wanderings of Oisín in the eighteenth century, text after text agrees. In the Hibernian paradise, that ideal land imagined by the early Irish, men and women assemble at a vast table for an exquisite and inexhaustible feast. Their cutlery is moulded from precious metals, their goblets scrolled with bright designs. Alcohol is so unrestricted that it courses in streams at their feet, and no single pleasure is got at the expense of any other. After eating and drinking, the women and men settle down to lovemaking. The most important aspect of their pleasure is that it is not sullied by any sense of guilt, blame, shame, or sin. They are equal partners in a series of sweet rituals culminating in the act of love. This is the not-so-secret vision of all early Irish literature, and it took many invasions and a half decade of famine to eclipse this glorious dream temporarily.

'And in our own time that ancient dream has certainly been bowdlerised. In an age of sexual indulgence, of easy gratification, the early Irish paradise could easily be misinterpreted as a celestial orgy, a glutton's delight, a land of instant pleasure unalloyed by emotional attachment. But to come to such a conclusion would be to trivialise a profound and mystical ideal. The Honey Plain is not a land of anonymous couplings, but a place where love in all its aspects is realised. In that way it is much closer to the Tantra than to Satyricon, to Indian mystical theory than to the Roman orgy.

'Let us examine for a moment the Hindu religion of love, so uncannily similar to our own ancestors' vision. The crux of it is the Mithuna doctrine, which maintains that human beings, when they make love properly, are participating in and echoing the divine act of creation. Natural, intimate, and ecstatic lovemaking can kindle male and female to an awareness of the great mysteries, and enable them to attain spiritual states. Shiva and Parvati, interlacing in their holy dance, embody this vision, in which the masculine and feminine principles, utterly equal, embrace in creative love to realise the rhythms which underscore all life.

'A curious yet compelling parallel to all this exists in the realm of psychology, in the concept, fundamental to Freudian psycho-sexual theory, of narcissism. Freudian theory contends that all infants pass through a primary phase during which they experience no distinction between self and other. The child cries for the breast and the breast appears; hands materialise to succour him, a voice to soothe him. The whole world is a reflection, and an extension, of his need. But as the child grows older and more conscious, he emerges from this primary narcissism through the slow realisation, borne of experience, that he is him*self*, housed in himself, separate from his parents, an other to their selves, and a self to their otherness.

'In healthy development, the child is then equipped to *connect* with other people, to engage with and journey into their separate selves, and thereby to express and realise his own self. In other words, he becomes capable of intimacy, and love.

'Tantric philosophy expresses a similar idea through the dance performed by Shakti, the female principle, when she is united in love with Shiva, the male principle. At first, Shiva and Shakti are so closely interlaced that neither can perceive the other as separate. But through Shakti's weaving dance the couple progress from this state of undifferentiated wholeness into separate entities. For a time they are cloven, isolated from each other, but ultimately their separateness itself becomes the means for a connection more profound than their original embrace, so that the

Chapter Eighteen

couple are once again whole, but not undifferentiated as before. They have attained a completeness which is the expression of a mystical union between self and other, and their sexual intercourse has become a microcosm of divine creation.

'Now, you are probably thinking that I have wandered alarmingly far from love in Early Irish mythology, but I have been eager to convey just how spiritually sophisticated, and how distant from traditional Western thought, the ancient Irish were. In the Honey Plain, the flesh is not mortified to advance the spirit, or, in the great words of W.B. Yeats, "body is not bruised to pleasure soul". The body and the spirit are not opposed in the Land of Honey; indeed, in that paradise, reverence for the divine is expressed through sexual intercourse, and, as I have stated, it is a pure expression, unencumbered by shame or guilt.'

Dermot looked up, and swallowed. He was as baffled as though he had just woken from a dream, and this vast lecture hall, dim against the harsh podium lights at his feet, did not help to moor him. He could see no one, only sense the audience, and now they were very still. What were they thinking? Had they liked his talk? He hadn't meant to say those things: the Tantra, Shiva and Parvati, my God! The words had crowded onto his tongue like gulls, squawking, flapping their insistent wings, and he was off, off, evoking Lady Gregory, the goddess Áine, Oisín, Freud, Shakti! He could scarcely believe it, but considered the possibility that he had been compelled to such wild diversions because, although he couldn't detect any one member of the audience, the room was fairly seething with possible presences. Fiona could be out there, along with Margaret Keogh and a battalion of Sheelas, as well as Doyle, since the Drumlin School had closed yesterday.

The Honey Plain's director, a forthright young woman called Blánaid, bustled up to ask for questions. At that moment the house lights flared on, and, simultaneously, the audience broke into applause — sustained applause, enthusiastic applause! — it seemed he had been a success, after all. Looking out at the crowd, he registered a sweep of red hair, perhaps Fiona's, though he couldn't be sure, and now a young man was asking him something so that he couldn't look again. But while he listened to the young man, one of those endearingly shy intellectual types with a complexion pale as whey and an enormous Adam's apple, he reflected that the ginger hair he had glimpsed might actually belong to Pamela Doyle, since, if Doyle had indeed travelled from Cavan down here to Lisdoonvarna, his furious spouse would almost certainly have dogged him.

The skinny young man (visibly excited by the daring connections Dermot had made, the skeins he had spun in the air) was not so much asking a question as expressing this excitement, and, when he stopped talking, other audience members proceeded to address *him*, offering their own responses to Dermot's talk, so that presently the audience were talking animatedly amongst themselves, a sure indication that he had succeeded in igniting their collective imagination.

Like a contented teacher indulging his bright class,

Chapter Eighteen

Dermot let them go on, glad that he could withdraw into the background while they fastened onto his ideas and soared with them. He had no desire to look amongst them for familiar faces; perhaps Talon, Fiona, Doyle, Maeve, and Cordelia of the random eyes were all out there, but he didn't want to know, and was glad that no official lunch had been scheduled for today. He and Grania could slip off to the pub now, and have some smoked salmon with a bottle of Meursault; then take this evening as it came.

They left while the audience was still talking. It was another warm day. Bees glinted in the air, which smelled of bruised grass and char from the smokehouse down the road. They were nearly in the pub door when they heard Doyle's voice behind them, crying, 'You two! Wait! Slow *down*! Please do not *compel* me to *scuttle* after you like a *dung beetle*! I thought we had become *friends*!'

'Shit,' muttered Dermot, who was indeed eager to talk with Doyle, only not just now. But they paused, having no choice, while a slightly rumpled but still dapper Doyle caught them up. There he was, oily Doyle, the same slender face and meagre beard, the same shrewd, lead-coloured eyes and haughty smile. Dermot was surprised by the stirring of affection he suddenly felt for the man. Well, he thought, sure, we have been campaigners together, and entangled in similar plights.

'Stopping for a nibble?' Doyle asked breathlessly. 'Excellent. I am quite hungry and parched myself. Superb talk, O'Duffy. Style *and* content. You are coming on, dear fellow. And how do *you* do, young lady? Let us go in. I have much to tell.'

'Bet you do,' mumbled Grania.

* * *

Pouring out the wine, Dermot said, 'Before you tell us anything, let me ask you one or two things, Doyle. First, is my wife here?'

Doyle, who had been buttering a chunk of brown bread, looked up, his knife arrested above his plate. 'Why, yes, old man, she is. At my hotel, actually. Quite a good hotel, really. They give a fine breakfast, and the restaurant across the road is rather splendid, though they don't hang the pheasant properly. A pity, but of course it isn't the season for game just now anyway, so you needn't trouble about that. And they have a more than decent claret—'

'Doyle, I'm not interested in Epicurean chatter. And I am not jealous or upset. I just want information. You did meet Fiona in Cavan, didn't you?'

Doyle narrowed his bespectacled eyes. 'You really are not jealous? You see, I should like to ascertain your emotional condition beyond a shadow of a doubt, since the last time that you and I were embroiled in a fracas, you clouted me in a most unseemly manner, and the young lady on your right gave me a thump in the bum which I do not imagine I shall soon forget. So it seems to me reasonable that you should offer me some reassurance before I launch into my exposition. If you see what I mean, O'Duffy.'

Dermot said promptly, 'I will always love Fiona,

244

ruefully and regretfully, as my former companion, and the person with whom I lived so much life. But our *active* love is over, and has been for some time. We are separate now, or nearly so, and I should like nothing more than for her to be happy — with someone else. There, Doyle. Does that satisfy you?'

Grania was grinning. 'And I promise not to thump you in the bum or any place else. Unless you revert to being an amorous ruffian, of course.'

Doyle sighed. 'All right, all right. Let us not conjure up unpleasant memories. Yes, Fiona came up to the Drumlin, with my Pamela. They were an imposing twosome, you can imagine, both so tall and flame-haired. And *angry*, it goes without saying. At first, I quailed, especially since a motley gaggle of Sheelas, including Beatrice, had also pursued me. Beatrice was a woman scorned, you see, or at least a woman evaded, since I had not said goodbye to her before hot-footing it up to Cavan, and I was afraid she would desire to *slaughter* me.' He took a deep breath. 'But matters did not develop as I had expected. First, Beatrice assured me that she had not come to the Drumlin School to exact vengeance. Oh, no! She had come because she wanted, in fact, to *defend* me, against those insufferable Sapphos. Sapphos, indeed! They are so *annoying*, my dear Dermot, so *shrill* and vulgar. Lesbians! Why in heaven's name would any woman choose to be lesbian? How anatomically tedious! And all that *equipment* they must use! So unnecessary, when the male is endowed with such an elegant baton. Anyway, even though Beatrice admitted her own bisexuality (ugh! can you imagine Dante's Beatrice engaging in such sordid confidences?) she actually agreed with me that the Sheelas of Sappho ought not to disrupt the affairs of our now more sedate Sheela-na-Gig Society.'

'I know all about that,' said Dermot. 'Cordelia Callaghan told us. She herself has become a Daughter of the Gig, I believe.'

'Yes, yes. A Dee of the Gee. What an unpleasant woman. Those eyes *pitching* in that crusader's face. It makes one sexually seasick.' Doyle shuddered; then continued to explain all that had transpired in Cavan over the past few days. Just when he believed the Daughters of the Gig had been thoroughly dealt with, who should arrive at the Drumlin School but Pamela and Fiona, accompanied by Big Truculent Finn. Doyle had been dreading Pamela's wrath, but, when they finally spoke, she was not only composed and cordial, she also offered him a revelation even more astounding than Beatrice's.

'Pamela told me that she was bisexual, also.' With his knife and fork, Doyle draped a coral frond of smoked salmon over a piece of bread. 'Of course I was appalled, and rather scandalised, I must admit.' Squeezing lemon on his fish, he did not seem in the least appalled, or even perturbed. 'Anyway, after Pamela finished explaining the nature of her erotic appetites, I could not even speak, I was so flummoxed. She went on to say that she supposed she had been bisexual all her life, only *she hadn't known it*, because our oppressive patriarchal culture had lowered her consciousness. Well!' He spread his hands in a gesture of dismay. 'How could I respond? I was stupefied. But—' He tilted forward, and gave them his scimitar grin. 'But then, almost immediately afterwards, I began to feel *relieved*. I realised that Pamela's anger, her tautness, her scorn, were, perhaps, *not my fault*, or at least not entirely, if you see what I mean. It was just her nature! She was never happy with men, it seems. Not even with me, and I am quite an adroit and rather sensitive lover, if I do say so myself, though one should not blow one's own horn, so to speak. But the truth was that Pamela's chilliness with me, her unhappiness, were all because she had wanted to make love with a woman!'

Dermot said, 'Is this the eminent hang-glider speaking? I thought that you and Pamela had worked out a cool, civilised arrangement. She cooked the *coq au vin* while you discreetly pursued chickens in the field. I have never heard you speak about her coldness, or her anger, as though you regarded those things as a problem. You never seemed to desire too much marital intimacy, Doyle.'

Doyle swallowed a mouthful of salmon. 'Ah, well, a fellow grows older, and begins to long for a measure of sweetness, as well as civility, in his life. Anyway, I needn't worry about Pamela now. She has decided to leave me.' He drank some wine; then bestowed his sickle smile on them again. 'Yes! She has decided to leave me — for *Beatrice*. They met up at the Drumlin, and almost immediately decided that they were made for each other. Can you imagine?'

Dermot looked intently at him. Was the man upset,

unnerved, disconsolate; was his jaunty demeanour veiling a deep dismay? It did not seem so. He was eating and drinking with gusto, and grinning all the while. And now he cried, 'Don't stare at me like that, Dermot, if you please. I am quite happy. Do you not see? This new arrangement gets both Pamela and Beatrice out of my hair. Marvellous! *Do* let us indulge in another bottle of this exquisite golden wine.'

Dermot said, 'What about Fiona?'

'Miss! Another bottle of the Meursault, please. What was that, dear fellow? Ah, yes, the indomitable Mrs O'Duffy.'

'That's right, old colleague. Seems you and she had a nice meal together in Cavan.'

'*Nice* is not quite correct. It is not possible to have a *nice* meal in Cavan. It was a half decent meal. Prawns in a kind of curry sauce; then roast—'

'Doyle! Stop talking about food. I told you I was not jealous. If Fiona is here now, I want to be prepared. Just tell me what has been happening.'

'Very well, old man.' Doyle paused, swirling the wine in his glass. 'I had never really met that good lady before, and it was a pleasant surprise to confront so poised and handsome a creature. At first she was very upset, with you, and with me, by proxy I suppose, but I managed to soothe her, if I do say so myself. Perhaps you never had the right *touch* with your lady wife, dear fellow, perhaps it was always just a matter of *touch*. Metaphorically, I mean, of course.'

'Of course.'

'Yes. Well. You see, O'Duffy, your Fiona is really very

simple.' He paused, surveyed Dermot warily, then plunged on in. 'My boy, perhaps you believe that throughout your marriage you conducted a sort of double life, trying to be a decorous husband at home, yet managing to sustain a bit of dalliance on the road, and so forth.' He sighed. 'But, dear man, despite all your amorous adventures, it seems to me that you never truly had the temperament for a genuinely rakish existence. I imagine that what you were always really longing for, whilst so feverishly stumbling from one romance to another, was the *Big Love*, that smarmy, awkward, messy thing which for some reason people seem to desire, with all its intimacies and revelations and vulgar displays.' He chortled. 'Do you not see? Of the two of you, it was actually not you, but Fiona, who desired the double life! She did not want too much of that cloying thing which you sentimentalists call intimacy. She just wanted a man who would behave himself, conduct his life with some elegance, and acknowledge her considerable beauty and wit. What her companion might do when not in her company was not her concern, provided, of course, that he managed his escapades with style, dignity, and tact. Not unreasonable, you must admit. Would you like raspberries and cream, or some cheese, perhaps?'

Dermot said, 'It seems you have learnt a great deal about Fiona's character over quite a brief period. You are certainly a fast worker, Doyle.'

'I shall take the raspberries. You two are not eating enough. What was that you said? Well, Mrs O'Duffy did require a sympathetic ear. She was, after all, a trifle distraught, though she remained marvellously tranquil in Cavan, and presented a stylish demeanour the whole time. A true lady. We did become quite close, as a matter of fact.'

Dermot gave him a level look. 'As another matter of fact, are you and Fiona here, now, together?'

Doyle caressed his tie. 'Well, yes. You see, old fellow, after she spoke to you in Cork, she took some time to reflect, and to right her balance. She began to realise, if you don't mind my presumption in saying so, that she would be better off without you. No more competing with you, her famous scholar husband who drew everyone's attention away from her, no more trying to restrain you or chasten you, no more of your boozing and womanising. Freedom! And then we talked, she and I, and Fiona herself proposed we come here, where we knew you would be speaking, in order to settle things.'

Grania spoke up for the first time. 'You mean that you and Fiona are intending to make a life together? You are an *item*, now, as they say in the gossip columns?'

Without asking permission, Dermot reached across the table and spooned up some of Doyle's raspberries, which looked delicious under their billows of cream. Anyway, he felt entitled to them. The crimson beads burst under his teeth like a kind of sweet caviar; he helped himself to more, and realised that he was quite shocked, but not unpleasantly.

'Doyle,' he asked, 'If what you seem to be telling us is true, how do you propose to address, with Fiona, the issue of your own boozing and womanising, which leave my exploits rather in the dusty rear? All she needs now is another rapscallion to harrow and disappoint her!'

'Help yourself, dear boy. Fine berries, aren't they? Ah, you know, I am not as young as I once was. The idea of a monogamous life with a felicitous companion begins to appeal to one after a certain age. Besides, I shall conduct my amorous affairs, if any do come about, with greater style and discretion than you have ever managed to do, O'Duffy. You do have a tendency to be *uncivilised*, when it comes to matters of the heart, or the part, if you know what I mean.' He produced a cigarillo, lit it with a flourish; then grinned. 'Fiona has explained to me quite convincingly that a significant aspect of her problem was your erratic behaviour, and at this point she is only sorry that she stuck with it for so long. She feels that she is now, finally, embarking on her real life, with somebody who really understands how to live!'

Dermot seized Doyle's glass and polished off his wine. Doyle smiled. 'Help yourself, old man. Shall I buy you a brandy?'

'No, thanks.' He didn't know what he was feeling. No, that was not true. He did know quite well: he was immensely relieved, but just as immensely annoyed. Fiona was off his hands; somebody else could deal with her now. But why had it been so easy for this smooth-talking popinjay to discover the formula, after all his own thankless years? And then there was the galling truth that he had indeed been less than a good husband. He had been insensitive, untender, gauche, too obviously unfaithful; apparently Doyle had always had far more *savoir faire* — on the other hand, his own wife had just left him, and for another woman!

'Doyle,' said Dermot bleakly, 'You are without doubt a canny fellow. But what are you going to do about your position as president of the Sheelas now?'

Doyle laughed. 'Beatrice and Pamela have agreed to take over, as co-presidents. I shall remain an honorary member of the society. But really it was all getting a bit too much for me. Such squabbling, and so many females. I am sixty, you know, nearly ready to retire. The Sheelas are being quite fine about my resignation, however. They are presenting me with a plaque at the party tonight. Surely Blánaid has told you about the party? It will take place at that lovely ruined church close to town, you know, the one with the sheela-na-gig *in situ*. Quite an imposing sheela she is, too, and it is always a thrill to see one intact, emblazoning an authentic old church, right above the portal. The Honey Plain people will place long tables on the grass within the ruined walls, for food and drink, and there will be music, Blánaid said. The two of you must come. Great *craic* will be had by all, I imagine.'

'What does *craic* mean?' asked Grania.

'Fun,' replied Dermot grimly.

Chapter Nineteen

When they said goodbye to Doyle (who had ordered a cognac for himself) and walked out into the road, the sky was azure and lambent, and the air pale gold and fragrant as the wine they had been drinking. People who had heard Dermot speak that morning greeted him enthusiastically. The men were coatless, and the women wore light frocks patterned with flowers, or cotton trousers and sandals, and sunglasses. Dermot said hello to some colleagues from Dublin, but the principal characters in his recent drama did not appear.

He and Grania went back to their room and talked about everything Doyle had said; she wanted to discuss his lecture, but he persuaded her to be quiet. It had been his experience that when people, including

253

himself, spoke idly about spiritual lovemaking, they invariably trivialised it, or rendered it into something false and mawkish, or else salacious. It was hard enough to lecture on subjects like Tantra, but at least the dry, hard light of intellectual scrutiny was a kind of tonic. When it came to informal discussion between lovers, however, it was far better just to *make love*, he told Grania, kissing her ear. She sighed, and brushed her fingers down along his body till he was groaning.

Later they lay on the bed, and talked about this party. 'Fiona will be there, probably,' said Grania.

He wound up her hair in his wrist. It was all too easy to bury his head in her hair with its rainwater smell, and to touch her body, warm from love and from the heat of these extraordinary summer days, and think of nothing. Doyle and Fiona, Beatrice Talon and Pamela! It was just too mind-boggling. But presently he said, 'Yes, Fiona might be there. But we should go, nonetheless. Probably she will be easier now, if what Doyle tells us is true. Anyway, I must speak to her about how to manage the legal issues. And you and I have not yet addressed what *we* should do, now. All the practical things, money and where to live, your career—'

Sleepily, she murmured, 'I want to live in Ireland, with you, and I want to paint.'

'That's good, darling, because I don't want to live in America, really.'

She hoisted herself up on her elbow and looked down at him. Her hair fell over his chest; in this light her eyes were a rich green. 'Neither do I. But we will go there for brief visits. You'll meet my mad family.'

'I should like that. But what will they think of me? Being so much older, and foreign. Taking you away from them, and from the great United States.'

'My father will like you. He'll think you're a bit dreamy, like me, but secretly he has always been pleased by that dreaminess in me. All his slithery friends make him a bit sick, sometimes, though he pretends to admire their hardness. He will like you, and he'll be glad to see me sort of settled.'

They slept, then, and Dermot dreamt that he was saying goodbye to Grania in one of those groined, vaulted stations familiar to him from films about the Second World War, families hurrying along platforms through watery blue light, through smoke and white steam, while uniformed men stare, and whistles blow forlornly. 'Goodbye,' Grania was crying, 'Goodbye.' And his heart was riven with anguish, with the unbearable knowledge of imminent loss, the loss of his love, his sweetness, his dear friend. A disembodied voice said contemptuously, 'You are too *dependent*, Dermot.' But he knew it wasn't so. He was not dependent, only wholly aware that Grania was the woman with whom he wanted to live, that in losing her he was losing something essential to himself, that he didn't want to see her sporadically, now and again, to be a gleaner in a desolate field, collecting dust and dry seeds, he didn't want a splintered life, he wanted to live entire, he wanted to live where love was, to move through his days with love, with her, but she was leaving. Then suddenly he was in some modern airport, and she was about to board a plane to America only he didn't want her to go, but she didn't know that, she thought he believed she must go away, and now he couldn't see her because a throng of tourists and Japanese businessmen had engulfed her. What could he do? Why, he didn't even have her phone number in Connecticut! Sick with panic, he began to hurry down an ugly, sterile corridor, looking for her, thinking, *In this kind of dream one is never fulfilled, I will stagger down corridors forever and she will never appear, I am lost, lost....* But then he felt a hand on his shoulder and it was Grania, wearing her pretty green frock and laughing. *This is not that kind of dream, idiot*, she said, and he answered softly, *You have been restored to me*, loving that word *restored*, feeling it as sweet on his tongue as one of Doyle's berries. *You have been restored to me....*

When he opened his eyes and looked at Grania asleep beside him, a voice in his head (perhaps his own voice, though he thought it was someone else's, and not recognisable) announced, *You have died, and come back to life.*

* * *

The church was a weathered husk, open to the sky; birds had made their homes in the crumbled grey spires, and the tombstones were softened with moss. The country all around was deeply green and sloping, and on this beautiful evening the whole place looked slightly enchanted, with the sky glimmering above the long party tables which were at once incongruous and festive, their cloths so vividly white against the grey stone and darkening fields. Blánaid, the Honey Plain's director, wearing a long ivory dress and with her fair hair drawn up, was stalking in her blunt way amongst the tables, inspecting the covered dishes, the array of bottles, the waiters in their white coats. And the music, provided by a piper and two fiddlers, floated towards Dermot and Grania as they made their way up to the green clearing where the tablecloths fluttered in the slight breeze; they were among the first to arrive.

The waiters were moving through the sparse crowd with platters of *hors d'oeuvres*: smoked salmon on brown bread; asparagus in a thick mustard sauce; grilled prawns; chunks of goat's cheese encrusted with peppercorns; leaves of Parma ham and crescents of melon; pâté on *croûtes* of French bread. And there were bottles of cold champagne and fragile white wine, and red wine and apéritifs, and deadly-looking martinis being made by a jolly barman behind a small table.

Dermot drew Grania over to the large portal where the sheela-na-gig was. She was a splendid sheela, fashioned from the same rough stone as the walls so that it was hard to distinguish her against them, until you looked more closely and saw how precisely made she was, a pagan frieze with her grimacing face, flaring thighs, and open vulva. And beneath her, in the loamy earth, were the lichen-mottled tombstones of generations of pious Catholics. 'Only in Ireland,' observed Grania affectionately, 'Womb and tomb.'

They went back into the clearing for a drink and some food. Fiona, Doyle, and the others whom they knew had still not arrived, but a vaguely familiar woman began walking towards them in a purposeful way. Her dark hair was coiled up on her head, and she was dressed in a turquoise sari that bellied out behind her like the canvas of some gaudy ship.

'*Hello*,' she cried, 'Don't you remember me? Cressida Rabitte, from Galway. I am the terrible woman who banished you because your wife had descended like a bird of prey.' She gave a shrill laugh which was itself like the cry of a bird. 'But now I am *so* sorry, especially after listening to your talk this morning, Dermot. My husband Owen and I were travelling through Clare and we stopped close to Lisdoonvarna last night, not even realising that the Honey Plain School was on. But when we learnt about it, and that you would be speaking, we decided to come in and attend the lecture.' She extended her slender hand. 'And I am so glad we did! You, Dermot, are my kindred spirit. Today, my dear Professor, you articulated something I had always been certain of in my deep heart, that there is a profound connection between the ancient Hindu and the ancient Irish. You see, for a long time I have been absolutely sure that I myself am the reincarnation of an ancient Irish female warrior, and I am equally sure that in yet another life I was an Indian princess!' She beamed at them. 'I am only sorry that I asked you to leave my guesthouse. But I was thrown off balance by that little bully Mr O'Reilly, who might very well have been Napoleon in a former life. And I must caution you—' She took a dramatically deep breath. 'I saw Mrs O'Duffy in the village today. She has followed you here!' She drank from her glass of champagne. 'You ought to be careful. She might come to this party in pursuit of you. It is a kind of open house party, you know, which is why waifs and wanderers like Owen and me were able to weave our way in. How's that for alliteration!' She gave yet another laugh.

'Thanks for informing us,' said Dermot, anxious to untangle himself from this glittering creature and get over to the drinks table. 'And I am sorry that Fiona disturbed you in your home. But we knew that she had come here, and, apparently she is calm now, and kindly disposed. Also, her father has gone away.'

'*That's* certainly good news. One sensed he was *not* a good influence. Do just let me thank you again. What you said about the Tantra was wonderful. Owen and I read it, and *practise* it, all the time.'

When they each had a drink and a plate of *hors d'oeuvres*, Grania said, 'I see what you mean about people reducing profound thoughts to something tawdry and trivial. Imagine using the Tantra as a sex manual! Oh, look, Dermot, there's Pat O'Driscoll, the Bard of Allihies!'

There he was, indeed, talking into the ear of an attractive silver-haired woman. The rounded gestures he was describing in the air, and the fact that his head was tilted back and his eyes half-closed, convinced Dermot that he was reciting one of his spontaneous poems. The lady into whose ear he was pouring his verses seemed pleased — she was smiling, and gazing raptly into the middle distance.

The sky was growing darker, and the curious stillness that accompanies twilight had settled over the fields: voices seemed hushed, laughter muffled. Under Blánaid's direction, a few young men were fastening floodlights onto the church walls. Dermot and Grania strolled up to the bar for another drink.

'Such luxury,' murmured Grania, 'and all of it *free*! I think I'd like a *kir royale*, this time.'

'And I'll take — let's see — a white wine, and some more of those grilled prawns. Good God, look at that woman genuflecting before the sheela. Is it — could it possibly be — *Talon*?'

Grania peered through the smoke-blue dusk, to where a large woman with gunmetal hair and immense glasses was kneeling on the grass beneath the great portal. 'Goodness, that *is* Talon. And she does seem to be genuflecting. Why, she must be offering homage to the sheela-na-gig!'

'Well, we shouldn't stare. It doesn't seem right to ogle someone who is praying. Anyway, at this moment I am not exactly eager to be pinioned by those particular talons. There is enough to worry about.'

As though this statement were a summons, Doyle suddenly appeared, strolling into the clearing which, thanks to the floodlamps, had become a shallow pool of gold light. He was wearing a light dress suit. 'Jesus,' muttered Dermot, half disdainful, half envious.

And behind Doyle walked Fiona, in a dress which was nearly the same lilac colour as the dimming sky. She saw Dermot and Grania almost immediately, and, after accepting a glass of champagne from the ebullient barman, strode over to them.

Grania, with a most welcome tact, murmured, 'I'll

just go over to the bar for my *kir royale*, and to talk to
old oily Doyle. See you later.'

She dipped into the thickening crowd just as Fiona
materialised before Dermot, looking formidably handsome, he had to admit. How was it that lavender and
violet suited redheads so splendidly? Of course the
auburn hair at her temples was stippled with silver
now, but she was still a lovely woman. The music
skirled and eddied about them; the guests laughed and
clinked glasses; he looked into the tapering eyes of his
old pal and old antagonist, his wife, his shadow. Goodbye, he thought, Goodbye, my friend, my girl, my one-
time love. But what he said was, 'How are you, Fee?'

'Fine,' she answered abruptly. 'Let's walk a bit. All
these *people*.'

They moved out of the pool of light and began
walking through a broad field. The trees were still
darker than the milky sky, in which a curlew suddenly
swooped. The air was damp, and smelled sweetly of
hay. Fiona said, 'I haven't my handbag.'

'What?' asked Dermot, not sure he had heard
correctly.

'I would like a tissue, but I haven't my handbag.
Doyle has it.'

'That's okay. Here's a hankie.' Clumsily, he thrust his
handkerchief, one she had, in fact, given him, into her
hand.

'Thanks,' she mumbled. Was she crying? He
couldn't tell in this gloaming, but suddenly she said
sharply, 'Don't look so concerned, Dermot. You know
how I hate that guilty look. It's only that I spilled

champagne on my frock.'

They walked through a mossy stile into the neighbouring field. From this distance the old stones of the church seemed honeyed with light, and the music was dim and sweet. A cow looked suspiciously at the two interlopers; then returned to her slow crunching of the thick grass. Dermot said, 'What's all this about Doyle?'

'He has become a friend to me. I think he will not let me down. Any objections?'

'No, no. And I suppose I have forfeited my right to object, even if I had wanted to.'

She frowned at him. 'You forfeited that particular right a long time ago, Dermot.' They walked on in silence for a while. Then she said, 'I suppose what troubled me the most over the years was how you always emanated *availability*, as though if you closed yourself off from the possibility of sex with *any* particular girl (whoever she might be) it would leave you utterly deprived.' Keeping her head averted, she gave him back his handkerchief. He had a sense that the deepening darkness was a kind of protection for her; they could barely see each other, now, and she was pouring her low, steady words into the air before her, almost as though she were alone.

He kept silent, and she went on. 'People *fancy* each other, of course, but it was always something else with you. You never seemed to realise that having so many affairs, being so reluctant to forego any possibility of dalliance, becoming so besotted so easily, and with so many creatures, well, you never seemed to realise that a person is diminished not by giving up such things, but by indulging in them. It was as if you had never left your early home, where there was such a poverty of love. As if you were persisting, feverishly, in trying to make up for that first loss. Oh, it was clearly always so new, so gratifying, so unexpected and delightful, to sport with Amaryllis in the shade!' She gave a harsh laugh. 'And you never seemed to see that indulging in affair after affair does not enrich or replenish one, not after a time. Profligacy closes in, becomes its own sort of prison, as constricting as any other, don't you think? Falling in love all the time, seeing the promise of love everywhere, in every remotely pleasant woman, why, that doesn't celebrate love, it cheapens it, surely! You are the expert, Dermot, you tell me: Is not love something rare and precious? And if so, shouldn't two people who love each other protect and guard and honour what they have, and not let anyone else encroach on it? And surely love is sometimes painful. But is that any reason to *bolt* into somebody else's arms?' She drew a deep, slightly tremulous breath. Then, to Dermot's astonishment, she said, 'But I suppose I was so distant and sad all the time, it was hard for you to feel at peace with me.'

He stopped. The field was quite dark now and there was no moon, so that her presence next to him was umbral, a cluster of shadows. Behind them, the church glowed like a great lamp.

'Why were you so sad, Fee?' he asked gently. 'It couldn't all have been my fault.'

She answered reluctantly. 'I don't know. I suppose you are right, it couldn't all have been your fault. A lot

The Honey Plain

of it must have been Daddy, all his designs and ambitions for me, and the fact that Mummy never protected me.' She paused, and Dermot sensed rather than saw her smile. 'I must say it felt rather good, to tell Daddy at the Drumlin that I no longer needed him, that he should go home. It left him at a bit of a loss, but honestly I don't feel sorry about that. He is well able to look after himself. Besides, his prize sow, Queen Maeve, has just been awarded a blue ribbon at the Cavan County Fair, which will be a new distraction for him. Now he intends to enter her for the All-Ireland.' She gave a low laugh. 'I suppose you might say he has transferred his ambitions if not his affections.' Again she hesitated. 'But it wasn't only Daddy, who made me unhappy. You did let me down, Dermot. I am emotionally fragile, as we all are, I suppose. And you asked too much of me. I could not live at the emotional pitch you had established for us. I needed steadiness, stability, *repose*.'

'Do you think Doyle can give you those things?'

'I hope so. It's interesting that he comes from Monaghan, so close to my home. I suppose the psychologists might say this means I identify him with Daddy. He certainly has been kinder to me than Daddy. And than you were.' They began walking back to the party. She continued, 'Anyway, I thought I might return to lecturing, and teaching, myself. After all, it would be a shame to let my perfectly respectable MA crumble into dust in some cupboard. I am a good tutor and lecturer, but in the past I was always too daunted, competing with you, the brilliant Professor O'Duffy.'

Chapter Nineteen

'But I didn't want you to feel competitive with me. I wanted us to encourage each other. We could both have been the brilliant Professor O'Duffy.'

'Perhaps, but I was too exhausted and depressed to try.' Another pause. 'Doyle has been rather nice about my career. He has contacts in the English departments all through Dublin, which would be a help to me, were I to return to the groves.'

They had passed over the stile back into the first field. The party seemed in full swing now. The lights were blazing, the music louder and merrier. As they approached the clearing Dermot saw that the waiters were serving platters of roasted meats and bowls of steaming potatoes and vegetables, and pouring wine into pewter flagons. Some of the guests had collected round the tables to eat, while others were settling on the tombstones with plates balanced on their knees. Fiona said, 'I imagine we should look for our respective new partners now.' She extended her hand in a manly way. 'Good luck, Dermot. Be kind to that girl.'

There was a thickness in his throat. 'You will never cease to surprise me, Fiona. Good luck to you, also, old friend. And Doyle had better look after you properly, or I'll give him another of my famous straight lefts.'

She looked puzzled, but at that moment Doyle appeared, and took her arm. 'Evening, O'Duffy. Your erstwhile distaff side is looking beautiful, is she not? I was just speaking with Beatrice and Pamela. They were on their knees, offering obeisance to that lovely girl Sheela. Extraordinary! You know, they intend to expand the Sheela-na-Gig Society, make it international.

And they have decided to call it the Global Sheela Society, because they like the idea of globes, which are circular, generous and female, like breasts and bellies, as opposed to the narrow, oppressive, linear structures which we males erect in celebration of our inferior appendages. Anyway, enough scholarship and politics! Let us partake of the fatted calf, Fiona. See you later, Dermot me lad.'

They disappeared into the crowd. Dermot gazed after them; then located Grania at the drinks table, proffering her glass to the barman. '*He's* Ganymede, this time,' she said, smiling at the man, who had rubicund cheeks, ginger whiskers, and a broad grin, like some Franz Hals portrait of a Laughing Barman. Dermot squeezed her hand, thinking he had never been so moved to see someone as he was just now, looking at his Grania with her chestnut hair and little face, laughing and extending her glass to the man behind the bar.

'It went well,' he murmured, drawing her into a darker corner.

'I'm so glad.' She brushed his cheek with her lips, and a flush of happiness coursed through him. 'And Dermot,' she said, 'I was speaking just now to Fergus Sweeney, do you remember him, the painter from Allihies? He told me he was very impressed by my work, and he would like to introduce me to some people who might arrange an exhibition for me! Also, he and his wife invited us to visit them in Allihies for a sort of holiday, after you have cobbled out a separation agreement with Fiona. Very kind of them, I thought.'

'That's splendid news, about an exhibition for you.

It would really launch you, Grania. And a holiday, as well. It will be nice to return to Allihies, and see people like Shay McCarthy and Pat O'Driscoll again.'

As though roused by the mention of his name, Pat O'Driscoll walked into the centre of the clearing. The musicians laid down their instruments, and the clatter of plates and glasses suddenly ceased. Even the church walls, burnished and rosy, seemed to tilt in towards the lawn as if to listen. Dermot regarded the celebrants at this strange festival: Beatrice Talon and Pamela Doyle, both looking aglow and quite lovely; Fiona with her hand placed serenely between the two hands of Doyle who was resplendent in his evening clothes, an elegant big bad wolf; Cressida Rabitte in a corner, her head on the shoulder of her husband — and was that Liam Cahill, embracing a smiling Cordelia Callaghan? Yes, it was indeed Liam, that hoor for the rococo, and indeed he was with Cordelia; no one else in the world could radiate such crooked beauty, those listing eyes in the fine face, like a glorious crazy pavement.

Pat threw his head back, raised his arms to the sheela in a hieratic gesture, and began to intone:

> 'Oh great warm vulva of the world
> From which Blake's fiery babe is hurled
> Alpha and Omega of our appetites
> Great bright Mother, shroud of night
> Secret wellspring of birth and death
> All hail to thee, magnificent orifice!
> Darkly the priests have cloaked your face
> But we recognise you as the fount of grace

The source of love, the ecstatic mould
Where all things are made, and hold.
To you we lift the circled glass in praise
That you may shower pleasure on all our days.
To live by love should be our common aim
So let the revels ring on the Honey Plain.'

* * *

Dermot and Grania walked away from the crush, to a small knoll behind the church where it was very dark, and the air smelled of peat and wet stone. 'You know,' he said, 'I think you ought to paint the figure, more. One can be as daring with the figure as with abstract things, it seems to me.'

She settled her head on his chest, and he caressed her hair. 'Grania,' he said, 'I've enjoyed the summer school circuit, despite all the tensions, haven't you? I think we should do it again, next year.'

'Which ones should we visit, next time around?'

He considered. 'There's a literary one in County Antrim conducted at a boarding school, which means that all the participants live in the dormitories, and eat together in the refectory. It creates an intimate, rather intense feeling, all these people bundled together for a week or so. And the food and wine are very good, so everything begins to centre on the meals. At breakfast they feed you this enormous Ulster fry, which for some reason just makes everyone hungrier. Then you proceed to the lecture hall to listen to a series of talks, but everybody's eyes are fastened on the clock above the lectern, waiting for it to be one o'clock, when lunch is served with buckets of wine and you can have amusing conversations with colleagues and pals. If the last morning speaker rambles on past one o'clock, everyone gets very annoyed, not because the lecture is boring, but because it has encroached on the lunch period, and all the stomachs in the audience are outraged and growling. Then the same happens before dinner, after the ritual hour in the bar. It's all very pleasant.'

Grania laughed. 'I'd like to go to that one. Any others?'

'Countless others. And the topics are becoming more obscure and strange. I hear there's to be a Civil War School next summer, with lectures by descendants of leaders from both sides, and since the English haven't woken up yet to the whole summer school phenomenon, a movement has been launched to celebrate any and all of their writers who ever ventured over here, though that could become a little tricky. Spenser wrote *The Faerie Queene* in North Cork, but he also advocated the extermination of the natives! So the locals might be reluctant to hear lectures about himself, and his pal Raleigh, from Youghal, who was also delightfully anti-Irish. But the Trollope Summer School promises to be highly successful, partly because it's being sponsored by An Post, since Trollope himself once worked in the post office at Banagher.'

'Very nice,' said Grania. 'Surely you and I could be Trollopes, next summer?'

They were quiet, then 'Darling,' he murmured, 'I mightn't be easy, you know. I don't think I will ever be a scamp again, but I'm still childish, in some ways. And the difficult years have embittered me a bit, I think, roughened-up my heart. I mightn't be easy.'

She laughed softly. 'What makes you think that I will be easy? I am stubborn and insecure and childish.'

'How terrible! If only I had known all those horrible things about you. And now here it is, too late.'

'Yes, too late. Looks like we are stuck with each other. As the postage stamp said to the letter.'

He gazed at the church walls, gilded with light, and at the revellers within, dancing, now, some of them, while others sang or drank or feasted, or walked arm-in-arm over the lawn. All his life, he thought, he had been afraid of a certain darkness of the heart, like some Victorian urchin who stares into the window of a lighted house where people in bright clothes are dancing. He had been afraid that he would be left out in the cold as couples swept by him, brushing him with the bottoms of their coats while they embraced each other for warmth, and hurried, laughing, through cold streets which for them were without menace. He had been afraid of the things in himself which were dark and fumbling, that they would be seen, and, once seen, condemned, and that he would be ostracised from the land of love, forever. What he had wanted all his life was grace, was to be known fully, and loved not only despite his faults, but for them, and to love in return, as abundantly and with the same freedom. And now it seemed he had found this kind of love with Grania. He believed she saw him whole, and that she would not waver. He had also come to believe that she had a gift,

270

and that something would come of this gift, slight, perhaps, but real.

'Grania,' he said, 'you are finishing your apprentice-ship, and I am entering my prime. I know it sounds terribly horticultural, but shall we try to be late-bloomers together?'

She smiled, he took her hand, and they walked back into the light.